RAINBOW'S END
AND OTHER STORIES

RAINBOW'S END
AND OTHER STORIES

For Sarah —

JOHN M. FLOYD

Best wishes!
John M. Floyd

**DOGWOOD
PRESS**

Library of Congress Control Number
2006927196

Printed in the United States of America

Jacket design by Bill Wilson
Author photo of John M. Floyd by Carolyn Floyd
First Dogwood Press edition: October, 2006

**DOGWOOD
PRESS**

DOGWOOD PRESS
P.O. Box 5958 • Brandon, MS 39047
601-919-3656
www.dogwoodpress.com

For my two Carolyns—my wife and my mother

ACKNOWLEDGMENTS

I would like to thank the following friends, authors, and editors for their encouragement: Janet Brown, Carole Bailey, Donna Huebsch, Ben Douglas, Margaret McMullin, Fran Gatewood, Tom McCurley, Robert Angelo, Nancy Horner, Tommy Wheeler, Jim Waltman, Susan Weatherholt, Martin Hegwood, Phil Hardwick, Jim Ritchie, Nevada Barr, Jim Fraiser, Johnene Granger, Linda Hutton, Babs Lakey, Linda Landrigan, Andrew Gulli, and Moira Allen. And many thanks to my publisher, Joe Lee, for his professionalism and for his confidence in me.

Special thanks to my wife Carolyn and our three children—Michael, David, and Karen—for their love, support, and patience. You're the best!

I would also like to acknowledge the magazines in which these stories were first published. "Teamwork," "Lindy's Luck," "Careers," "Hardison Park," "The Bomb Squad," "The Blue Wolf," "The Pullman Case," and "Battleground" first appeared in *Alfred Hitchcock's Mystery Magazine*. "The Jumper" was first published in *Crimestalker Casebook*, "The Early Death of Pinto Bishop" in *Writer's Block Magazine*, "Survival" in *Orchard Press Mysteries*, and "King of the City" in *Murderous Intent*. "The Proposal" and "Murphy's Lawyer" first appeared in *The Strand Magazine*. "Guardian Angel," "A Gathering of Angels," "Henry's Ford," "Ladies' Day," "Family Business," "A Stitch in Time," and "Rainbow's End" were first published (the first three under different titles) in *Woman's World*. "Lucy's Gold" and "Della's Cellar" made their first appearance as serialized stories in *Grit*. "The Messenger" was first published in *Futures*, "Vital Signs" in *Red Herring Mystery Magazine*, "One Less Thing" in *The Rex Stout Journal*, "Saving Mrs. Hapwell" in *Dogwood Tales*, and "Newton's Law" in *Reader's Break*. "Creativity" and "Night Work" first appeared in *Mystery Time*.

CONTENTS

TEAMWORK

"Where'd you go, Martin?" Shorty asked.

Martin Rhodes was sitting in the passenger seat of the Honda, hunched down into his overcoat, watching the foggy night go past. "What?" he said.

Alton Purvis—Shorty to his friends—kept his eyes on the road, his hands clamped to the wheel. "You heard me. Back there at the office, while Steffy and I were hauling the box out of the safe, you disappeared. You left us without *cover*, Martin." Shorty paused, his jaw muscles twitching. "Where'd you go?"

Martin studied him for a moment. "Didn't Steffy tell you?"

"Tell me what?" As if on cue, both men turned and glanced into the back seat, where Stephanie Purvis lay sleeping. She had been sleeping for the past fifty miles or so, ever since the three of them had ditched the Ford and stolen the Honda. "Didn't tell me *what*?" Shorty asked again.

"I went to the back door," Martin said. "I thought you

knew that."

"The back door," Shorty repeated. "Very interesting." Keeping his eyes on the misty highway, he reached over to turn on the defroster. "You know why that's interesting, Martin? The back door didn't need watching. The back door was locked, from the inside. I found that out in about two seconds, from the lady in charge of the vault; you should've been able to find that out yourself, in the two days you and Steffy spent casing the place."

Martin just looked at him, saying nothing. Shorty Purvis was an ex-wrestler, and tough as nails; Martin was a much larger man, especially in his baggy overcoat, but not nearly as aggressive. It had always been understood that Shorty was the boss. "What we found out," Martin said finally, "was where they kept the goods."

"True enough," Shorty admitted, reaching down to touch the cold steel of the strongbox on the floorboards beneath his knees. "But the fact is, you *left* us, Martin. The back door wasn't part of our plan. In the time you were gone, one of the office guys could've hit me in the head from behind, or shot me, for cryin' out loud."

Martin turned to stare through the windshield. "Well, nobody hit you, or shot you either. Let it go."

Both men fell silent. For several minutes, the only sound was the hum of tires on the pavement. The lights of a town appeared ahead, fuzzy and yellow in the fog.

"We were supposed to be a team," Shorty murmured. "You and me and Stef. But a man who won't follow orders . . ." He shook his head. "Something about you scares me, Martin."

Martin was quiet a moment. "I think what scares you about me," he said, "is asleep in the back seat right now."

Shorty looked at him sharply, started to reply, then

12

changed his mind. Martin's face was an eerie yellow-green in the glow of the dashboard lights. After a pause Shorty said, "She's *my* wife, Martin, not yours. And now that you mention it, you two have been spending a lot of time together lately—"

"Casing the office was your idea, Shorty. Remember? You asked us to do it, and we did."

"You sure that's *all* you did?"

A long silence passed. Martin studied the driver's profile as the words hung there in the air between them. When he spoke again, his voice was low and tight.

"You want me to leave, Shorty? Is that what you want?"

Shorty didn't answer. Outside, the fog was thickening.

"I thought we trusted each other," Martin said.

Still no reply.

Martin turned away, his face darkening. "There should be a truck stop just ahead," he said. "Let me out there."

Shorty sighed. "Look, Martin—"

"I said let me out, okay? There it is, on the right."

The brightly-lit building looked like an island in the shifting fog. Shorty turned the wheel, eased the Honda in beside a bank of gas pumps, and cut the engine. In the rear seat, Steffy stirred once and was still again. Her rhythmic breathing was the only sound.

"What about your share?" Shorty asked.

Martin Rhodes was buttoning his long, bulky coat. Without looking up, he said, "What about it?"

"We'll have to cut the lock off the strongbox. That'll take time, and a safe place."

Martin thought that over. "When it's done," he said, "just send my share to my dad's house, in Atlanta. Steffy has his address." He opened the car door and turned to look one last time at the sleeping form on the back seat. "Tell her goodbye for me, Shorty. She was a good friend."

"Martin—"

"So long, Shorty."

Martin got out of the Honda and shut the door. Shorty watched him walk through the chilly mist toward a group of men leaning against a row of parked tractor trailers. Gathering his coat close about him, Martin spoke for a moment to the truckers; the first two shook their heads and pointed north, but the third nodded. A minute or two later, Martin and the third man walked together to one of the big rigs, where Martin, smiling his thanks, climbed up and into the passenger seat. With a low, throaty rumble the eighteen-wheeler pulled out of the station and onto the highway, heading south. It vanished into the fog.

Shorty sat there for a long time, staring at the spot where he'd last glimpsed the truck's red taillights. In his mind's eye he could see the intersection with I-59, a half mile away. A right turn there would lead to New Orleans, a left to Meridian and Birmingham; straight ahead was the Gulf Coast. He had no way of knowing which way the truck had taken.

Not that it mattered now, he thought. The important thing was, Martin was gone.

Shorty drew a deep breath and let it out slowly. With a last glance at his sleeping wife, he got out of the Honda, filled the tank, made sure the doors were locked, and walked into the building to pay for the gas and visit the restroom. When he returned to the car, Steffy was awake and sitting up front in the passenger seat.

"Well," he said, climbing in. "Welcome back to the living. You feel okay?"

She stretched like a cat, then looked at him and grinned. "I feel rich," she said.

"That's because you *are* rich. At least you will be, once we convert it all to cash."

Her smile widened. Though she was past thirty, Stephanie Purvis still looked like a sixties flower child—straight blond hair, granny-glasses, no makeup. As Shorty watched, she took a plastic barrette off the dashboard, put it between her teeth, and reached up with both hands to pull her hair back.

"I've been thinking about that," she mumbled around the hairpin, "and I've decided that anybody who'd believe for two days that Martin and I were security consultants"—she stabbed the barrette into her hair and smoothed it out—"deserves to be robbed. What do you think?"

"I couldn't agree more," he said, trying to sound casual.

She yawned, then looked around. "Where is Martin, anyway?"

Shorty hesitated. "Inside, I guess. He's been in there a while, though . . ."

"He'll be back," she said. She stretched again, then leaned back and propped her bare feet on the dash.

"How do you know?"

She turned and frowned at him. "What?"

"How do you know he's not planning something? Calling his buddies, maybe, to gang up on us?"

"Because I know him, that's how. If we trust him, he'll trust us."

Shorty said nothing. Their eyes held for a long moment.

Then, suddenly, her frown vanished.

"You think there's something between us," she said, looking amused. "Between me and Martin."

He just stared back at her.

With a sigh, she said, "Martin's a friend, Shorty. Nothing more. Besides, he's leaving in a day or two anyway."

Shorty blinked. "He's leaving?"

"That's what he told me."

"Alone?"

"I guess so. Unless you're planning to leave with him." For the first time, there was an edge to her voice. Shorty realized it was time to back off.

"Okay," he said. "Sorry. But how is it you know his folks?"

"His folks?"

"He told me you have his father's address."

Steffy laughed. "Well, I don't."

"You don't?" As that news sank in, Shorty's face changed. His eyes took on a dreamy, faraway look.

"Then there's nothing I can do," he thought aloud. "If there's no place to send it—" A slow, cunning smile appeared on his lips. "We get to keep it all . . ."

"What are you talking about, Shorty?"

He blinked, and his eyes cleared. "What I meant was— well, he really *has* been in there a long time, Stef. I don't think we should hang around here much longer—"

"Well, we can't just leave him." She turned to check out the lighted station. "We're a team, Shorty, you said so yourself. And a team sticks together."

"Like today?" he asked.

She looked at him. "What?"

"Why'd he leave us today, Stef? Why'd he go to the back door?"

That caught her off guard. "He didn't tell you?"

"Tell me what?"

She studied his face. "My God, you really don't know, do you? I thought Martin had told you, and he must've thought I had—"

Shorty's cheeks reddened. "Just *tell* me, dammit!"

She stayed quiet a moment, watching him. "Let me ask you one thing, first. Why do you think we haven't seen any cops tonight?"

"Cops? What do you mean?"

"Think about it a minute," she said. "Why is it we haven't seen one single sign that they might be after us?"

"I don't know." He frowned, unsure of what she was getting at. "We switched cars, for one thing—"

"That helped, sure. But the fact is, three people don't just put on ski masks and walk in and steal a million bucks' worth of rare diamond jewelry from a museum office and get away that easy. There should've been roadblocks all over the state by now."

He just stared at her, waiting.

"They're not all that worried about catching us," she said patiently, "because they don't know we stole the jewelry. They think we stole a boxful of bricks from their safe."

"*Bricks?*"

"The diamonds weren't kept in the safe, Shorty. That's what Martin and I found out yesterday. They were hidden in a broom closet, beside the back door."

Shorty's mouth dropped open. "You mean—when Martin left . . ."

She nodded. "He went to get the diamonds. You and I were the diversion."

Shorty's eyes, wide as golfballs now, drifted down to the strongbox. "But if the diamonds aren't in *there* . . ."

Steffy nodded again. "That's the beauty of it. When the three of us left together, all they saw us take with us was the strongbox. They're probably still laughing, and don't even know yet that their precious jewels are gone. Pretty good, right?"

"That's not what I mean," he blurted. "If they're not in the box—where are they?"

She grinned. "In Martin's overcoat," she said. "You could hide an elephant in those pockets."

John M. Floyd

THE EARLY DEATH OF PINTO BISHOP

"I know you have my grandpa's gun," Eddie said.

The tall man sitting beside him on the wagon seat didn't appear to have heard him. Eddie wasn't surprised. Tom Dolan didn't say much under the best of circumstances, and today—at least ever since they'd left town ten minutes ago—he looked a little preoccupied. *Moody*, Eddie's father would have said. As Eddie watched, Tom Dolan pushed his hat back with his right hand and rubbed his forehead. His left hand held the reins.

"I saw him give it to you, out in front of the store," Eddie continued. "You put it under the driver's seat."

Finally Dolan turned and regarded him a moment, leaving his worn brown hat cocked back on his head. As always when he looked at Eddie McCartle, Dolan's face relaxed, his eyes softened. In the two months since he had come to work for Eddie's father, Dolan and the boy had formed a kind of bond, and each enjoyed the other's company. Eddie's dad said Dolan was probably in his early thirties, but he looked older than that.

I expect he's seen hard times, son, Will McCartle had explained. *He probably needs us even more than we need him.*

Tom Dolan settled his hat back in place and faced the road. "If you saw him give me the gun," he said, "then you saw me ask him not to. He made me take it."

Eddie heaved a sigh. He didn't doubt that a bit. It was, in fact, the only thing about Tom Dolan that he couldn't figure out. Every man Eddie knew—every man or boy he had ever known—liked guns; his schoolmates, the hands at the ranch, his father, everybody. Except Tom Dolan. Dolan didn't like guns or knives or violence of any kind, and didn't mind saying so. He had already backed down from several fights in the bunkhouse. Eddie still liked him—most everyone did—but he found the whole matter hard to understand.

As usual, Dolan seemed to read his thoughts. "I'm a cook, Eddie," he said. "What would a cook know about guns?"

Eddie started to reply, then changed his mind. Both of them watched the rutted road awhile, saying nothing. Lurching and groaning, the wagon eased down into a dry wash and up the other side. They were halfway home now; thick stands of birch and pine began to appear on both sides, hugging the road. Tom Dolan stared straight ahead, both hands holding the reins, both elbows propped on his knees.

"I think I know why he gave it to you," Eddie said. "I think he was afraid we might need it, on the way home."

Dolan turned again to look at him, but this time his eyes stayed hard and watchful. "What exactly did you hear, in town?" he asked. Then, with a frown: "Did you sneak into the saloon again? I promised your dad I'd look after—"

"The saloon's not the only place people talk," Eddie said, in the all-knowing manner of a twelve-year-old. "I heard it at the feed store, from Jack Langston. He said everybody in town knows about it."

A silence passed. The wagon bumped steadily along. Somewhere far away, thunder rumbled.

"What exactly did you hear?" Dolan asked again.

Eddie swallowed hard, excited that at last he was about to say the thrilling words. "I heard Pinto Bishop's close by. That somebody saw him in Cimarron a while back, heading this way."

Dolan nodded. "That's mostly what I heard," he agreed. "But 'a while back' could mean anything. For all we know, he could've come and gone by now."

Eddie shook his head. "Jack said Bishop robbed a stage outside Blue Mesa, two days ago."

This drew another frown. "How do you know it was Pinto Bishop?"

Eddie was thinking that over when a covey of quail burst from the weeds beside the road. "Here's my point, kiddo," Dolan said, watching their noisy flight. "Folks see strange things, when they're scared. Sometimes they see what they want to see. If Pinto Bishop had done everything people say he's done, he'd have had to be in a hundred places at once. Why, nobody even knows for sure what he looks like—"

"He's tall and thin, with a bushy mustache," Eddie said. "He smokes cigars, he wears black clothes, and when he shoots at something he never misses."

"Is that so." This time Dolan couldn't keep from grinning. "You've seen him yourself, then?"

Eddie gave him a look that only a youngster can give a grownup. "I heard that from Danny Hobbs, who heard it from four different people."

"Well, it must be true, then," Dolan said solemnly. Before Eddie could tell if he was kidding or not, he added, "But my advice is, don't worry too much about Pinto Bishop. If you need something to worry about, there are bears in these woods that are a lot more dangerous to you than—"

A shot rang out somewhere ahead of them.

Dolan leaned back, reining the team in. As he and Eddie sat staring, a tall man on a bay horse emerged from the woods on their left. He wore a black hat and vest, black pants, and long leather boots. A cigar jutted from beneath a drooping mustache, and his eyes were as cold and narrow as a lizard's. But the two riders on the wagon were looking at none of these things. They were looking at the smoking pistol in the man's right hand.

"Hello boys," the stranger called. He stopped his horse twenty feet away, just ahead and to their left. "No sudden moves, now."

The warning was unnecessary: Both Eddie and Tom Dolan were as still as statues. "What do you want?" Dolan said.

The man's laugh was so loud and sharp the McCartle horses jumped in their traces. "Don't you know who I am?" he asked. "What I want is money, my friend. And I want it now."

Tom Dolan just stared at him. "This ain't a stagecoach, mister. We got no money. We been to town, to get supplies."

The stranger studied them a moment, stroking his mustache. "I don't know whether to believe that or not, but I do know the brand on them horses." Looking at Eddie, he said, "You're Will McCartle's boy, ain't that right?"

Eddie just sat there, numb with fear.

"Get down off that wagon, kid. Come over here."

Tom Dolan blinked. "Now, just a minute—"

The stranger's gun, which until now had been aimed at Dolan, shifted to point at Eddie. "I said come over here, boy!"

Without taking his eyes off the gunman, Tom Dolan reached out and squeezed Eddie's hand. "Go on, Eddie. Do as he says."

His young heart hammering, Eddie climbed down and walked around the front of the team to stand before the stranger.

As Dolan watched, helpless, the man spurred his horse forward, reached down, grabbed Eddie by the straps of his overalls, and hauled him up onto the front of the saddle. Holding him close with his left hand, he pressed the gunbarrel to the boy's temple.

Tom Dolan had half-risen from his seat. "Don't hurt him, mister. Please don't hurt him."

Smiling broadly, the man in black shook his head. "No promises, there. But I got a feeling Mr. Big Shot McCartle might pay dear to get his kid back. You just tell him"—he paused for a second, thinking—"you tell him to bring five thousand dollars to Wildhorse Canyon tomorrow at sunup. Tell him to come alone, or I'll kill the boy. You got that?"

"Wait!" Dolan blurted. "I lied to you. I lied about the money. We do have some, left over after the supplies. I'll give you that, if you'll leave the boy alone—"

"Well, I'm much obliged. But I believe I'll take the boy and the money too." Keeping the gun to Eddie's head, he added, "Hand it over."

"It's under the seat," Dolan said, and glanced at Eddie. Just for a second, their eyes met. "I'll have to dig it out."

"Just make it quick. And you hold still, kid, this gun's got a hair-trigger."

Eddie held his breath as Dolan leaned forward and poked his arm into the compartment underneath his seat.

"Let me get this right," Dolan called, intent on his search. "Noon tomorrow, you said?"

"*Sunup* tomorrow."

"Oh. Right. And—Blackhorse Canyon?"

"*Wild*horse Canyon!" The stranger glared at him.

"Sorry," Dolan murmured, still groping beneath the seat. "I'm new here. Where is that, exactly?"

"Over *there*," the man said. Exasperated, he raised his pistol and pointed east. "About five miles—"

The man in black never finished the sentence. As soon as the gun moved away from Eddie's head, Tom Dolan's hand came out from under the seat. Three shots split the silence, three shots fired so lightning-fast they sounded like one, and before Eddie knew what was happening he was free of the man's grasp, free and on the ground and running for the wagon. Only when he got there and turned around, panting and sweating, did he see what had taken place.

The man on the horse sat as still as a stone, his mouth open in shock and his gun still pointing east as if it had been frozen there. Only three things looked different: his hat was off and lying in the road twenty feet behind him, and both his earlobes were gone. Bright blood dripped from the bottoms of his ears and onto the shoulders of his fancy black vest.

Very slowly, as if in a dream, Eddie turned to look up at Tom Dolan, who was down on one knee beside the wagon seat, holding the reins of the nervous horses in one hand and Eddie's grandfather's pistol in the other. The gun was cocked and smoking and rock-steady, and pointed at the head of the man on the bay horse.

"Drop it," Dolan said, and the stranger seemed to awaken—he actually blinked a couple of times. Immediately his right hand opened and the pistol fell to the ground.

Eddie stood there by the front wagon wheel, awestruck.

"I'll know you now, if I ever see you again," Dolan was saying—only later did Eddie realize he was referring to the man's ears—"and if I were you I'd make very sure that never happens. Is that clear?"

The man in black just sat there, mouth agape, eyes as wide as hen's eggs.

"Is that *clear*?"

Apparently it was. The stranger nodded vigorously, blood spattering both himself and his horse.

"Go," Dolan said, and watched as the man wheeled his mount and raced away down the dirt road. Within seconds he was out of sight.

With a sigh Dolan lowered the gun and looked at Eddie. "You all right, kiddo?" he asked.

Eddie swallowed. Without a word, he climbed up and onto the seat and buried his head in Tom Dolan's chest. Dolan hugged him tight, then held him at arm's length and looked him over. "I said, are you all right?"

"I think so." Eddie drew a long breath and let it out. "I was so scared—"

Suddenly a thought hit him.

"Do you know what just happened?" he blurted. "Do you realize who that was? You just whipped *Pinto Bishop* in a *gunfight*. You shot off his hat and his ears! I can't believe—"

But then he stopped. Part of it was the calm, knowing look on Dolan's face, and part was Eddie's vivid memory of the way Dolan had moved in that split-second between life and death. The way he had whirled and fired, the speed of his hands, the accuracy of the shots—

Eddie blinked, his mind racing now. He found himself remembering the box of cigars he'd seen under Dolan's bunk, the dark shirt and pants in his bedroll, the patch of pale, untanned skin between his nose and his upper lip the day he arrived at the ranch looking for work, as if—

As if he had just shaved off a mustache.

Their eyes held for a long time. At last Eddie turned and looked down the road, at the place where the stranger had vanished from sight.

"That wasn't Pinto Bishop at all," Eddie said quietly. "Was it."

Dolan shook his head. "No."

And suddenly Eddie felt scared. Not scared of Dolan—

he'd never be afraid of Tom Dolan. He was scared of what would happen to Dolan now. It was all too much to try to understand.

"Eddie?"

Slowly, the boy turned to face him.

"Eddie, for what it's worth, Pinto Bishop is gone. He doesn't exist any more." A long pause. "I'm Tom Dolan now. I work for your daddy, I cook pancakes for his cowboys, and I'm a happy man. The past bothers me sometimes, but I've changed my ways."

Eddie just sat there, not knowing what to say.

After a pause Dolan sighed again and gazed into the distance. "You know how you can be sure that's true?" he asked. "The old Pinto Bishop would never have let that fellow ride out of here." He looked Eddie straight in the eye. "Do you understand what I'm saying?"

Eddie swallowed, turning that over in his mind. Finally he nodded, and a weight seemed to lift from his shoulders. "Yes," he said. "I do understand that."

For several minutes, neither of them said a word. In the trees beside the road, a crow cawed. One of the horses swished his tail at a fly.

"So what do we do now?" Dolan asked.

Eddie frowned, still a little dazed. "What do you mean? We go home."

"I mean what do we do about this?" Dolan waved vaguely toward the gun on the ground, the hat in the middle of the road, the scene in general. "What are you going to tell your father?"

Eddie thought that over, then said, with great conviction: "I won't tell him anything, yet. Maybe later. Maybe we can— ease into it."

Dolan nodded. "Fair enough."

He was about to pick up the reins again when he noticed Eddie's grandpa's pistol, lying on the seat beside him. "What about this?" he asked, hefting the gun in his palm. "I was told to give it to your dad when we get home."

"So?"

"So he might wonder why three rounds were fired."

Eddie pondered that for a moment. "We'll say we saw the cougar that's been stealing our calves. You shot at him, but you missed."

Dolan looked amused. "I missed?"

A slow smile broke out on Eddie's face. "You're a cook," he said. "What would a cook know about guns?"

THE PROPOSAL

With a long sigh, Jordan Cain leaned back in his chair, slipped off his Gucci loafers, and propped both feet on the edge of his leather desktop. His glasses dangled by one earpiece from his right hand; his left massaged his forehead, the fingers moving so slowly they seemed to be tracing the worry lines to see where they went.

Jordan Cain was a weary man. Weary of his job, weary of his wife, weary of life in general. In fact, there was only one thing that kept him from being a truly unhappy man. That thought made him smile.

Cain slid his glasses into place and opened his eyes. Behind him, the last rays of the sun filtered through the blinds, daubing the toes of his socks with gold and painting a ladder of yellow stripes across the office's east wall. Cain's gaze climbed them, one by one, until he was staring at the ornate clock perched on a shelf near the ceiling.

It was 4:33. Less than two hours until his meeting with

Diana. His smile widened into a grin.

Content once more, he plucked the afternoon newspaper—the Christmas Eve edition—from atop his credenza and snapped it open to the sports page. As an afterthought he pressed a button beneath the desktop. Three matching lamps, strategically placed throughout the room, flickered to life.

Lighted, the office was a showcase. Accessories of gold and brass reflected the glow of the lamps, and leather wingback chairs sank two inches deep in the Bigelow carpeting. The gleam of polished mahogany was everywhere. Bookshelves ran half the length of the south wall, flanked on one side by a Schefflera tall enough to hang a swing in and on the other by a marble fireplace. Above the mantle was a portrait of Sam Houston; other paintings and prints, elaborately framed, covered the opposite wall. The entire room exuded wealth like an aroma.

The only inconsistencies were small ones: a coiled lariat on a peg in the corner, a miniature windmill made of copper wire, several dogeared copies of Louis L'Amour westerns stacked alongside the works of Shakespeare on the bookshelves. They were remnants of Cain's past, reminders of the days on the sprawling ranch outside Waco.

The Rolling C. It had a nice ring to it, even now. The irony of the name—considering the location, which was at least two hundred miles from the nearest large body of water—had had a great appeal to his father. And indeed the place had rolled, at least for a while. At one point it surpassed ten thousand acres, with fat red-and-white herefords spread out as far as the eye could see.

But cattle—and land—had been only a part of Benjamin Cain's dream.

In the fall of '66, after years of surveys and arguments and indecision, he finally took the leap, going deeply into debt to sink two wells a mile apart, both within sight of the main house. Close enough, in fact, that all the windows on the east side were blown out six months later by the explosion at #1 that killed him and two of his workers. Close enough, also, that on a sunny morning in November of '67 his widow and their son Jordan felt their breakfast table begin to tremble under their plates, and saw through the kitchen window a roaring black geyser that climbed three hundred feet into the air.

The strike at #2 would become the fifth largest in Texas history. To Jordan and his mother, who had risked everything to continue the drilling, it was a godsend. Money began to roll in, a lot of it, and young Jordan, who had turned twenty-one the week before the gusher, channeled most of it back into the operation. Soon there were bigger wells—and bigger money. Riding the wave, he traded his range boots for wingtips, his ponies for Porsches, his bandannas for Dior neckties. Along the way he lost his mother and married Margaret, and now, more than thirty years later, Jordan Cain was one of the richest oilmen in South Texas. And though he insisted that he'd lost touch with the Old Days, his colleagues still joked that during speeches he would often pause and stomp his foot to kick imaginary cow manure off his shoes.

Cain finished the paper, tossed it onto the desktop, tucked his feet back into his loafers, and swiveled his chair to face the window. It was almost dark now. Listening closely, he could hear a tinny P.A. system version of "Deck the Halls" over the murmur of traffic three stories below. 'Tis the season to be jolly, the words reminded him.

Well, he fully intended to be, in just a little while now. Looking at his Rolex—it was almost five—he wondered again if his wife had believed the story he'd told her about having to work late tonight. She undoubtedly had; Margaret was as gullible as a field hand. But he'd have to be cautious just the same. If she ever found out about Diana—

"Mr. Cain?"

Startled, Cain turned toward the voice. For a fleeting instant, he had feared it was that of his own conscience.

Twenty feet away, a man was standing in the open doorway. He was tall and dark, with the arrogant good looks one might associate with a cologne commercial. His suit and tie were expensive, his pocket hanky arranged just so. A gold collar pin added the final touch, winking in the lamplight.

"Your secretary seems to have left early," the man said. "I hope I'm not imposing."

Cain stared at him without speaking. The corner of his eye caught his open appointment book. The page for Wednesday afternoon, December 24, was as clean as Kleenex. Cain was mildly irritated. "Do I know you?" he asked.

The stranger pushed the door shut and strode across the room, totally at ease. "No. We've not met." He paused just short of the desk, his hands out of sight in his pockets. "My name is Ross."

The oilman leaned back in his chair, watching his visitor. He had decided, for the moment, to hold his temper. "All right, Mr. Ross," he said, "what can I do for you?"

The man pursed his lips. "Actually, it's what I can do for *you*, Mr. Cain." He waved a hand toward one of the armchairs facing the desk. "May I?"

"Help yourself." Cain continued to study Ross's face as the younger man settled into the chair. The two of them sat there staring at each other.

Cain cleared his throat. "I assume this won't take long," he said, glancing at his watch. "I have an appointment at—"

"At the Hilton?" Ross said. "Room—let's see—305, isn't it?"

Cain looked up, stunned. He felt the blood drain from his

face.

"I know all about Diana Hartman, Mr. Cain. And quite a bit more, actually."

Cain felt dizzy; his pulse pounded in his ears. This couldn't be happening. He'd been so careful—

A single word popped into focus in his brain:

Blackmail.

He managed to clear his throat again. "Exactly how much *do* you know?"

Ross crossed his legs and brushed a speck of lint from his trousers. "It's not so much what I know," he said, "as what I've concluded." He frowned for a moment at the crease in his pants leg. "And I've concluded, Mr. Cain, that this is probably the second worst mistake you've ever made. The first"—he raised his head and looked the older man in the eye—"the first was allowing your wife to see your private records. Don't you agree?"

Cain's stomach, already uneasy, seemed to turn over. "This can't be," he croaked. "No one else knows about—"

"That's not exactly true, I'm afraid. I have my sources."

The oilman closed his eyes and took several deep breaths. He tried desperately to organize his thoughts.

The diary. Someone must have gotten to my diary.

It had been four years ago. He was sitting in his study late one night, looking over some files he'd brought home from the office, and dropped off to sleep in his chair. When he woke, Margaret was standing beside him in her bathrobe, a cup of tea in her hand. She was staring at the papers spread out on his desktop. The papers—notes, actually—were reports of income from a string of Venezuelan oil leases.

She hadn't really understood all of what she had read, he found, but she'd seen enough to ask him some pointed questions, and had eventually cornered him into admitting what she had suspected all along: the fact that oil wasn't the only commodity his drilling crews were shipping back from South America.

From that night forward, her knowledge had been an ever-present, though unspoken, threat. For their marriage had long since gone sour, at least as far as he was concerned. He tolerated her, and that was about all. Ironically—and for no logical reason that he could see—her love for him seemed to be as strong as ever. It proved how irrational she was, Cain reminded himself. But she was also impulsive, and unbelievably possessive. He was convinced that if he ever tried to divorce her, or if she ever found out—God forbid—that he was having an affair, she'd ruin him with the information she had. She'd darken the skies with so many incoming narcs and lawyers that he'd be in court for months and prison for years.

Because the one thing he hadn't done, in all his miserable years of marriage, was be unfaithful to her. Not once.

Until now.

Cain opened his eyes and looked across the desk at the younger man. Ross was tapping a cigarette against a flat gold-plated case he had taken from his coat pocket. Without asking, he lit it with a matching gold lighter.

Cain couldn't have cared less. Secondhand smoke was the least of his problems right now.

"How much do you want?" he asked, his voice hoarse.

Ross exhaled a plume of smoke and shook his head. "You're jumping to conclusions, Mr. Cain. I meant what I said earlier: I'm here to help you, not threaten you. Your secrets are safe with me."

The long silence was broken only by an occasional honk or squeal of tires from the rush-hour traffic below the window. Very slowly, very cautiously—as if his visitor might be provoked by any sudden movement—Cain removed his glasses and took a monogrammed handkerchief from his hip pocket. He used it to mop his forehead. Sweat had begun to creep downward from beneath his styled gray hair.

"If that's true," he murmured, "then why have you told me all this?"

"Two reasons," Ross said. "For one thing, it's important that you take me seriously. That you respect my talents." His face turned grave. "You see, I'm very thorough, as are my associates. You might say we're the best in the business."

"The business?" Cain put his glasses back on. Some of his composure had returned, but he was still shaken. He was watching Ross as if he were a tiger in a flimsy cage. "What business? Exactly why are you here?"

The tiger leaned forward, his elbows on his knees. His eyes were blue ice.

"I'm here," he said, "to make a proposal. To ask you one question. If your answer is no, then I'll walk out that door and you'll never see or hear from me again. If it's yes . . . well, then we'll proceed from there. Get into the details, I guess you'd say."

Cain sat motionless in his chair, thinking. A moment ago he had run a restless hand through his hair, and as a result a long graying comma hung down over his left eye. It made him feel old. Tired.

"I don't follow you. What kind of question?"

"Let me put it this way," Ross replied, stretching back in his armchair. "I told you I had two reasons for telling you what I know. The first, as I said, was to assure you of my competence. The second—" He paused and examined the ash on his cigarette. "I had to find out just how scared you are of your wife."

Cain glared at him. "I'm no fool, Mr. Ross," he said. "The information she has could destroy me. It's something I have to live with."

"That's where you're wrong," Ross said.

Cain frowned. "What do you mean?"

Ross hesitated. "How would you like to get rid of her?" he asked. "For good?"

Cain felt his eyes narrow, then grow wide as the meaning of Ross's words sank in. In a strained voice he said, "That's your—what did you call it? Your *proposal*?"

"That's it."

"Surely you're not serious—"

"I'm serious. I know how it can be done."

The oilman sat and stared at him. "I don't believe this. You're asking me to take out a *contract*? On my *wife*?"

Ross shrugged. "I have certain . . . resources," he said. "I'm asking if you'd like to use them."

Cain's gut tightened. He eased forward in his seat, placed his hands flat on the desktop, and glowered at the man in the armchair. "I could have you thrown out of here," he said.

The younger man looked bored. "Come now, Mr. Cain. You don't need to impress me. I told you before, all you have to do to get me to leave is say no, you're not interested." He stubbed out his cigarette in the ashtray. "Is that your answer?"

Cain frowned, saying nothing. A nervous tic that hadn't bothered him in months had suddenly returned, tugging like an imp at his left eyelid. Perspiration chilled his forehead. Across the desk, Ross sat and waited. He somehow managed to look amused without actually smiling. It occurred to Cain that a man like Ross might not know how to smile.

The oilman rose from his chair and walked to the window. He stood there in silence for a long time, his back to the room and his hands stuffed deep into his pockets. When he finally spoke—still looking out into the darkness—his voice was low.

"What do you mean by *resources*?"

"Experts," Ross said. "Professionals. Secrecy would be guaranteed."

Another silence. The faint sound of Christmas music drifted up from the street.

"How—" Cain coughed. "How would it be done?"

Ross shook his head. "I need your answer first. Yes or no."

Jordan Cain licked his lips and swallowed. His mind was spinning. How many times in the recent past had he tried to imagine what life would be like if he were married to Diana rather than Margaret? Dull, jealous, homely, trusting Margaret, who knew so little about most things and far too much about others. And for the past four years, since she'd seen the records, her very existence had been a threat to his career, his freedom, his life.

He deserved better.

And even if the impossible were to happen—if she one day had a complete change of heart and decided to grant him a divorce—it was entirely possible that he would have to give up Cain Enterprises as part of the settlement.

A voice interrupted his thoughts. "Yes or no," Ross repeated.

Cain stood there a moment longer, then turned.

"Yes," he answered. "Yes. I'm interested."

Ross regarded him for several seconds. "It'll cost."

"Doesn't matter. I'm interested."

Ross nodded. "All right. We have a deal."

Cain moved back to his chair, never once taking his eyes off his visitor's face. A drop of sweat ran into his eye, and he blinked. He whipped out his handkerchief again, swept it over his forehead, and stuffed it into his pocket. He lowered himself into the chair in slow motion, as if he were sitting on eggs.

Ross lit another cigarette. "I imagine you have some questions," he said.

Cain nodded, tried to collect his thoughts. "When would it happen? And where?"

"Tomorrow. At your house."

Cain blinked. "But I'll be there then."

"You'll be out. I'll go over that in a minute. Your wife will be home alone."

"But . . . the servants—"

"Tomorrow's Christmas Day," Ross said. "They won't be on duty."

Cain frowned a moment, then nodded. Ross was right. Margaret always gave the staff the day off so they could spend Christmas with their families. But how had he known that?

"I checked," Ross said. "I've checked everything, Mr. Cain. You have nothing to worry about."

Cain licked his lips. He was beginning to feel better. The younger man's confidence was contagious. "Go on," he said.

"Tomorrow morning at nine-thirty sharp you'll receive a phone call," Ross continued. "It'll be me. I'll say your full name once and then hang up. You'll tell your wife you've been asked to come down to the office—one of your freighters is in trouble in the Gulf. Rescue operations are underway. You'll be back as soon as you can."

Cain stared at him, absorbed.

"Exactly forty-five minutes after you leave the house, a man in a business suit will ring the front doorbell. He'll say he's a friend of yours, and will show your wife a card identifying him as the manager of a well-known jewelry store downtown. You called him at home half an hour ago, he'll say, and asked him to find a little something for her—a sort of peace offering for having to leave her alone on Christmas morning." Ross tapped the ash off his cigarette. "You've . . . done that kind of thing before, haven't you?"

Cain scowled. "What do you mean?"

Ross shrugged and said, "You know—sent her gifts and so forth. Unannounced."

"Occasionally." Cain had the distinct feeling that Ross had already known the answer. "What kind of gift?"

Ross switched the cigarette from his right hand to his left, leaned sideways, and reached into one of the outer pockets of his jacket. A delicate gold chain appeared; it was entwined around the fingers of his right hand. At the end of the chain hung a flat round pendant, also gold, about an inch and a half long and three quarters of an inch thick. It gleamed in the lamplight. At the bottom of the pendant was a tiny clasp.

"A locket," Cain murmured. He glanced up at Ross's face.

"Right. But a rather unusual one." Ross reached forward and placed the locket and chain on the desktop. "Take a look."

Frowning, Cain picked it up. He examined it, turning it over in his hands. It was quite heavy, he found, and yet elegant. Designs of intricate detail covered most of its surface. Intrigued, he unfastened the clasp with his fingernail and opened the cover.

The inside was even more unique. Nestled in the center of a blue velvet background was a stone approximately half an inch in diameter. Cain recognized it as a fire opal, professionally facet-cut and mounted. He had seen a number of them years ago in Mexico and Honduras, though none had been this perfect. Vivid shades of red, yellow, and orange—the colors that gave the stone its name—flashed and changed from one to the other as he tilted the locket back and forth. Gingerly he touched the stone's rounded surface. It felt as smooth as silk. Inside the opal, the fires danced and flickered.

"What do you think?" Ross asked.

"It's magnificent." Cain touched the stone again. "It even *feels* expensive."

"Good," Ross said, nodding. "That's what we're counting on."

The oilman looked up. "What do you mean?"

"I mean, Mr. Cain, that the locket you're holding is exactly like the one your wife will be given—with one major difference." He paused and added, "How much do you know about opals?"

"Not a lot. Why?"

"They're porous," Ross said. "They absorb liquids very readily. Finished stones, I'm told, are often coated with water or films of oil until they're sold to protect them from cracking or losing their color."

"So?"

"So we took advantage of that. The opal inside the locket we'll use tomorrow will be saturated with enough poison to kill an elephant."

Cain blinked. To his surprise, he felt a thrill of excitement move up his spine. "What kind of poison?"

"A fluid from the oscolio blossoms of eastern Africa. Lethal. Better than curare because it's absorbed directly through the victim's skin, on contact. That's what I meant earlier, about feeling the stone." Ross studied his cigarette. "All Mrs. Cain has to do is touch it once, for only a second or so. It takes effect immediately."

Cain swallowed. "How long exactly?"

"It varies. For sure, less than ten minutes after contact. When it happens, it's quick."

"And it leaves no traces?"

"None. Looks like a coronary."

Cain thought this over. "Who'll do the job?" he asked. "You?"

Amusement flickered again in Ross's eyes. "I negotiate. Someone else does the heavy stuff."

"Who?"

Ross hesitated. "His name is Pickett."

"Pickett," Cain repeated. "I take it he knows what he's doing?"

"He's the best. There'll be no mistakes."

Cain stared at the younger man for a full minute, still thinking. Smoke from Ross's cigarette curled lazily toward the ceiling.

"I just thought of something," Cain said. "The locket can't be left at the scene. Your man's going to have to take it with him when he leaves."

Ross shrugged. "So?"

"That means he'll have to try to stand there and make small talk until the poison takes effect." Cain leaned forward, worried. "What if, after touching the stone, she decides to thank him and show him the door so she can get back to whatever she was doing? That'll ruin everything."

"Mr. Cain," Ross said, "the one thing we don't want is to cause any sign of a struggle. I don't think he'll have any problem stalling for time, but if he does have to leave before the time's up, he'll leave. He'll already have made sure he saw her touch the stone. All he'll do then is wait outside, out of sight, until it's over. Then he'll go back in and retrieve the locket."

"What if he can't find it?"

Ross seemed about to smile, but didn't. "He'll find it. Mr. Pickett is rather industrious. This wasn't his first line of work, if you get my drift."

Cain let that one pass. Finally he asked, "What about the telephones? If she should happen to make a call in the meantime—or if someone should call her—there's a chance she might mention the gift. That could raise some awkward questions later."

"That won't happen," Ross said. "The phones will be temporarily out of service."

"He's going to cut the lines? That doesn't sound very smart—"

"I didn't say they'd be cut, I said they'd be out of service. Among other things, Pickett knows his way around a junction box. He'll disconnect the lines when he gets there and reconnect them when he leaves."

Cain shifted in his seat, trying to remember whether the box terminating the underground lines could be seen from the house. He decided it couldn't. And the property was remote and heavily wooded; the odds were slight that a neighbor or passerby would notice anyone on the grounds. The plan sounded good. Absently, he snapped the locket shut and tossed it onto the desktop.

He had a sudden thought. "Hold on. If he does have to leave without the locket . . . how will he get back in again? She always keeps the house locked."

Ross flicked the ash off his cigarette. "You'll see to that," he said. "I know all the doors have different locks. When you leave, take the key to the kitchen door with you. Hide it someplace where our man can get it if he needs it."

"Where?"

"In the mailbox, all the way to the back. Remember, it's the postman's day off too."

Cain felt he had missed something. "Why the kitchen door?"

"It's the only one without a chain latch. Correct?"

It was true. The chain had come loose a month ago and hadn't been replaced. "I'm impressed," Cain said.

Ross nodded. "You should be."

The two men fell silent. The room was dead quiet; the sound of the holiday music outside the window had stopped.

Cain studied his folded hands a moment, thinking hard.

Ross checked his watch. "Well," he said. "If there are no more questions, Mr. Cain—"

"I want her to know," Cain said.

Ross frowned. "Pardon?"

Cain looked up at his visitor. "Tell your man—Pickett— that I want him to give her a message. I want her to know who's doing this." He paused. "How long did you say the poison takes to work?"

"Eight or nine minutes, max."

"And you said there's a good chance he'll be with her when it takes effect?"

"That's right. What are you driving at?"

Jordan Cain leaned back in his chair. He felt a delicious little tingle in his gut. "Tell him to watch the time very carefully," he said. "When she's just begun to feel the effects, and when he's sure she has only seconds left, I want him to tell her"—he thought a moment—"I want him to tell her: 'Regards from your husband.'"

Ross looked intrigued. "Regards from your husband," he repeated. "How thoughtful."

"Just tell him," Cain said. "I want her to *know*. I want it to be the last thing she hears."

Ross nodded. "All right. I'll pass it on."

Ross glanced again at his wristwatch and rose to his feet. "I'm afraid I really have to be going." The locket still lay on the desktop. He picked it up and replaced it in his pocket.

"Wait a second," Cain said, surprised. "Don't you want to discuss the money?"

Ross stared at him. "Oh, I don't think that'll be necessary. To be perfectly honest, Mr. Cain"—Ross gave him a benign look—"I've already been paid."

The oilman blinked. "What are you talking about?"

"Remember my proposal, Mr. Cain?" Ross stooped down

and crushed out his cigarette in the ashtray. "You should have said no. I was instructed to leave if you said no."

Even before the meaning of the words hit him, Cain remembered something else: the way Ross had picked up the locket off the desk.

He had only touched the chain.

Cain felt his stomach clench.

It was all clear to him now. There would be no murder tomorrow, no contract on his wife.

Ross had been stalling for time.

Frantically Cain reached for the telephone, snatched the receiver to his ear—

The line was dead.

A wave of nausea swept through his body; he couldn't seem to get his breath. The first blue jolt of pain hit him in the chest. The phone slipped from his grasp and landed with a thump on the leather desktop.

Cain stared at it vacantly, then raised his eyes.

"Who *are* you?" he whispered.

Pickett had made it to the door. He paused and turned, his hand on the knob.

"Regards from your wife," he said.

And smiled.

THE JUMPER

"The smartest thing?" I asked.

"That's right," Rufus said. "What's the smartest thing you've ever done? Simple question."

I thought a moment. Ten feet beyond the log where Rufus Olson and I were sitting, the muddy waters of Lake Beaudark lay flat and still in the midday sun. The black swamp on the far side shimmered in the haze. It was July in Georgia, and hot as the hinges of hell's door.

"You mean like *wise* smart?" I asked.

Rufus smiled and tossed a pebble into the water. "I mean like *clever* smart. What's the cleverest thing you've ever done?"

I had to think about that awhile. Clever wasn't something I knew a lot about. If I'd been clever, I probably wouldn't have been sitting there on a log beside the lake with Rufus Olson.

"I don't rightly know," I said. And then I asked him the question I knew he wanted me to ask. If he hadn't, he wouldn't have brought up the subject in the first place.

"What's the cleverest thing *you've* ever done, Rufus?"

He pursed his lips and stared out over the lake, as if actually trying to remember.

"I guess it was something that happened when I lived in Atlanta," he said, after a minute or so. "There was a jewelry store downtown, I forget the name, but I walked in there one Christmas and asked to see some of their finer merchandise. Wanted to buy a little something for the wife, I said."

He paused, scratching his chin.

"The salesclerk was a little baldheaded guy with glasses. As soon as he heard the words *finer merchandise* he pulled out a big flat box, set it down on the countertop, and opened it up. Inside that display box, Raymond my boy, was the fanciest jewelry I ever saw. At least a dozen diamond necklaces, lined up so they overlapped each other in the case, gleaming and winking like a million crystal chandeliers.

"'Perhaps one of these,' the clerk says, real prissy. 'Perhaps,' I told him. I took my time, looking at each one. Pretty soon, when he figured he had me hooked, he offered me a silver cigarette case—everybody smoked back then, you know. I opened it and took one out, and he lit it with a matching silver lighter. Then I went back to studying the necklaces, trying to remind myself not to dust my ashes on the carpet.

"About that time, just as a clock in the corner was striking the hour, we heard a commotion outside. We turned around to look, and saw through the big storefront window that a crowd was gathering, and was staring straight up at the tall buildings on the other side of the street. All of a sudden a woman called: 'Look out!' and we heard a scream—a long, horrible, bloodcurdling scream.

"'Oh Lord,' the clerk says, under his breath. 'It's a jumper.'

"And sure enough, a second later, the crowd outside scattered like leaves in a storm, and those of us in the store saw a body falling through the air. There wasn't a lot of traffic right then, and we actually saw the body hit the ground. It didn't bounce or splatter or anything, it just landed—WHUMP—on the far sidewalk.

"Right quick after that, half a dozen bystanders ran to the body, gathering around it in a huddle, almost. The two other men in the store groaned and shook their heads. My clerk was pale as a ghost, his eyes glued to the window."

Rufus paused again, staring down at the ground between his workshoes.

I sat and waited.

"That was when it happened," he said. "All of a sudden, as all of us watched through the window, the crowd around the body began to spread apart. They all backed away together—and they looked . . . scared. No, more than that; they looked terrified. And when they had backed away far enough, we could see the body again."

I stared at him, absorbed. "And?"

Rufus raised his head and looked at me. "And it moved."

In the sticky heat of the July sun, I felt a cold shiver run down my backbone.

"It what?"

"The body moved," he said. "First one leg, then the other, then a hand fluttered a little. Finally, as we stood there with our mouths hanging open, the man on the sidewalk rolled over, propped himself up on one elbow, and looked around."

I swallowed. "You're not serious."

"I am. And I'll tell you, Raymond my friend, you would not believe the reactions of the people around me. One of the men in that store fainted dead away, and so did most of the women outside, and everybody started running in all directions. Every place of business in shouting distance emptied like the

45

whole block was on fire. I guess that was to be expected—this was the city, after all, and crazies do jump from buildings. But coming back to life, afterward? Now, that's something to see.

"And that's just what he did. After a minute or so he sat all the way up, an average-looking guy in a gray suit, blinking at everybody like he just woke up from a nap. He didn't seem to have a scratch on him. Pretty soon he stood up, wobbled for a second, smiled real dopey-like at everybody, and just walked away. The crowd parted for him as if Jesus Himself had returned to earth and was setting out to gather the righteous."

Rufus fell silent again. I stared at him a moment, stunned. "Then what?"

He glanced at me. "Beg pardon?"

"What happened then?" I asked, exasperated. "That's not *all*, is it?"

"No, that's not all. The crowd finally broke up, looking a little dazed. Several people stopped to help those who had fainted."

"And . . . everybody just went back to what they were doing?"

"Well, not everybody," he admitted. "I, for one, walked down to the corner of Peachtree and Ellis, and hid for a while inside a hotel restroom. I had, you see, the big flat box from the jewelry store tucked inside my overcoat."

I stared at him in disbelief. "*You stole the necklaces?*"

He smiled. "You bet your booties. I figured I deserved it."

"Deserved it? What do you mean?"

His smile widened. "The jumper," he said, "wasn't a jumper at all. He was a dummy, made out of rags sewn inside a gray suit, and its head was a painted sack stuffed with Styrofoam. It was thrown from the roof of the Hamilton Building by a man named Willy Maddox, who should have been an opera singer. His was the scream we heard." Rufus stopped a moment, remembering. "As soon as the dummy hit the sidewalk, six of our partners, dressed in trenchcoats, ran to the body and gathered close around it while they cut it apart with pocketknives and stuffed the rags and pieces of suit underneath their coats. Within seconds the jumper had completely disappeared."

I shook my head in confusion. "Wait a minute. If that was what happened—who was lying there afterward? Another of your men?"

Rufus nodded. "A guy named Gus Fedderman. He was the first to run up to look at the body, and under the cover of his partners it was easy for him to strip off his trenchcoat—he had on a gray suit underneath—and lie down on the sidewalk while they dismantled the dummy. When they let others through to look, and the new 'body' began to stir a little, they backed away together and vanished into the crowd."

I sat there on the log for a minute or more, staring at him in awe.

Then a sudden thought hit me.

"How did you clear a profit?" I asked. "All the recruiting, the planning, the setup—and at least eight of you to split the take—" I studied him. "Was it worth it?"

He smiled. "The way we did it, it was. You see, there were two more jewelry stores nearby, and a couple of ritzy shops. One man in each place did the same thing I did, at exactly the same time. Three days later, at a park in Marietta, twelve of us split more than seven hundred thousand. The six sidewalk men got half shares because of the lower risk, the rest of us cleared eighty grand apiece. Not bad for those days."

Not bad at all, I thought. And he was right: The whole idea was just about the cleverest thing I had ever heard of.

I was quiet for a long time, watching his profile as he squinted at the calm waters of the lake.

"What went wrong?" I asked him.

He turned and regarded me solemnly. "An oversight," he said with a sigh. "A small lapse of concentration."

It took me a minute to figure it out. "The clerk's cigarette case?"

He nodded. "My prints were all over it."

Both of us fell silent.

"At least you're almost done," I said. "One more year, isn't it?"

"Ten months. It's something to look forward to, all right."

Behind us, a deep voice called out: "Break's over, boys. Back to work."

We rose stiffly to our feet, picked up our swinging-blades, and followed the trusty up the hill toward the road crew. Our leg chains clanked and jangled with each step.

Halfway there, I put a hand on Rufus' arm, and he turned and looked at me. The guard had gone on ahead.

"One more thing," I said. "They got *you.* Did they get the money, too?"

A slow grin spread across his face.

"You're pretty clever, too, sometimes," he said.

Smiling, we trudged together up the hill toward the others.

LINDY'S LUCK

In the very center of the mall, at the top of the down escalator, beside a display of World Book encyclopedias, Lindy Zeller was tying her shoes. They were old white Reeboks, and went well with her gray sweats and baggy windbreaker. After a moment she stood up, smiled at her male companion, and stepped onto the escalator.

They made an unusual couple. In her casual outfit she looked rather plain, a pale blonde with hazel eyes and no makeup. He was short but dapper in a navy sportcoat and Dockers. You could see your reflection in his shoes.

Neither of them said a word on their way down.

They got off on the first floor and headed for the west entrance.

Twenty feet from the escalators the woman stopped in her tracks, staring straight ahead. Another young lady, heading in the opposite direction, froze as well. Both their mouths fell open at the same time.

"Lindy?" one said.

"Mary Nell!" the other cried.

And before the man knew what was happening, the two women were hugging and giggling like schoolgirls. After a moment they separated, and looked each other up and down.

"My God, Lindy, what has it been? Ten years?"

"At least—and you haven't changed. Not a *bit!*"

During all this, the man in the sportcoat studied the second woman—Mary Nell—more closely. She was attractive but a little tacky; the eye shadow was too dark, the hair too orange, the jeans too tight. Her earrings were as big as tennis balls. He decided she was either a hooker or a TV evangelist.

He suddenly realized she was staring at him. "Lindy, I don't think I've met your, uh, gentleman," she said.

The first woman blinked, then looked at him. "Oh. I'm sorry—"

"Sam Rollins," he said to her friend. "Pleased to meet you."

"I'm Mary Nell Hartsfield," she said. Without looking away, she asked, with open approval: "My, Lindy dear, where did you find *him?*"

Lindy looked embarrassed. "We met in a night class. Sam's a good friend. Now, tell me about you. Didn't you move to Memphis? And how are your folks?"

Mary Nell Hartsfield pried her eyes from Sam and focused again on Lindy. The two of them rattled on for a few minutes about everything from school to clothes to the failed marriages of their old friends. Finally Sam glanced at his watch. Both women noticed.

"I guess we should be going," Lindy said sadly. She turned to Rollins. "Where are you parked, Sam?"

The question surprised him. "Just outside Dillard's. Why?"

Ignoring him, Lindy turned to Mary Nell and took her hand. "I'm so glad you're back in town. How about lunch sometime? Ruby Tuesday, maybe?"

Mary Nell grinned. "Let's do that." She gave Lindy another hug. "I can't wait to tell Mother I saw you. And so nice to meet you, Mr. Rollins."

"You too," he said. As she walked away they turned and continued down the corridor. After a moment Lindy looked at him.

"Thank you for that," she said.

He shrugged. "Your friends'll find out soon enough. No point in rushing it."

"And thanks especially for the handcuffs."

He fetched a sigh. "That was a mistake, probably. Rules say you should be wearing them right now. And you will be, when we get downtown."

She frowned. "Sounds stupid to me. I'm not a murderer or anything."

They reached the mall entrance. He followed her out onto the sidewalk beside the parking lot. The sun was almost down now, and it had been raining.

"What you are," he said, "is a shoplifter who's been caught red-handed, in the biggest jewelry store in the city." He shook his head as they walked. "If we find out this isn't your first offense, Lindy Zeller—or whatever your real name is— you'll soon be shopping from the warden's pushcart."

This time she didn't reply. Looking glum, she pulled up the collar of the windbreaker and tucked her hands into its pockets. Sam pointed to an empty unmarked car parked twenty yards away, near the entrance to Dillard's department store. She left the wet sidewalk and started toward it; he followed a few steps behind.

"On the other hand, if you're telling the truth about this

being your first time, there's a chance the judge—" He looked up to see her moving away to the left. "Hey! Where do you think you're going?"

She kept walking, making a wide detour around a pool of brown water twenty feet across. Then she calmly turned and looked at him, her hands still in her pockets.

"I may be a criminal," she said, "but I don't have to get my shoes wet."

Detective Rollins couldn't think of a single response to that. Frowning, he also skirted the puddle and they continued on to his car.

"Get in," he told her.

"Where? In the front, or in the back like the guys you see on the news?"

Sam heaved a sigh. "Get in the front. Unless maybe you want to drive, too."

She walked around, climbed into the passenger side, and shut the door. He took out his keys and sat down wearily behind the wheel. He put the key into the ignition, rested his left arm on the wheel, turned to say something to her—

And saw the gun.

It was a little nickel-plated automatic—a lady's gun—and she was holding it with both hands. It was aimed directly at his head.

"I really am sorry about this," she said. She didn't seem nervous in the least. Or sorry, either, for that matter.

At first he couldn't imagine where she had gotten the gun. He had searched her himself, at the scene, just after he arrived. Had he overlooked it somehow?

Then he remembered.

"Mary Nell," he said.

"Afraid so." She glanced down at his sportcoat. "Let's have it. Slowly. Keep your right hand on the wheel."

Very carefully he reached underneath his coat, took out his revolver, and handed it to her butt-first. She tossed it onto the back seat.

But at least she touched it, he thought. Now we'll have her prints.

And then he saw the gloves. Thin, brown leather gloves. When had she put those on? He had seen them before, of course—in the pocket of her jacket during the search. But he was certain she hadn't been wearing them in the mall, and he'd have noticed if she put them on later; it was too warm today for gloves.

Then he remembered falling behind her as she went around the puddle in the parking lot. Afterward, she had kept both hands in her pockets.

She's smart, he told himself. And quick.

"Okay," Lindy said, "start the car." He did. "Now back up, slowly, into that little alcove back there, by the dumpsters." She held the gun on him, rock-steady, until it was done. When he cut the engine this time, the car was well hidden, parked tail-first in the shadows between a row of tall shrubs and a eight-foot-square garbage container.

She put the ignition keys in her pocket.

"Still too bright in here, don't you think?" She leaned forward to look at the floorboards, then smiled and pulled a folded cardboard sunshield from under the seat. She tossed it in his lap. "Fix it."

Under the watchful eye of the gun Sam unfolded the cardboard and spread it across the length of the windshield. It shut out the rest of the world as effectively as if a curtain had been drawn. On the side, facing in, were the words CALL POLICE—NEED HELP. Sam didn't find it funny.

"Handcuffs," she said.

He took them from his pocket. Watching him closely,

Lindy made him snap one end of the cuffs to his left wrist, then reach through the steering wheel and snap the other to his right. When that was done she pitched the key out the window, put the gun in her pocket, and had him lean his head back against the headrest at the top of the driver's seat. Then she unwound his shoulder seatbelt and wrapped it snugly around his neck and the headrest, binding them together. Any hope he might have had of leaning forward enough to get to his doorhandle or the radio was gone. He was trussed like a pig.

"Tying your shoe at the top of the escalator," he said. "That was the signal. Right?"

"You're learning," she replied.

With an effort, he turned his head to watch her. She was rummaging through the glove compartment, looking for heaven knew what. After a moment he saw her take a pair of pliers from a jumble of tools in a back corner of the compartment. The pliers went into her jacket pocket.

She drew a deep breath, let it out slowly, and looked around the inside of the car, taking stock. Her gaze stopped on his wristwatch. It was a gold Bulova, a gift from his father. She reached across him, unbuckled the leather band, and put the watch alongside the car keys and pliers in her pocket.

She was about to shut the open glovebox when she saw something else inside, among the odds and ends. Smiling, she reached forward and plucked it out.

It was a beautifully carved silver cigarette lighter, heavy and solid. It gleamed like a star in the fading light. She flicked it once, and a thin yellow flame leaped out. Apparently satisfied, she snapped the cover shut and pocketed the lighter.

She looked around again, thinking.

"You were lucky," Sam said quietly. He was staring straight ahead, at the covered windshield. "You know that, don't you?"

Lindy smiled again. "I'd rather have luck than talent, Sammy boy. But I'm glad you spoke up—it reminded me of something."

Moving swiftly, she reached down and unlaced his right shoe, took it off, removed its shoestring, and pulled off his sock.

"Say ahhh," she said, opening her mouth wide.

"Ahhh."

She stuffed the rolled-up sock into his mouth and tied it in place with one of his shoestrings. Then she leaned across his legs to pull the lever that sprung the hood.

Again she checked her surroundings. She seemed pleased. Looking him in the eye, she said, "I really must be going. I usually don't leave quite so soon after removing a man's socks, but I have a lot of things yet to do today." She gripped the doorhandle and grinned at him. "Maybe my luck'll hold."

She got out and shut the door.

Sam heard her stop and lift the car's hood, and a moment later heard the click of wires being cut. Then the hood was eased back down and she was gone. It took him a minute to figure out what she had done; when he did he verified it by pressing one forearm against the pad on the front of the steering wheel. Sure enough, there was no sound. The horn was dead.

Outside, in the parking lot, it was almost dark.

Sam Rollins sighed and closed his eyes.

***

Mary Nell Hartsfield was parked where Lindy had asked her to be, in her parting comment—just outside Ruby Tuesday, on the mall's southwest side.

"About time," she said, as Lindy climbed into the passenger seat.

"I've been busy," Lindy said. "Let's go."

The blue Ford Escort pulled away from the curb and into the parking lot, heading for the exit. Thunder grumbled somewhere in the distance.

Lindy leaned her head against the window glass and stared blankly at the windshield. She was exhausted.

"What happened back there?" Mary Nell asked. "I was getting really worried."

Lindy didn't answer right away. She just sat and stared out at the traffic. "Thelma dear," she said finally, "you've never been really worried about anything in your entire life."

"I've never been caught, either. The closer I come to it, the more worried I get."

Lindy grinned. Keeping her head propped against the window, she swiveled her neck to look at her friend. She studied her a moment in silence. Mary Nell's real name was Delores McClellan, but—like Lindy—she had had so many aliases she scarcely remembered the original. Ever since a movie they rented last summer—a film about a couple of wild women joyriding through life—they called each other Thelma and Louise.

"It wasn't your neck on the chopping block," Lindy said. "I was at ground zero, remember?"

Mary Nell frowned at the road. "And you think he's forgotten about *me*? Look, honey, I don't know how you got away from him, but I doubt your beauty struck him helpless. And unless he's brain-dead, he knows by now where it was that you got the gun." She coasted to a stop at a red light. "Besides, he got a good long look at me."

Lindy's smile widened. "Oh he did, did he?"

Mary Nell shot her a glance. "Sophisticated men," she said wisely, "don't like women who dress like Russian weightlifters. Not to mention women who are taller than they are."

"You're not so dainty yourself," Lindy pointed out. She had just remembered her pockets, and was going through them one by one, placing their contents on the dashboard.

"The difference is, I am a woman of obvious refinement."

Lindy held the watch up to the light and examined it thoughtfully. "You look like a waitress in an all-night diner," she said.

Mary Nell chuckled as she accelerated. "The hair is a little much, isn't it? But it worked. Columbo proved that if you look dumb enough everyone takes you for granted. If I'd been dressed like Barbara Walters we couldn't have made the transfer. He'd have been suspicious."

Lindy put the watch back into her pocket, picked up the cigarette lighter, and returned to her thoughts. She ran her thumb back and forth over the lighter's surface. It was fully dark outside now, and the traffic was thinning. They left County Line Road and cloverleafed onto the interstate.

"You never did tell me what happened."

Lindy shrugged. "We had a nice chat. He wants to meet my folks."

"Tell me you didn't shoot him."

"You didn't hear the shots?"

Mary Nell sighed and merged into the left-hand lanes. "What happened in the store?"

Lindy grimaced. "I almost made it. I had the salesgirl fooled, the necklace was in my hand, and I was on my way out. A guy I hadn't even seen, all the way in the back of the store, blew the whistle on me. He shouted to the manager, who jumped over the display counter like it wasn't there and held me down till the cops arrived. Or cop, in my case. An off-duty detective who'd stopped by the mall on his way home." She shook her head. "Just my luck. All the jewelry stores in the city and I pick one that has eagle-eyed employees and a halfback for a manager."

Neither of them spoke for a while.

"At least you got lucky with the cop. He seemed like an

okay guy."

Lindy nodded. "He was. If he'd cuffed me at the scene, the way he should have, I'd probably have four or five new roommates downtown tonight."

"Worse than that. You might have had the next few years to get to know them better." Without taking her eyes from the road Mary Nell said, "Not that we're famous or anything, but I'm told our likenesses are hanging in more than one post office in this state." She gave her partner a long look. "You really did-n't shoot him, did you?"

"Not anyplace important." Lindy leaned back and studied the tiny scrollwork on the lighter. "He'll be fine."

***

Ten miles away, Sam Rollins was anything but fine. Sitting there in the darkened car, he had time to ponder his mistakes.

And they were many. Granted, there was no way he could have known about the signal at the top of the escalator, but he could certainly have prevented what happened later. The gun, for instance. He should have caught that. For crying out loud, it had changed hands less than six feet in front of him. And the gloves. For that matter, the girl should have been cuffed in the first place. The chief would be thrilled.

There was, of course, one bright spot in all this.

It was an experimental project, begun last month. The department had purchased twelve silver cigarette lighters and twelve battery-operated monitors from a German surveillance firm.

The project was based on two theories. The first was that there are certain things that thieves simply cannot resist, just as a monkey cannot turn his back on a peanut even if he's full. If something looks valuable and it can be easily hidden and transported, it's fair game—and the fancier the better.

The second theory was based on fact. According to recent studies, seven out of every ten criminals are smokers.

Thus, the lighters.

The homing device inside each of them had an effective range of two hundred miles.

Sam looked down at the dashboard, where the digital monitor was ticking off the direction and mileage between itself and Lindy Zeller. He smiled grimly. His car had no siren—and no horn, thanks to Lindy—but it had been easy enough for his bare right foot to reach the button that activated the little battery-operated display. Just as it had reached the headlight switch.

Once every thirty seconds or so, he gripped the switch with his toes and blinked the car's headlights on and off again. The alcove was dark now; soon someone in the parking lot would see his lights and come to investigate.

So he sat and watched the numbers change on the display screen, just as he had watched them for the past fifteen minutes. The homing signal inside the woman's pocket was beaconing merrily away. According to the screen, the direction was now southwest, and the distance was increasing at the rate of about a tenth of a mile every five or six seconds. That meant her vehicle was doing just over sixty, which meant the interstate.

God, if he could only get loose.

Painfully he crossed his legs, positioned his right foot, and blinked the headlights again. Then he went back to watching the monitor: 11.9 miles—12 miles—12.1—12.2 . . .

***

"What's that?" Mary Nell asked.

Lindy looked up at her, then down at the lighter. She held it up. "What the hell does it look like?"

"Throw it away."

"What? Why?"

John M. Floyd

"Because it's dangerous, that's why. A fancy lighter like that one's unusual these days. It attracts attention, and we don't need attention. It could be traced." Mary Nell paused. "Wipe it clean, then throw it away."

Lindy frowned at it doubtfully.

"Now," Mary Nell said.

Obediently Lindy polished it with a Kleenex, then cranked down her window. The wind whooshed in, tossing her hair about like a yellow scarf. She threw the lighter, tissue and all, out into the darkness. It landed in the tall grass between the interstate and the frontage road. She rolled the window up again.

It was very quiet in the car. Lindy didn't mull over her loss; Mary Nell always knew best about those kinds of things. And what she had said earlier was right—they'd never been caught yet.

"So what now?" Lindy asked.

Mary Nell checked her mirror. "Another town, I guess. Houston, maybe?"

"How about New Orleans? Next week's Mardi Gras—"

"You talked me into it." Mary Nell opened her purse with one hand and pulled out a fifth of bourbon. "We might as well start getting in the mood, old girl."

Lindy took the bottle, twisted off the cap, and grinned. "Call me Louise," she said.

***

Sam Rollins blinked.

The numbers on the monitor had stopped.

Sam held his breath, narrowed his eyes. The display, still pulsing, said 18.2 miles.

Maybe she was just sitting at a red light, he thought.

Minutes passed. The numbers didn't change again.

Sam felt his heartbeat quicken. The woman named Lindy

Zeller—and probably her friend Mary Nell too—had stopped. Hopefully for the night. And only eighteen miles away.

It made sense, he decided. There were plenty of motels south of town. No one knew her real name, her car, or her location. Why not get some rest and stay off the roads until morning?

Now, if he could only get loose, he could have her in no time. The little green numbers on his display would guide him straight to her.

Suddenly he heard something. The sound of voices, and approaching footsteps.

Looks like your luck's run out, Lindy, he thought.

Sam Rollins grinned around the sock in his mouth.

***

Half an hour later, three cruisers and six police officers arrived at the office of the Great Southern Motel on the west frontage road of I-55. Though the names in the register didn't match, the descriptions and the check-in times did; within minutes the two occupants of Room 126 were arrested on a variety of charges.

As the others filed out, Officer Sam Rollins and one of the suspects stayed put, staring at each other in silence.

"How'd you find us?" Lindy asked him. She looked more puzzled than worried.

"You were greedy," he said. He held up the tiny monitor he had unscrewed from his dashboard. The display was still on; the blinking message now said 0.0 MILES.

Her confused look vanished. Understanding dawned.

"The lighter," she murmured, half to herself. Then she frowned again. "But . . . I threw it away. Miles from here."

Sam nodded. "He said that you might."

Lindy blinked. "What?"

"Well, not you specifically. He just said a lighter might

not be a good choice."

"What are you *talking* about?"

Sam couldn't help smiling. "My dad's a retired cop. When I was issued the lighter last month, he questioned the logic. He said no matter what the studies showed, it was too fancy for a crook. Too conspicuous to use and too risky to sell. I agreed."

"So?"

"So he removed the homing device. In mine, at least." Sam shrugged. "He used to be a jeweler, he still had the tools. He took out the workings."

She was beginning to understand. "And put them into . . ."

"My watch." Sam jingled the bag that held the contents of Lindy's pockets. "I think it was your only mistake."

A patrolman's voice, from outside in the lot, called: "You comin', Sam?"

Lindy sighed, long and deep. "I guess we should be going, huh?"

"Well," he said, "this time you know where I'm parked."

And this time he used the handcuffs.

SURVIVAL

Ross and McLane stood together on the grassy ridge, looking down at the coastline.

"If he left this morning," McLane said, "he should be back by now."

"He'll be back," Ross said.

"I don't know. He told Susan there might be pirates about." McLane was leaning on a crutch he had made from a tree limb, and gazing at the spot where the beach disappeared around a peninsula a mile to the west. They knew which way was west, at least, from the sun. That was about all they knew.

"Let's just hope he finds the boat."

McLane nodded. "Or more survivors. Right?"

"Wrong. We don't need more survivors. There's barely enough food for the four of us. What we need is the boat." All of them had seen it, just before dark last night—an empty rubber lifeboat, drifting in somewhere beyond the peninsula.

"What if he finds it," McLane asked, "and leaves us here?"

"I don't think that's a problem." Ross turned to glance at Susan McLane, who was standing fifty yards away. She also was looking west, her hands on her hips and the sea wind rippling her hair.

"What do you mean?"

"I mean I saw your pretty wife leave the campfire last night, while Antonio was out in the jungle somewhere. She stayed gone quite a while."

McLane's face reddened. "You're a fool, Ross. I may be old, but Susan's too smart to fall for Antonio, or for you either. Which has also crossed your mind, hasn't it?"

Ross made no reply.

Watching him, McLane adjusted his crutch and said, "When did he leave, exactly? And what was he wearing?"

"What?"

"Antonio. When did he leave?"

Ross frowned. "I told you, he left at sunup. In that red shirt of his, and jeans."

"You're certain of that?"

"What's that supposed to mean?"

"Maybe he didn't leave at all," McLane said. "Maybe you just told me and Susan that, so we wouldn't be suspicious."

"Suspicious of what?" Suddenly Ross blinked. "You think I *murdered* him?"

"You said yourself, there's barely enough food. One less mouth wouldn't hurt. And if I were next, you'd have Susan all to yourself."

Ross glared at him. "Well, maybe that's—"

"There he is!" Susan shouted. She was down in a crouch, one hand shading her eyes, the other pointing west.

Both men turned to look. Sure enough, a yellow lifeboat had rounded the peninsula and was coming this way. Inside it, paddling with what looked like a long piece of driftwood, was a man in a red shirt. Susan waved; Antonio waved back.

All of them watched until the boat disappeared beneath the brow of the ridge. The same thought was in all their minds: they were saved. Or at least they had a chance now. They knew their directions, and if they could find and pack enough water and food and row east, they would eventually hit the mainland.

Susan ran up to the men and said, breathless and grinning, "It'll take him a while to get up here. Come on, I want to show you both something."

They followed her to a spot further inland, near where she was before. Here, the ridge ended in a sheer cliff.

"Look down there," she told them.

Carefully the two men walked to the edge and peered over. A hundred feet below, dark rocks covered the valley floor.

"What is it?" McLane asked.

Suddenly, without warning, Susan McLane snatched her husband's crutch away and shoved him over the cliff.

For a moment Ross stood there stunned, gaping at her. Then, very slowly, his face changed. He broke out a smile.

"I knew it," he said. "Now all we have to do is get rid of Antonio and take the boat. Right?"

Susan's face was flushed. "You don't think he'll suspect anything, do you?"

"Why should he?" Ross stepped cautiously to the edge and looked down again. "We'll just say—"

The heavy crutch caught him just behind the right ear. It didn't knock him cold, but it was enough. A second later he toppled over the edge.

Susan stared down at them both a moment, breathing hard. With a loud laugh she threw the crutch after them and turned away. Antonio was already walking toward her along the top of the ridge.

"It's done," she cried, running to him. "Now we can—"

She stopped. The man in the red shirt wasn't Antonio at all. He was older and leaner, with a world-weary face and tattered trousers. As he approached he pulled a short, ugly pistol from his waistband.

Susan backed away, tripped on a rock, and sat down hard. The man stopped five feet away.

"Are you a pirate?" she whispered, her eyes wide.

"You've been watching too much TV." He waved the gun. "Stand up."

She stood up. "Who are you, then?"

"I'm with the cruise line. Assistant head of security. Three of us—two crewmen and I—washed ashore a few miles away. We thought we were the only ones who made it, till your friend showed up."

"Why do you have his shirt on?"

"Because I didn't have one, and he was unconscious when I left. Dehydration. He'll be fine." The man studied her a moment. "He told us there were four of you."

"The other two aren't here."

"I know. I saw them leave."

Susan swallowed. "Oh." She looked about, ran a hand through her hair, then faced him again. "Does this mean I'm under arrest?"

"You will be. I'm sure the search planes are out, and we found flares in the lifeboat. Someone should get to us soon."

She looked him up and down, thoughtfully. "I don't suppose there's anything I could do to . . . change your mind about this?"

"You could try to push me over the cliff too, but I wouldn't advise it."

Her face darkened. "In case you're wondering," she said, "Antonio was in on it, too."

"I'm sure he'll be glad you told me." He stepped back and

motioned with the pistol. "Let's go, Ms.—"

"McLane. Susan McLane. And you don't need the gun." She raised her chin. "I'm a corporate executive, believe it or not."

"Oh, I believe it," he said.

He kept the gun on her all the way to the beach.

John M. Floyd

KING OF THE CITY

Martino Ramirez was already there, waiting in the grassy clearing at the edge of the overlook, when the tall man arrived. Ramirez turned and watched, his elbows propped on the wooden railing behind him, while the man walked through the last of the trees and out into the sunlit clearing. As he approached he took something from his coat pocket and held it at his side—the object was large and black and rounded, and had a strap attached. At the sight of it Ramirez tensed, then slowly relaxed. It was only a pair of binoculars. The tall man stopped at a distance of ten or twelve feet, and for several seconds the two of them stood facing each other in silence.

"So you're the famous Mike Valenti," Ramirez said.

The tall man didn't reply. Instead he turned to the wooden barrier and, like Ramirez, leaned against the top rail. Below them, the city was spread out like an aerial map, the valley stretching away into hazy blue distance. The guidebooks said you could see fifty miles from here—the old guidebooks, that is. The road to the overlook had been closed for ten years.

The man called Valenti raised the binoculars and studied the view. Without turning, he said, "Thanks for coming. I know it was short notice."

Ramirez removed a thin cigar from his vest pocket. Keeping his eyes on Valenti, he lit the cigar with a gold lighter and inhaled.

"I suppose I should be honored," Ramirez said, letting out jerky little clouds of smoke along with his words. "I'm told you don't often come out of hiding."

Again the tall man didn't bother to reply. He kept his eyes to the glasses, his elbows on the railing. The only sounds were the sighing of the wind in the pines and the occasional faraway honk of a car horn.

"Actually I'm a little surprised," Ramirez added. "You don't look as much like a thug as I thought you would."

Valenti gave him a bored glance. "You don't look like a man who might be about to die in a few minutes, either," he said. "Appearances can be deceiving."

Ramirez blinked. He was not accustomed to hearing threats—at least not firsthand. He took his cigar from between his teeth and smiled.

"Who should I be afraid of?" he asked. "You?"

Valenti lowered the glasses and stared at him. "I doubt you have sense enough to be. But yes, you should."

Ramirez laughed out loud. "You got some thick bark on you, Valenti, I'll give you that. Coming up here all alone, talking to Martino Ramirez that way—"

"I'm not alone," Valenti said. "A guardian angel watches over me." He turned to the view once more, as if studying a rare work of art. "A short angel, with a bald head and one eye." He scratched his chin. "An eye sharp enough to put that cigar of yours out at a hundred yards, if I tell him to."

Ramirez's grin faded. Moving only his eyes, he looked up and past the tall man's profile, up into the dark forest on the slope above the clearing. Ramirez's gaze stayed there a minute, searching. "You're lying," he said. "Shorty's still in Quentin. With three years to go."

"Not any more. He's here now. Working for me."

"I don't believe you."

Valenti nodded. "I figured you might not. He and I talked about that. So we agreed on a signal. A little demonstration, let's call it. Problem is, you're not wearing a hat today, so I'm not sure what part of you he might choose to shoot off." Valenti set the binoculars down on the top rail and held both hands down at his sides. "Would you like me to show you?"

Ramirez licked his lips. His smile was gone now. He had known Shorty Robinson well, had even done a job or two with him over the years, and had seen the feats he could perform with a highpowered rifle. As a result Ramirez found himself faced with a dilemma. On the one hand, he doubted that Valenti—even with his obvious connections—would be able to get a man like Shorty Robinson out of a maximum-security prison. On the other hand, Ramirez had grown fond of most of his body parts, and preferred to keep them intact.

"You're forgetting something, Valenti," he said. "I'm not all alone up here either."

"Oh yes you are, Martino. I know you're not used to it, but you are."

Ramirez frowned. Without looking away, he turned his head and called, "Pedro! Luis! Come out here."

No answer. Somewhere far away, a train whistle blew long and mournfully.

"Boys!" More loudly now. "Get out here!"

Silence.

After a moment Valenti said, "Your friends are fine,

Martino, they're just catching a little nap. That's why I was late. If you behave you'll be able to stop and pick them up on your way out." He sighed. "Good help's hard to find, isn't it?"

Ramirez's face darkened. He started to take a step forward.

"Hold it," Valenti said. "Just stop right there."

Ramirez stopped.

"Long as we've started on the ground rules, let me finish them up. I'd advise you to listen." Valenti held a hand out in front of him and wiggled his fingers. "Anytime during our little meeting here today, if I raise my hand over my head with a forefinger extended, you will be wounded. A kneecap, probably. Also if you try to run away." He paused. "If I raise my hand flat, with the palm out and all five fingers extended, you will die. Immediately. You'll also die if you make a sudden move toward me, or try to pull a weapon. Understood?"

Ramirez stood there glaring at him, chewing the thin cigar. His eyes flicked past the tall man again, scanning the forest, then returned to Valenti's face. "I'll kill you for this," Ramirez said.

"Maybe later. You have other issues right now."

Ramirez was quiet a moment, watching the other man's eyes. "What is it you want? Why are you doing this?"

"I want information," Valenti said. His hands were tucked into his pockets now. He looked like a businessman who'd decided to take a stroll through the park on his lunch break.

"Information?"

"A name and a place. If you give them to me you can go. You'll find your buddies in a ditch just down the path a ways, tied up and snoozing like babies. I'm afraid you'll have to load 'em into the car yourself, though."

Ramirez's face tightened. He took out his cigar and flung it aside in disgust. "Forget it, Valenti. You're not gettin' anything from me, now or ever."

"I truly hope you don't mean that, my friend."

"Damn right I mean it. Have your man kill me if you're going to, I'm not telling you nothin.'" He glanced once more up into the trees. "Do it now, if you're so damn smart. Go ahead!"

The tall man sighed. "I was afraid of this," he said. "Typical macho Mexican. But if you don't care about your own life, maybe you do about someone else's."

Ramirez's eyes narrowed. "What?"

"Your brother, for instance. You want your stubbornness to hurt him, too?"

"What are you talkin' ab—"

With one smooth motion Valenti swept the binoculars off the rail and tossed them through the air to a startled Ramirez. "See for yourself."

For a moment Ramirez just stood there holding the glasses. Then, puzzled, he turned to the overlook and brought the binoculars to eye level.

"The railyard," Valenti said. "North end, behind the old packing plant."

It took Ramirez awhile to find it and get the glasses focused. When he did he squinted and leaned forward an inch or two, as if that would be enough to show him he wasn't really seeing what he thought he was seeing.

Far below and almost two miles away, his brother Carlo was standing beside a black Cadillac in a deserted parking lot near the back corner of the city railroad yard. With him were two other men. All three wore dark suits and sunglasses. As Ramirez watched, his brother said something to one of the others and looked at his watch.

"They're waitin' on something," he said, as if to himself.

"They sure are," Valenti agreed. "They're waiting on twenty pounds of cocaine, which should arrive in about"—he glanced at his watch—"ten minutes."

"What?" Ramirez turned to look at him. "How do you know that? I didn't even know that."

"I have connections, Martino. I won't bore you with details."

"But . . . why are you showing me this? What's going on?"

The tall man studied him. "What you're seeing, my friend, is a setup. A sting, in movie lingo." He paused. "The coke will be there in ten minutes, the cops'll be there in twelve. To see it change hands."

"*What?*"

"I said I had connections; they're not just in the under-world. The cops have been in my pocket for years now, you should know that. They want Carlo, and want him bad—so I gave him to them. On a platter." He smiled again. "The kicker is, I can also get him out of it. Or, to be exact, you can."

Ramirez was holding the binoculars to his eyes again, his fingers white-knuckled. Nothing much had changed. Carlo and his compadres were standing near the car, talking soundlessly and kicking cans with the toes of their thousand-dollar loafers. At Valenti's last statement, Ramirez looked up at him.

"Me? What do you mean?"

"All you have to do," Valenti said, "is tell me what I want to know. If you do, I'll abort the sting. Or at least spoil it. There's plenty of time yet—your brother'll get away clean."

"But . . . how—"

Valenti reached into the left pocket of his coat and removed a cell phone. "Two of my men are parked in an old tan Ford, in the field beside the packing plant. The number of their car phone is stored in this one. I press one button, I'll be talking to them. I'll just say one word—Go!—and they'll let loose a burst of machine-gun fire. Carlo and his friends are only fifty yards away—they'll make a little water in their pants and then take off like a bat out of hell. And when the dealers arrive they'll find nobody there. Neither will the cops."

Ramirez stared at him, breathing hard. Confusion and fright had swallowed his anger. Beads of sweat gleamed on his forehead. He snatched up the glasses again. Sure enough, concealed behind some tall bushes near the plant he could see what looked like the top of a tan-colored car.

His mind spun. His tongue had gone dry.

He turned to Valenti. "What do you want to know?" he blurted.

"I want the name of Eddie Del Vecchio's accountant, and where to—"

"What? Del Vecchio?"

"—and where to find him," Valenti said. "I already know he has all the records with him. Falsified tax returns, invoices for arms shipments, everything. They can be requisitioned. The machinery's in place—if I can point the cops to him they'll put Del Vecchio away forever, just like Capone. It's the last link." He paused. "Think what that would mean, Ramirez. The King of the East End would be out of business. Dethroned. In fact there'd be no more king of this or king of that around here. I'd run it all. And my organization would be no more a threat to yours than Del Vecchio's was. You and Carlo have never branched out any further than drugs anyway."

It was suddenly very quiet in the clearing.

"That's the information I need," Valenti said again. "But I need it now." He checked his watch. "Five minutes till show-time."

The silence dragged out. Ramirez looked at Valenti, then at the scene below, then at Valenti again.

A drop of sweat stung his eye, and he blinked.

Eddie Del Vecchio, he thought.

If Ramirez finked on Del Vecchio and Del Vecchio found out about it, Martino would soon be wearing lead galoshes, and he knew it. But why should Del Vecchio find out? At least half a dozen people knew the connection between Del Vecchio and his shyster bookkeeper. At least that many. Nobody could pin the leak on Ramirez. And besides . . .

Besides, his brother was a cooked goose if he didn't. Carlo had four priors, and a bust like this would send him up for good. That is, if they didn't have a shootout right there in the parking lot—in which case Carlo might wind up in a coffin instead of a cellblock.

Ramirez made up his mind.

"Okay," he said, and swallowed. "I'll give you the name, you sound the alarm."

"And the address."

"Yes. And the address."

Valenti raised the phone and held a finger above the buttons. "Remember—I'll know enough about this to know if you're lying."

Ramirez hesitated another moment, then took a deep breath and let it out in a whoosh.

"The bookkeeper's Toler," he said. "Benjamin Toler. Fairview Apartments, fourth floor. I don't know the number, but he lives with a gal named Bonnie Sims, he'll be easy to find."

Valenti's face went blank as he processed the information. "Of course," he murmured. "The Sims woman was—"

"Come *on!*" Ramirez shouted. "I did my part. Call your men."

The tall man pressed a button—and stopped. He turned the phone in his hands, examining it. He put it to his ear, frowned, looked at it again.

"What're you doing?" Ramirez said. "Make the call!"

Valenti looked puzzled. "Ain't that a note? The batteries

don't seem to be working."

Ramirez's mouth dropped open. Frantically he snatched the glasses to his eyes and focused on the scene below. The Cadillac was still there, his brother was still there. No sign of another group. Maybe the whole thing had been a hoax, he thought, maybe there would be no bust . . .

Then, as he watched, another Caddie pulled into the yard, this one gray. It stopped ten paces from the first. Four dapper-looking dudes piled out, money and drugs exchanged hands. A moment later, during the transaction, half a dozen police cruisers wheeled into the lot, their tires spraying gravel. Doors popped open, cops popped out, hands reached for the sky. Carlo Ramirez had purchased his last gram of cocaine.

Martino lowered the glasses and turned to face the tall man, who stared back at him calmly.

"Japanese phones," Valenti said, with a sigh. "You just can't trust 'em."

Keeping his eyes on Valenti, Ramirez's arm slashed out and to the right. The binoculars went spinning out into space. Far below, the sound of metal on rocks floated back to them.

"You never intended to stop it, did you," Ramirez murmured. His face was hot, his head roaring. "You never had any guys down there at all."

Valenti seemed to ponder that. "I would have, but they had other commitments. Something about a special at Wal-Mart."

"I'll kill you for this," Ramirez said. His voice was deadly quiet. Every muscle in his face seemed to have taken on a life of its own, twitching and jerking.

"Now you're repeating yourself," Valenti said. "A sign of a limited vocabulary, Martino. You should try to read more—"

Suddenly Ramirez's right hand, which had tightened into a fist, uncurled again and slid into his pants pocket. As it did, he took a step toward Valenti.

The tall man raised his own right hand, palm out.

"Hold it, Ramirez," he said. "One more step, you're a dead man."

Ramirez paused, frowning. His eyes flicked up again at the trees behind Valenti, combing the slope for some kind of sign. He saw nothing.

A moment passed.

Then Ramirez smiled. The doubt seeped away.

"A bad mistake, Valenti," he said. "You held up your hand just now, remember? You held up your hand like you were stopping traffic, with all fingers extended—the signal for Shorty to kill me, I believe you said. Isn't that right?" His grin widened. "And nothing happened, did it? Nothing happened because nobody's up there." And then he let the smile fall away.

Ramirez took his hand from his pocket. The switchblade snapped open, flashing in the sun.

"You made a mistake," he repeated, "and now you're going to die."

He stepped forward.

Mike Valenti said nothing. He just dropped the phone and raised his fist toward the sky. Only his forefinger was extended, as if showing this misguided drug-pushing child of God the direction to Salvation.

At that instant, so sudden it seemed magical, Ramirez's right kneecap exploded. A split-second later he heard the gunshot. It came from somewhere in the thick woods above and behind Valenti.

Martino Ramirez fell like a tree, both hands clasped around his ruined knee. Blood was everywhere. He rolled back and forth, moaning and cursing with every breath.

The tall man walked over, picked the switchblade up off the ground, and threw it over the railing. Then he squatted and watched with interest as Ramirez writhed like a snake in the dirt.

Finally Ramirez quieted down a bit. He lay with his eyes closed and his breath whistling through his clenched teeth. Both hands gripped his bloody kneecap.

"Look at me, Martino," Valenti said.

Ramirez opened one eye and glared at him.

"You made a mistake too," Valenti said. He held out his palm and flexed his fingers. "I'm left-handed."

They stared into each other's eyes a moment, then the tall man rose to his feet. "I'll call some of your goons and tell 'em where to find you," Valenti said. "It's anybody's guess whether they'll come or not."

Ramirez swallowed, almost delirious with pain.

"I'll . . . kill . . . you . . . Mike . . . Valenti," he whispered.

Valenti regarded him for a second or two, then checked his watch. "Afraid I can't stay and chat, Martino. Duty calls. Say hello to Pedro and Luis for me." He turned and strode away.

"I'll have you killed, Valenti," Ramirez shouted after him. "You'll be dead by tomorrow night, I promise you that!"

The tall man crossed the clearing and disappeared into the trees. Behind him, Martino Ramirez moaned and cursed and screamed his name.

***

Six hours later the tall man sat in the study of his home north of the city. On the right half of his desk were his stockinged feet; on the left was a stack of paperwork he'd shoved over to make room for them. On his mind were the events of the afternoon.

It had been a productive day.

Just after leaving his noisy meeting with Ramirez he had driven for ten minutes along the winding forest road. He stopped near a pine thicket near the top of the mountain. Shorty was there, packing up his rifle and scope and grinning like a kid who's just been down the longest water slide at Six Flags. They talked a bit, the bald marksman accepted a thick envelope for his services, and they parted. The tall man then drove downtown to his office to make a few phone calls, and now—at just past seven o'clock—he was leaning back in his swivel chair, looking out between the V of his propped-up feet at the gathering twilight outside the window of his study.

The tap of footsteps in the hallway roused him from his thoughts. He turned and smiled as his wife opened the door and approached his desk. Her hair glowed like spun gold in the light from the desk lamp.

"You must've had a good day," she said. "You look . . . satisfied."

He studied her a moment. "They picked up Eddie Del Vecchio this afternoon. He's going to prison."

Her mouth dropped open. "That's fantastic."

"It's a start," he agreed.

She came around the desk and stood beside him, her eyes searching his face. He draped an arm around her waist.

"Jack Warrington," she said with a smile, "you're going to be the best police commissioner this town's ever had. Only a month on the job, and—how many already? First Charlie Zizack, and now Del Vecchio . . ." She paused. "At this rate maybe somebody'll shoot Mike Valenti, and people could feel safe on the streets again."

Commissioner Warrington's eyes twinkled in the lamplight.

"Who knows?" he said. "Anything's possible . . ."

John M. Floyd

CAREERS

It was almost noon when Chicago detective Ed Parker entered the main terminal of Narita Airport. He was directed to a room off the south concourse, where he was greeted by Officer Tashiro Kasaki of the Tokyo P.D.

"I know you are on holiday, Edward," Kasaki said, "but this is strange case. Involves three Americans." He held up a revolver in a plastic evidence bag, then nodded toward a sheet-covered body on a stretcher. "That is one of them. Other two are suspects, held under guard in next room. Medical examiner is on his way."

Parker took off his coat and draped it over a chair. "What's strange about it?" he asked.

"One of the suspects, who always tells truth, says he killed victim. Other suspect, who always lies, says *he* did *not*. Very confusing."

Parker frowned. "Wait a minute. What do you mean, one guy always tells the truth?"

"He's a priest," Kasaki said.

"Priests don't always tell the truth, Socky."

"This one was Eagle Scout in his youth."

"Ah. I see what you mean. And he says he killed the guy?"

"Right."

"So you believe him?"

"What choice do I have? He never lies."

"What about the other suspect?" Parker asked.

"He always lies."

"So you said. How do you know?"

"He is used car salesman," Kasaki explained.

"Well, actually, used car salesmen don't *always* lie—"

"This one also studying to be lawyer."

"Ah. I see what you mean. And he says he *didn't* kill the guy?"

"That's right."

"So you think he *did* kill him."

"Right again. Because he always lies."

Detective Parker sighed. "That is confusing," he agreed. "What about the victim?"

"He is schoolteacher, from Los Angeles. At least he was."

"What else do you know about him?"

"Well, he owned the gun, for one thing. Also owned plane they came in. Private jet. The two suspects, old friends of victim, had been his guests on trip to Hawaii. He went scuba diving while they fished. On flight here today, the three were playing poker in main cabin when incident occurred. None of crew were close by."

"When did all these things happen?" Parker asked.

Kasaki took a notebook from his pocket. "Let's see . . . they arrived in Honolulu from L.A. on seventeenth. Spent night at victim's beach house. Took boat out the next afternoon, when victim went diving near Hanauma Bay. Then all three flew here this morning, the twentieth. Crew heard gunshot during flight, victim died shortly after."

Parker pondered that a moment. "A beach house and a private jet?"

"Correct."

"On a teacher's salary?"

"His son is a plumber," Kasaki said.

"Ah. I see what you mean." The detective sighed again. "Okay, I'll talk to the suspects and take a look at the body. I'll also need to see the inside of the plane, and interview the crew." He paused, thinking. "And see if you can get me a map."

"A map?"

"Of the Western Pacific." Parker walked over and opened the door to the adjoining room.

***

Ten minutes later Parker came out again and spoke with the M.E., who had arrived and was examining the body. Then he left the terminal, boarded the victim's aircraft, and took a moment to check the map Kasaki had provided him.

Finally, looking satisfied, Parker reentered the terminal. He found Kasaki at one of the west windows, studying the distant white cone of Mount Fuji.

"Okay," Parker said.

"Okay what? Have you figured it out?"

"I think so."

"Holy Macao," Kasaki blurted. "You know who killed him?"

"Well," Parker said, "I don't think the priest did it. I realize that a holy man who's an Eagle Scout would always tell the truth, but in this case he was liquored up a bit. I don't think he knew what he was saying."

Kasaki shook his head in wonder. "A drunkard priest," he

said, "who also plays poker."

"But not very well," Parker observed. "The cabin crew said all the chips were on the victim's side of the table."

"Maybe priest did kill him, then. For cheating, possibly."

"No, the bullet entered the victim's right side. According to the crew, the priest was seated to the left of the victim."

"So the salesman killed him?"

"Well," Parker said, "the salesman's exact words were: 'For once, I'm telling the truth: I didn't shoot him.' I agree that since he sells used cars and plans to be a lawyer, he would certainly lie, so the statement that he's telling the truth was in itself—"

"—a lie," Kasaki said.

"Right."

"So the salesman *did* kill him."

"Not exactly. He just shot him."

"What?!"

"The coroner says the gunshot wound wasn't the cause of death," Parker said. "My guess is that he died from D.C.S. Decompression stress."

"You mean the bends? Like when you surface too fast from a deep dive?"

"Or fly too soon afterward. Especially at the altitude required by that jet."

Kasaki considered that, then said, "But there was plenty of delay. Victim went diving on eighteenth; flight here was on twentieth, two days later."

"That's right, it was—in calendar time. Real time, he lost a day." Parker held up the map. "In flying from Hawaii to Tokyo they crossed the international date line. The time between his dive and his flight was less than twenty-four hours."

Kasaki thought that over, nodding. "So he actually killed

himself," he murmured.

"In a way. He was just careless." Parker picked up his coat. "Gotta go," he said. "I have a plane to catch, myself."

"Home to USA?" Kasaki asked, as they shook hands.

"Not yet. The wife and I are going to our place in Singapore."

Kasaki blinked. "On a detective's salary? You must have son who's a plumber too."

Parker grinned. "A lawyer," he said.

THE MESSENGER

Joe Perry was a happy man. His divorce was final, his new BMW had been ordered, and he was certain he would win the murder case he'd been arguing for the past two days. His client was guilty as sin, of course, but that was beside the point.

Perry plopped down on an empty park bench outside the courthouse and took his cell phone from his pocket. He was about to punch in a number when a voice at his elbow said, "Mr. Perry?"

He almost dropped his phone. A man with a felt hat and rimless glasses was sitting beside him on the bench.

"Sorry," Perry said. "I didn't see you sitting there."

"I wasn't," the man said.

"I beg your pardon?"

"I wasn't, when you arrived. I . . . what's the word? Materialized."

Perry's eyes narrowed. "Materialized," he said.

"Right. It means—"

"I know what it means." Perry studied the man and said, "Do we know each other?"

"No. You can call me Norman. I have a message for you."

"A message?"

"A choice, really. I was sent to offer you a choice."

Perry frowned. "What do you mean, a choice?"

Norman adjusted his glasses. "Two events are about to take place, Mr. Perry. One will involve you, the other someone else. One also involves a great deal of money. You have been selected to determine who participates in which event."

"Selected? By whom?"

"By my superior. Your recent, ah, activities have attracted his attention."

"My legal work, you mean?"

"Among other things."

Was this guy for real? Perry found himself wondering whether to feel worried or honored.

"Honored," Norman answered. When Perry blinked, Norman added, "I can also read minds, providing the mind isn't overly bright." He smiled pleasantly.

Jack Baker, Perry thought. Baker was behind this—he had to be.

"Who *are* you, exactly?" Perry asked.

"I told you. I'm a messenger. And the sender is highly impressed by certain aspects of your character."

"Is that so."

"You have many, you know. Arrogance, ruthlessness, a total lack of integrity . . ." Norman leaned closer. "Think of it as Santa Claus in reverse: he wants to reward you for being a very naughty little boy."

Perry regarded him a moment. "I think I get it, now. Your employer—"

"My superior."

"Your superior," Perry said, "is the devil. Right?"

Norman shrugged. "He is known by many names."

"And you are one of his henchmen. Is that what I'm supposed to believe?"

"We prefer *angels*."

"Of course," Perry said. "You ride motorcycles, I suppose."

Norman turned to face him. "I realize how all this must sound, Mr. Perry. But I assure you, this is legitimate. I have been sent here for one purpose: to offer you the choice of events I described." He took a small notepad from his pocket. "At least allow me to give you the details."

Perry was silent a moment. "Is this what you do, full time? Go around delivering messages?"

"Pretty much."

"Sounds like easy duty."

"I wish. Next week I'm in Detroit and Buffalo."

Perry nodded. "My condolences."

"I hate cold weather," Norman murmured, as if to himself. "How long, in all these places?"

"Just long enough to state the choices, and see that they're carried out." He held up the notepad. "Speaking of which . . ."

Perry sighed and glanced at his watch. "Okay. Why not?"

"Event number one," Norman began, reading from the pad. "A man goes into a phone booth. As soon as he makes a call, the phone starts spitting out silver dollars. It keeps spitting them out, one after the other. The final payoff is almost half a million dollars."

"How amazing," Perry said dryly. "I didn't know pay phones used silver dollars—or that they would hold that many."

"You don't know my superior," Norman said with a grin. "Event number two. A man stands at the bottom of a well thirty feet deep. Water begins to pour into the well. Like the silver dollars, the water doesn't stop until the well is full."

Norman put the notepad away and stared at him. Perry waited.

"That's it?" Perry asked.

"That's it. Those are the two choices. You must pick one for yourself, and designate someone else for the other."

Perry snorted. "I've heard enough." He pocketed his cell phone and started to rise.

"Don't leave," Norman said. For the first time, he seemed alarmed. "If you leave, my superior gets to make the choice for you, and believe me, that's not what you want."

Something in the man's voice made Perry hesitate. After a long pause he said, "Show me why I should do what you say."

"I've told you already."

"I said show me."

"Ah," Norman said, brightening. "A demo."

"Is that a problem?"

"Certainly not." Norman looked around for a moment, then tipped his head toward an old office building across the street. A window washer was hard at work on the seventh floor. "See that man up there?"

Perry nodded.

Norman casually pointed a finger, and the man's safety harness snapped. He fell backward into space, the rope-and-leather harness trailing behind him like a kite's tail.

Perry stood and gasped.

Then, as they watched, the flapping harness snagged on a lion's-head sculpture that jutted from the second floor of the building, breaking the man's fall at the last moment. Seconds later, he emerged from the thick shrubbery that lined the side-walk, shaken but unhurt.

"Darn," Norman said.

Perry was stunned. He stared openmouthed at the staggering workman. "I can't believe it," he whispered.

"I can't either," Norman said, looking vexed. "I'm only allowed three of those a year, and I just wasted one."

Perry sagged onto the bench and swallowed. He turned to study his companion with new respect.

"Okay," he said. "I'm a believer."

"Then choose," Norman said.

"You mean . . . either the well or the phone booth?"

"Those are the choices."

"What's the catch?"

Norman shook his head. "There's no catch."

They stared at each other a moment.

"I choose the phone booth," Perry said.

Amusement flickered behind the glasses. "Rather be rich than drowned, huh?"

"Wouldn't you?"

Norman took out a small electronic device and pressed a key. "Done," he said.

Perry swallowed again. "What's next?"

"Who do you want in the well?"

"Excuse me?"

Norman looked up at him. "You get the phone booth," he said. "Who gets put in the well?"

"I have to name somebody?"

"Technically, no. But you can if you want to."

Perry paused a moment, thinking. "Dave Fairweather."

"Dave Fairweather?"

"He's a partner in my firm."

"I know who he is," Norman said. "Has a pretty wife, too, doesn't he?"

Perry's face darkened. "This mind-reading thing could get irritating."

"Sorry," Norman said, typing in the name. "Fairweather it is."

Perry studied the device. Besides the keypad, it had a tiny color display. "How does all this work?" he asked.

"Did you ever see *I Dream of Jeannie*? Remember when she'd blink and Roger Healey would wind up in the Gobi Desert?" Norman pushed another button. "Same principle."

Perry leaned over the man's shoulder to see the display. Staring back at him from the screen was Dave Fairweather in a blue suit and striped tie, standing knee-deep in water and screaming. More water cascaded over his head and shoulders.

"Wow," Perry murmured.

Norman pursed his lips as he watched the screen. "I always wanted to be a lawyer, myself, when I was alive," he said thoughtfully. "I was an insurance agent, you know." He glanced at Perry and grinned. "I was also"—he spread his fingers and ticked off each item—"an embezzler, a forger, a car thief, an adulterer . . ." He paused, holding his little finger. "There's something else, too, what was it—"

"Let's get on with this, okay?"

"Of course." Norman tucked the device into his pocket and looked at the courthouse. "Just inside that door are three pay phones. Help yourself."

Perry followed his gaze. "Which one?"

"Doesn't matter." Another smile. "He has all the numbers."

Perry looked uncertain. "So I should just pick one?"

"Walk right in, sit right down."

"Are you going with me?"

"Afraid not." Norman touched the brim of his hat. "Goodbye, Mr. Perry."

Suddenly Perry was alone on the bench. He blinked and looked around, but Norman was gone. He had dematerialized, Perry said to himself.

A bit shaken, Perry rose and crossed the street to the

courthouse. Inside, in the hallway, he saw that Norman had been right: though Perry had never really counted them before, three phone booths stood against the wall.

He took a deep breath, opened the folding door of the first booth, and stepped inside.

It was old-fashioned, with wooden sides and no seat. The only glass was in the door, which he slid shut. Then he removed the receiver, inserted coins, got a dial tone, punched in a number, and waited. Instead of an answer, however—or even a ring—he heard a rattling noise deep inside the phone.

A fat silver dollar clinked into the coin return and rolled out onto the floor.

As Perry watched in amazement, another dollar came out, and then another, and another.

He picked one up, looked at it. It was real.

"Unbelievable," he said.

More dollars poured out. The rate had increased now; there was an almost solid flow of silver into the booth. The noise was deafening. Perry plunged both hands into the growing pile and let the coins sift through his fingers.

He stopped long enough to glance through the glass door. The hallway was empty. He wondered if Norman had had anything to do with that.

Heavy coins continued to flood from the phone. The level had risen past his knees, pinning his feet and legs in place. Frantically he began stuffing the dollars into the pockets of his suitcoat and shirt and trousers.

Suddenly a thought hit him. He was waist-deep in coins now; things were getting a little cumbersome. Groping through the pile, he found the doorhandle and pushed.

Nothing happened.

Perry frowned. He held his breath and pushed again.

The folding door didn't budge. It was blocked by the wall

of coins in the booth.

The rising flood of silver dollars was up to his chest. Sweat dotted his brow. His stomach began to churn. He thought of his cell phone, but he couldn't reach his pocket. Since his arms and hands were free, he pounded on the door glass and called for help.

No one heard him, or saw him.

He was trapped.

"Norrrrmannnn!" he shouted.

Somewhere in the back of his mind, he realized that the level shouldn't still be rising—the phone itself was long since buried. The coin-return slot should be blocked. But it wasn't. Somehow more and more dollars were coming in. The floodtide was up to his neck now.

And all of a sudden Norman was there, on the other side of the door glass, his face inches from Perry's.

"You rang?" he asked.

"Thank God!" Perry yelled, above the rumbling of coins. *"Get me out of here!"*

Norman looked surprised. "That's forbidden, I'm afraid. I just thought you might like an update on Mr. Fairweather." He held the device up to the glass. "Seems he finally stopped screaming and just treaded water until it rose to the top of the well." On the tiny screen, a man in a soaked blue suit was trudging across a field toward a farmhouse. "Looks good as new, doesn't he?"

Perry's face had gone pale. "But . . . you said there wasn't a catch!"

Norman blinked and snapped his fingers. "That's it!" he said, pointing at Perry. "That's what else I was trying to think of." He leaned closer, looking embarrassed. "I was also a liar."

Perry's eyes, as he struggled to keep his nose and mouth above the pile of coins, suddenly cleared. He understood.

"You were sent to kill me," he blubbered.

"No. I was sent to test you. You'd have lived if you'd refused to put anyone in the well."

Perry groaned. "And the window washer? You planned that, didn't you? He lived because you broke his fall."

"Afraid so. My boss is strict about demos. No casualties allowed."

"So . . . so you're not a devil's angel?"

Norman shook his head. "Just an angel."

***

He watched silently as the booth filled to the top. The rumbling stopped. There was no sign of Joe Perry.

After a moment Norman removed a laminated sign from inside his coat and hung it on the booth's doorhandle. Printed on the sign were the words DONATIONS FOR THE HOME-LESS, and beneath that a passable rendition of the governor's signature.

Just before leaving, Norman took out a pocket calendar, flipped a page, and checked his next stops. Sure enough, Detroit and Buffalo. He hadn't lied about that, he thought sadly—or about his sentiments.

He really did hate cold weather.

John M. Floyd

LUCY'S GOLD

"What did you do?" Lucy asked.

The young man in the seat across from her made no reply. He just sat there, staring out the window of the stagecoach.

A while ago, when Lucy Roberts climbed into the stage in Heritage, she stumbled a bit on the step, and he had leaned forward to take her hand. Their eyes met then, but he didn't speak—in fact he'd hardly looked at her since.

But she had looked at him. The truth was, she'd scarcely taken her eyes off him. He was intriguing, Lucy thought—sandy hair, square chin, blue eyes. And about her age, nineteen or so. She found herself wondering if this feeling, this—fascination, almost—might be more than just a passing interest. If it was, there were two things here that could prove to be a little inconvenient. One was that she was already engaged to be married; the other was that he was wearing a pair of handcuffs.

Whatever the case, Lucy thought, he should have the courtesy to answer her question. But just as she opened her mouth to ask him again, he turned from the window and looked at her. She snapped her mouth shut.

"Did I miss something?" he asked. His voice was deep, his eyes tired.

Lucy cleared her throat. "I asked you a question."

"Would you care to repeat it?"

"I asked you," she said, with a glance at his handcuffs, "what it was that you did."

Another long pause. Then: "They say I robbed a railroad office." The tiredness in his face seemed to deepen, and he turned again to the window.

"What do you mean 'they say'? Did you or didn't you?"

Again, no response. They rode on in silence.

Finally the third passenger—the man sitting beside the prisoner—spoke up.

"His name's Charlie McCall," the man said. "He was outside, holding his two friends' horses, when the two ran out of the office with the stolen money. They were both shot dead, and McCall here was charged as their accomplice." He paused, then added, "He said he hadn't known anything about a robbery."

Lucy studied the older man a moment. He was burly, with a red face and mustache. A sheriff's star was pinned to his vest.

"Are you telling me he's innocent?" she asked.

The sheriff shrugged. "Don't matter what I tell you. We're on our way to Dodge, to let the judge decide. It's what he'll tell us that matters."

Lucy nodded in Charlie McCall's direction. "I want to know what *he* would tell me."

The big sheriff chuckled. "He won't tell you anything, unless he's looking at you when you ask him."

"What?"

"He's deaf," the sheriff said.

She blinked. She turned to the young man again, watching him watch the plains roll past outside the stage's long window. She remembered now: His eyes had been fixed on her lips as she spoke to him.

"His pa was killed in a mine blast, years ago," the sheriff said. "Young Charlie was with him at the time. The boy survived, but could never hear again. Came to live with his aunt outside Heritage." The sheriff squinted. "You're from Heritage yourself, ain't you? A clerk at the bank?"

She nodded, looking at the sheriff but still thinking about Charlie McCall. "Until it closed," she said. "Mr. Larrabee's opening a new bank in Dodge, and said I could work for him again. I'm on my way there now, with the last of his move."

"His move?"

She hesitated. "I'm bringing the rest of his gold. It's in a strongbox, up top." Lucy was aware that the young man had turned from the window and was watching her as she spoke. She found it hard not to look at him.

"You mean you're making the delivery yourself?" the sheriff said.

"Yes. Are you surprised?"

"Well, I don't know. It seems strange—"

"To have a woman doing a man's work?"

The sheriff scratched his mustache. "Let's say I would've thought you'd be happier at home somewhere, married, than escorting a gold shipment for Ben Larrabee."

Lucy Roberts felt her face grow warm. "I can do most anything a man can, Sheriff. Ride, plow, shoe a horse. When I was little, on my pa's farm, I could kill a prairie dog with a rock at forty yards, every time."

"Well, the kind of varmints I'm thinking of are a sight bigger than prairie dogs, missy."

Lucy set her jaw and forced a deep breath.

"I should mention," she said, "that my wedding is next

week, in Dodge. So I'll soon be home, *and* married. Does that please you, Sheriff?"

"Does it please *you?*" Charlie McCall said, from out of nowhere.

She blinked and looked at him. "What do you mean?"

The young man shrugged. He hadn't intended to be rude, she could see that—he just appeared curious. "The way you looked just then," he said, "you don't seem too happy about it."

She felt herself flush again. "I'm perfectly happy. Billy Ray Feeny is a fine man, and he'll make a fine husband. Not that it's any of your business."

McCall lifted his manacled hands. "My problem's none of your business, either," he said. "But it felt nice to know you're interested."

She regarded him for a long moment, feeling her anger drain away. She hadn't really been all that upset anyway: McCall's comment had been too close to the truth. She'd been having doubts about Billy Ray—and her feelings for him—for weeks now. What bothered her even more, at this instant, was her feelings for this mysterious stranger. Even the sheriff seemed to realize something unusual was afoot here, as she and the young man stared into each other's eyes.

Suddenly the window darkened. For the moment, the rolling countryside was blocked from view; the stage had entered a small and scarce grove of trees. Just before they broke into the open again, something THUMPed on the roof of the coach. All three passengers looked up.

"One of the boxes tipped over, I expect," the sheriff said, as the stage began to slow down.

When they came to a full stop, he rose and stepped through the door. Lucy heard voices outside. Thirty seconds later the sheriff returned to the doorway, his face pale. "You two best come outside," he said.

The handcuffed man rose first, stepped down, then turned and helped Lucy down behind him. As soon as her feet touched ground she froze. Two men in tan dusters stood in the road near the front of the stagecoach, guns drawn and bandannas pulled tight over their lower faces. One of the men, tall and dark-haired, stayed close to the sheriff, whose own gun was missing from its holster. Three saddled horses were tied nearby.

"Line up right here, folks," the tall man said, waving his gunbarrel at the side of the stage. As they obeyed, Lucy noticed a third bandit, also masked. He wore a black hat and vest, and appeared to be unhitching the team from its traces.

The tall man—the leader, Lucy decided—was studying the three passengers. His gaze stopped on her. "We won't keep you long, Sheriff," he said, his eyes still fixed on Lucy. "All we want's the gold."

Lucy stiffened, which was apparently just what the tall man had been watching for. He looked at the second bandit and nodded. The second man climbed quickly past the driver's seat and onto the top of the stage. Lucy could hear him above and behind her as he rummaged through the bags and cases stored there. A minute later he stepped down again, carrying the banker's strongbox.

"Good," the leader said. "Tie it down and mount up." He then glanced at the bandit in the black vest, who was unhitching the last of the team. As everyone watched, the man slapped the horse's rump and fired several shots into the air, sending all four horses thundering away into the hills north of the road. Within seconds they topped a rise and were gone.

"Where's our driver?" the sheriff asked. By now Lucy had figured out the noise they'd heard earlier—one of the thieves must have dropped from a tree limb onto the top of the coach. "I didn't hear a shot," he added.

The leader nodded to the east, the way the now-horseless

stagecoach had come. "He got whacked on the head and fell off. He'll live, I imagine."

The sheriff's face hardened. "I'll find you, you know. Dodge City's no more'n twenty miles away. I can walk there by dark, and you'll be caught before the week's out."

"Is that so," the tall man replied, amusement twinkling in the eyes above his mask. Without saying more, he turned to Charlie McCall, and looked him up and down. The handcuffs were hard to miss. "Well, well. Seems we have a friend in the crowd."

McCall stared back at him.

"Hold out your hands, boy," the tall man ordered, cocking his pistol.

McCall's hands were clasped together in front of him, the insides of his wrists resting on his belt. When he made no move to obey, the bandit raised his gun and thrust its muzzle against the handcuff's chain—and McCall's belt buckle.

"You want my help or don't you?" the tall man asked.

"He can't hear you," Lucy said, alarmed.

The gunman ignored her. The two men looked into each other's eyes a moment, then McCall seemed to understand. He held his hands out to one side and stretched them apart. The gun roared, the chain separated. Still watching the leader's eyes, McCall rubbed his chafed wrists.

"Go," the leader said, with another wave of the gunbarrel. McCall gave him a final look, then turned and headed east, toward the grove of trees they had just passed through.

Once more, the tall man fixed his attention on the sheriff. The second bandit had secured the strongbox behind his horse's saddle and was mounted now, ready to leave. The third man— the one wearing the black vest—strolled over to the group and stood watching.

"You might walk out of here, sheriff," the leader said, "but not in half a day."

"What do you mean?" the lawman growled.

The leader nodded to Black Vest, who cocked his pistol and shot the toe off the sheriff's right boot. The big sheriff grunted once and fell heavily to the ground beside the stage. He lay still for a second or two, his eyes squeezed shut and both hands clutching his wounded foot. Though horrified, Lucy made no sound; she just knelt beside him and held him as he groaned through clenched teeth. She gave the black-vested man a glare of pure fury.

Without a word the bandit holstered his gun and backed away. The leader stepped forward and studied the fallen sheriff.

"That should slow you down a bit," he said. "I think a decent head start is only fair, don't you?" He glanced once at Lucy, then nodded to the others. The man with the gold spurred his horse south; the leader swung into his saddle and followed. Black Vest stood where he was for a moment, watching Lucy and the sheriff with casual interest. He said, speaking for the first time: "Have a nice stroll, folks."

At the sound of his muffled voice, Lucy's narrowed eyes opened wide. Her face went slack.

"*Billy Ray?*" she said.

The black-vested gunman, who had already begun to turn away, froze where he stood. His eyes widened also, as he realized his mistake.

He and Lucy stared at each other for several long seconds. Finally he turned and almost ran to where his horse was tied. Behind him, Lucy rose unsteadily to her feet, pale with shock. He fumbled with untying the reins, and seemed to have trouble getting his foot in the stirrup. Once mounted, the bandit raced away in the direction his friends had gone.

He had covered only a short distance when Lucy's shout stopped him. Her face was flushed a fiery pink now, and she stood alone in the road twenty feet from the stage, one hand behind her back.

"Billy Ray!" she called.

He reined in, then wheeled his horse around so he could look back at her. He was between thirty and forty yards away.

She was ready. Her left arm was already extended, her right arm cocked back; in one smooth motion she snapped her upper body forward as hard as she could. The lemon-sized rock caught Billy Ray Feeny in the center of his forehead, and made a sound like an axe hitting the trunk of an oak. He flung both arms wide, opened his mouth in a perfect little O, and toppled backward out of the saddle. His riderless horse shied a step or two, then stopped.

Lucy watched the man fall and lie still. She was breathing hard, and barely heard Charlie McCall walk up behind her. He was half-carrying a dazed and bloodied old man she recognized as the stagecoach driver. Gently McCall propped the old-timer against one of the coach's wheels and gave the sheriff a glance. The big lawman had managed to get his boot off, and was tearing strips from his shirttail to use as bandages. Lucy blinked a few times, getting her bearings, then rushed to the sheriff to help him.

McCall said nothing to either of them. He started walking south, moving neither slowly nor quickly, toward the spot where Billy Ray Feeny's horse stood grazing beside his sprawled form.

"Where's he going?" the sheriff said, his face pallid and sweating.

"Let me do that," Lucy said, kneeling beside him.

"Where's he *going*? *McCall!*"

This time Lucy raised her head. Charlie McCall was still striding away, the broken handcuff chains swinging from his wrists.

"He's getting away," the sheriff murmured. "He's getting *away*." He turned to her, his eyes wild. "Get my rifle. It's up top, in a brown pack."

"What?"

"Get it," he said, then shouted, "*McCallllll . . .*"

"He can't hear you," she said, staring after him, her mind whirling with a dozen disjointed thoughts.

Suddenly the sheriff pushed her away, and she sat down hard in the dirt. Muttering to himself, groaning with pain, he tried to hoist himself to his feet—

And then stopped. He was staring past her at McCall. She turned to look, and at first didn't understand what she was seeing.

Forty yards away, Charlie McCall had put on Billy Ray Feeny's black hat and vest and gunbelt and was mounting Feeny's horse. Without a single look back, he took off at a gallop, heading south across the rolling green hills.

"He's gone," the sheriff said, as if he found it impossible to believe. "He's gone with them."

Lucy stared into the distance until McCall had vanished from sight, then looked again at the sheriff. She didn't know what to think or believe anymore, after the events of the past twenty minutes. She could understand McCall's escape, and taking the gun, but why had he bothered with the hat and vest? He already had a hat.

She decided not to worry about it right now. What she did instead was help the sheriff scoot back into the shade of the coach and then tend to the gash on the old driver's head. After examining and cleaning the cut, she hurried to a gully she'd seen beside the road to get mud for a poultice for the sheriff's foot. Half an hour later both men were in considerably better shape, though she was covered with dirt and blood and sweat.

And then, just as suddenly as he had left, Charlie McCall

rode into sight. He was leading a saddled horse and carrying two extra pistols in his belt. And on the extra horse was the strongbox of Ben Larrabee's gold.

He dismounted and tied both horses to the rear of the stage. "How's the foot?" he said.

The sheriff was speechless, and so, for the moment, was Lucy. She stared at McCall as if he were an apparition.

"What . . . what happened?" she asked.

He tipped his hat back. "With the other guy's horse and clothes, I was able to get close enough to get the jump on 'em. They thought I was him." He pointed with his thumb. "I left them tied to a big oak beside a pond, about three miles south. They'll be okay till we ride into Dodge and get help." He added, with a disgusted look, "The other horse got away."

The sheriff was still gawking at him. "I . . . I thought—"

"I'm no criminal, Sheriff," McCall said. "I'll go with you, like before, but I'm no criminal."

The sheriff swallowed and nodded.

McCall turned then to Lucy, and their eyes held for what seemed a very long time. "There's one more thing to do," he said. "Get the rope off that saddle, would you?"

It took only a short while to drag Billy Ray Feeny's limp body back to the stage. He was still out cold, but he was alive, with a blue knot the size of a fist just above his eyes. "I saw you throw that rock," McCall said, when he finished tying the man's hands and feet. "Not bad."

"Well, he is a dog, and this is the prairie," she said. She managed to keep her tone light, but she was all too aware that this outlaw sprawled on the ground at her feet was the man who, until an hour ago, she had intended to marry. It was still a bit of a shock. She could see that the sheriff also knew. McCall, of course, didn't know; he had been down the road, attending to the driver, at the time she'd recognized Feeny, and of course couldn't have heard her call his name.

Lucy was also aware that she was at least partially responsible for this whole mess. She remembered now: Billy Ray Feeny had been in the bank, visiting with her, when Mr. Larrabee asked her to escort the gold to Dodge City for him. It didn't take a genius to figure out the rest.

Even so, she was secretly grateful it had happened. Not only had she discovered, and corrected, what had almost been the biggest mistake of her life—she had also met a man totally unlike anyone she had ever known before.

"You probably saved our lives," she said. "And my job, and my boss's gold."

McCall looked surprised. "You knocked the guy off his horse," he reminded her. "I couldn't have done anything without the horse."

"I guess we make a good team, then." She smiled, searching his eyes.

To her delight, he blushed a little. "I guess so," he said.

The plan, such as it was, didn't take long. She and Charlie McCall would ride into town on one horse and the driver on the other. The sheriff would stay here, in the shade of the stagecoach, with the still-unconscious prisoner, until they could return with the local law and a doc. "Besides," the sheriff said, "I have to stay. If this guy wakes up I intend to shoot him in the foot."

Within ten minutes they were ready. With McCall's help, the stage driver was boosted onto the one horse, and he and Lucy climbed onto the other. Before leaving, while the sheriff was making himself comfortable and the driver had already started out down the road, McCall turned to Lucy and said to her, over his shoulder, "Guess you heard the sheriff say he'd speak for me? To the judge?"

She smiled and nodded. "He told me the charges were

sure to be dropped."

McCall looked thoughtful. He didn't appear as happy about it as she thought he should be. "I suppose that means I'll soon be headed back home to Heritage, then," he said.

A silence passed. She just watched him, waiting.

"About your wedding . . ." he said, and swallowed. "When's it supposed to be, exactly?"

She hesitated, studying his face. From the direction of the stage, the sheriff was humming a tune. It occurred to her that Charlie McCall wasn't able to hear it.

Very carefully, making sure he was watching her lips, she answered, "The wedding's off."

He blinked. "What?"

"It's off. I'm not getting married."

"Isn't that kind of sudden?"

"You have no idea," she said, with a smile.

He frowned and cleared his throat. "Does that mean . . . could that mean you'd come back home too, then? To Heritage?"

Lucy felt a terrible weight on her heart. Just as she was about to speak, the driver called from up ahead, to see what the delay was. When she glanced ahead, past McCall's shoulder, he turned to follow her gaze.

"I'll have to stay in Dodge, Charlie," she answered, as he waved the old man on. "After all, my job's there."

But then she realized, as they faced each other again, that her words had gone unheard. He stared at her for a second, then asked, "Did I miss something?"

She swallowed. "I answered your question," she said.

But then something happened. The look in his eyes, at that moment, was so intense, so full of concern and expectation and emotion, it made her skin tingle. Suddenly the weight lifted, and Lucy knew for certain what this strange feeling in her heart was. She knew it as surely as she knew her own name. Out here in the middle of nowhere, sitting on a horse that had belonged to a man she thought she had known but hadn't known at all, sitting behind a man she had only just met, she realized she had finally found her gold, and it wasn't the kind you buy or steal or put in a strongbox.

"Would you care to repeat it?" McCall asked. He looked as if he might be holding his breath.

She reached up and brushed a wisp of hair off his forehead. "What I said was . . . I won't be staying in Dodge after all. I'm coming back home, to Heritage."

Very slowly, both of them grinned.

Up ahead, the old-timer was still staring at them, waiting. McCall glanced at him, then turned again to Lucy.

"Guess it's time to go," he said, still smiling.

"Well, let's go then. You're driving."

Behind them, in the shade under the coach, the sheriff started up a new tune.

CREATIVITY

After the tall dark-haired woman lifted the Hartmann bag into the overhead compartment, the young blonde in the aisle seat moved her knees so the older woman could squeeze past her to sit by the window. The seat between them was empty. Outside, the tarmac baked in the noonday sun.

"Thanks for helping me with my bags," the blond woman said. She held a matching leather briefcase on her lap.

"Glad to." The tall brunette glanced at the case. "I see your husband is a physician."

The young woman looked down. DR. STUART FREE-MAN III, the laminated tag announced. The accompanying photograph showed a bald, plump man of about fifty.

"He was," she said.

She offered no further explanation. Instead, she leaned back, closed her eyes, and rubbed them with the back of her hand. The diamond on her ring finger would have choked a horse.

When they were airborne, the older woman turned to her and said, "I'm Olivia Smith Banks, by the way."

"Suzie Freeman," the blonde murmured.

"What do you do, Ms. Freeman?"

"I'm a designer."

"Of course. A creative mind. Dresses? Kitchens? Software?"

"Landscapes."

"And your office is . . . ?"

"Here, in L.A. I'm going to Dallas for a seminar."

A silence passed.

"I'm sorry," Olivia Banks said. "About your husband, I mean."

Freeman stared at her. "You know my husband?"

"No, but you said—"

Freeman looked uneasy. "I'm afraid I misled you. My husband is fine. At least he was when I kissed him goodbye this morning." She leaned back again and shut her eyes.

"So he's been visiting you?" Banks asked.

"I beg your pardon?"

"Visiting you. Here in Los Angeles."

"If that were true, why would I have his luggage?"

Instead of answering, Banks gave her a smug look. "May I ask you a personal question?" she said.

Freeman paused. "I suppose so."

"How old are you?"

"Twenty-nine."

"And your husband. Is he a tall man?"

"Not very. Why?"

"How tall?"

"About my height. Maybe a little shorter."

"I see." Banks turned to stare out the window at the passing clouds, then asked, "How do you feel, Ms. Freeman, about all this?"

"Excuse me?"

"Is there anything you want to tell me?"

"I don't know what you're talking about."

Banks turned to face her. "Your luggage tags say your husband Stuart lives in Ontario."

"That's right."

"And you've lost a button off the front of your blouse."

Freeman glanced down at it, surprised. "So?"

Another smug look. "Ontario is 2000 miles from L.A., Ms. Freeman. And any husband you kissed goodbye this morning would have told you, before you went out in public—unless he was too blind or too tall to notice it—that you have a missing button. Especially if you were young enough to be his daughter."

Freeman made no reply.

"What I think," Banks continued, "is that you and your rich doctor husband were here on vacation. And frankly, I think you might have left him in no condition to critique your outfit, or anything else."

Freeman blinked. "You think I *killed* him?"

Banks just stared at her.

"You do," Freeman said. "Don't you."

"Did you?"

A silence dragged by. As they sat there watching each other, a flight attendant stopped his service cart in the aisle beside Freeman's seat. "Would you like a drink?" he asked.

Very calmly, she ordered coffee, with sugar. So did Banks. When the steward had placed the cups and two white packets on Freeman's lowered tray, she opened her purse and fiddled with her compact. "Who are you?" she said to Banks. "The police?"

"Please. Give me some credit."

"Who, then? A lawyer? A reporter?"

"A psychologist. I was here to present a paper."

"Of course." Freeman's hands were steady as she dusted sugar into their coffees and passed Banks's cup to her. "A creative mind."

"I like to think so."

"But what you've created," Freeman said, "is a fantasy."

"In what way?" Olivia Banks took a swallow of coffee.

"Well, for one thing, Ontario isn't two thousand miles from L.A., it's twenty miles."

"Ontario, Canada?"

"Ontario, California."

"There is no such place."

"Really? I'll tell that to our mayor, when I get home."

Banks raised her chin. "I don't believe you."

Suzie Freeman shrugged and sipped her coffee. "Why should you? After all, I'm a murderer."

Both of them stayed quiet for a while.

Finally Freeman asked, "How do you think I killed him?"

Banks studied her a moment, looking pleased with herself. "Any of a dozen ways. A pillow over his face, possibly. You look strong, and if he's short—"

"Short doesn't mean weak, Ms. Banks."

"Maybe a blow to the head, then, as he was putting on his shoes, or brushing his teeth."

"This is disappointing," Freeman said sadly. "And you call yourself a psychologist?"

Banks' face reddened. "All right then, how *did* you kill him?"

"An arsenic compound," Freeman said. "A white powder. I sprinkled it into his coffee, instead of sugar."

It took a moment for that to register. Suddenly Banks tensed and stared into her cup.

"It's very effective," Freeman said, with a smile.

Banks looked wide-eyed at Freeman's tray, at the two packets of sugar. A third opened packet, also white, lay beside them.

"My *God*—" Dropping her cup, Banks struggled to her feet. Freeman barely had time to raise her tray table before Banks blustered past her and into the aisle. Once there, she ran gagging and green-faced toward a group of flight attendants at the rear of the plane.

Still smiling, Freeman took the in-flight phone from its cradle on the back of the seat in front of her and punched in a number. After a pause, she said, "Stuart? It's me. How was your first morning as a retiree?" Her grin widened. "Yes, I'm fine. I'm just calling to tell you I found your glasses after I left, in my purse. I'll FedEx them to you from the hotel. And by the way, you know that headache powder you sent with me today?"

She turned and looked back down the aisle at the commotion.

"It works wonders," she said.

HARDISON PARK

"How'd you find me?" Cash asked. He was sitting in the passenger seat of the police car, staring sleepily out at the passing night. His wooden crutch was angled in beside him, its rubber tip propped on the dash.

The man behind the wheel gave him an amused look. "I called your mother, in Salinas. She's still my aunt, remember?" They eased to a stop under a red light, and the driver shook out a cigarette and lit it while they waited. "I would think you'd be proud to have so many cousins around to keep track of you," he added, exhaling word-sized chunks of smoke.

"I'm thrilled," Cash murmured. "Give me quantity over quality any day."

The driver grinned again, holding the cigarette between his teeth like a cigar. Philip Meeker was Chief of Detectives, and fairly good at his job, but he looked like a bouncer in a cheap nightclub. "You'll feel better once you hear about the case," he said. The light changed, and they headed west on Palo

Verde. It had been raining most of the night, but the sky was clearing now; the rearview mirror showed the first gray streaks of dawn.

"Ah, yes. The case." Cash sighed. "It's a sad thing," he said, "when a man can't come back to his hometown to visit friends and fish a while in his daddy's pond without being called out of bed to do consulting work for the local cops." He stopped talking long enough to stretch. "Besides, I'm retired. I'm small-town now; this is the big city. I've tried to forget about it, Phil. It, and the way it operates."

"Well, we haven't forgotten about *you*," Meeker said. He glanced at his passenger's profile a moment before turning back to the road. The old rascal hasn't changed a bit, Meeker thought. Faded sweatshirt, blue jeans, cowboy boots—he looked the same as he had when he left the force ten years ago, right down to the sad eyes and the game leg and the frizzy gray hair. Hard to believe, from his appearance, that this was the man who had cracked the Hollingsworth case. Solved it in two days, Meeker had heard, after the FBI had been on it for two months. "Or the way you operate," Meeker added, with a note of respect.

Cash responded by leaning back against the headrest and gazing blearily into the side mirror. Behind them, the gray horizon had turned to pink. Sunrise was twenty minutes away.

"I should be watching it from the pond bank," he mumbled.

***

The conference room was at the end of the hallway on the third floor of the station house. It contained a long wooden table, ten chairs, no windows, and three detectives. Two men, one woman. All of them stood when Cash and Meeker entered the room. Introductions were brief, but all eyes lingered on the newcomer as he set down his crutch and sagged into his seat. There was no resentment or suspicion in their gazes—just curiosity. None of them knew Lando Cash, but almost everyone knew of him. The Hollingsworth case was being taught at the Academy now.

When everyone was seated, Philip Meeker took a second to glance around the table. "Anything new?" he asked.

One of the men, a thirtyish fellow with a crewcut and an ID badge that said LESTER RILEY, nodded toward the papers on the desk. "Since you left, we got statements from all three suspects and a preliminary coroner's report. Nothing earthshaking."

Meeker pondered this a moment, then turned to study the faces of the others at the table—one a young black woman who had been introduced as Riley's partner and the other an older man in a wrinkled blue workshirt and jeans. He looked tired. "Either of you need to add anything before we start?" Meeker asked. Both shook their heads.

Meeker took out a cigarette, lit it, and leaned back in his chair. Despite the earlier reprieve, rain had started to fall again; they could hear it on the roof, above their meeting room. Fixing his gaze on Detective Riley, Meeker tipped his head toward Cash. "Brief him," Meeker said. "I've only hit the high points, so far."

Riley hesitated. "Has he been to the crime scene?"

"We stopped there on the way in," Meeker said. "Brief him."

As Riley began speaking, the Chief of Detectives puffed thoughtfully on his cigarette, tilted his chair onto its back legs, and watched his cousin through the cloud of smoke. He had been right in his earlier assessment, Meeker noticed. As soon as the story began, Lando Cash became a new man. His posture didn't change, nor did the expression on his face; what was different was his intensity, his focus. All traces of tiredness seemed to fall away, leaving him as cool and alert as a dog on point.

Sitting there watching him, Meeker felt good about his

decision. The murder victim in this case was an important man, and there would be a lot of pressure to make a quick arrest. It was fortunate for all of them, Meeker thought, that Lando Cash had been nearby, and accessible.

Philip Meeker and Landingham Cash had grown up right here in this town, had played cops and cowboys and pirates in the shallow caves of the cliffs beside the ocean. Meeker was even the one who had given him his nickname, after they had gone together to see the movie *Hondo* at age eleven. Even then, Cash had been Meeker's hero. Eventually the name Lanny was phased out and Lando in, to such a degree that almost everyone he knew began to call him that.

But there was more to Landingham Cash than an intriguing name. His schoolteachers noticed it early on, and were always trying to get him to skip grades or take on accelerated studies. Lando refused. He excelled in the classes he liked, which were few, and did just enough to get by in the rest; at graduation he held a low C average. His grades, however, were little indication of his talents, and everyone who knew him knew that. Lando Cash was easily the most brilliant mind Ramona County had ever produced. This was the man who, after only three years on the police force, compiled enough evidence to convict Surly Dan Surlacio, pinpointed the whereabouts of the Two Moon Bay strangler, and rescued a senator's daughter from terrorists at LAX without a single civilian casualty. It was an Iranian's bullet during that incident that made Lando Cash a cripple.

It also made him a hero. A month later, with the new rank of Inspector, Cash was paired with former USC linebacker Butch Carrigan, and after a two-year span their partnership produced more arrests and convictions than the rest of the department combined. With unerring regularity, Cash would solve the crime, Carrigan would break down the doors, and bad guys would get caught. "Cash and Carry," as they were known, soon became nationally known—at one point they were featured on the cover of *Newsweek*. And all this in addition to the Hollingsworth extortion case.

And none of these things had happened because of luck or bravado; they had happened because Cash was smart. He could think fast and accurately, and had an unbelievable talent for organizing facts in his head. Simply put, he saw things that others didn't. If anyone in the free world had a chance of solving this case and solving it quickly, Phil Meeker said to himself, it was this man sitting next to him now.

And the case was a challenge, no doubt about that.

The scene of the crime was an isolated piece of wooded land on the west edge of town. Hardison Park, as it was called, was a public nature area located on a five-acre peninsula that jutted out like a pointing finger high above the choppy waters of Renaissance Bay. It was bordered on three sides by steep rocky cliffs and a guardrail and on the fourth by a ten-foot-high wooden fence with a single entranceway set squarely in the middle. Twenty yards inside the entrance gate was the only man-made structure in the park: a lighted pavilion housing a row of benches, several vending machines, a water fountain, and an ATM for Merchants & Mariners Bank.

According to Detective Riley's account, the first call had come in around 2:20 a.m., from a woman named Rosemary Fernandez, a private duty nurse, at a kiosk pay phone in the gravel lot just outside the park. She had reported, in a whispered but terrified voice, that she had just witnessed an attack on someone at the park's covered pavilion. Later questioning revealed that she'd had a flat tire near the roadside parking lot on her way home from work, and had seen the mugging through the entrance gate as she walked past it to get to the pay phone to call a garage. She had screamed once, involuntarily and loudly, and had seen the figure of the attacker turn to look in her direction and then move away into the shadows.

After making the frantic call to the police, Ms. Fernandez raced back to her car, got in, and started the motor—she had decided that riding on a flat would be just fine under the circumstances. It was as she switched on the headlights that she saw a man on foot, standing directly in front of her car. He stared at her a second, momentarily blinded by her lights, then hurried around to her open window. She sat frozen, too shocked to even put the car in gear—

"—and that's where Gustavsen comes in," Riley said, nodding to the man sitting next to him.

Gordon Gustavsen was in his late fifties, an overweight but otherwise average-looking fellow with a round face and glasses with Coke-bottle lenses. Though he was also a cop, his workshirt and baggy jeans gave him the appearance of a common laborer. If Meeker looked like the bouncer in a bar, Gustavsen looked like the guy who came to fix the jukebox. According to Riley, Gustavsen had been off duty last night when Rosemary Fernandez had turned on her headlights and pinned him like a deer in the middle of the road.

"She scared me as much as I scared her," Gustavsen began. His voice held an apologetic tone, as if he were embarrassed to have been caught with his guard down. "I was driving down Hardison Loop on the way to a drugstore to get some Pepto-Bismol when I heard the scream. My window was down and the wind was blowing, but I heard it clear as a bell. It sounded like it came from near the park, so I pulled over just south of the parking lot. I noticed two cars in the lot when I got there, but didn't see anyone around. I was on my way past them, on foot, when the lady's headlights came on. She told me later her dome light was broken, which is why I didn't see her get into the car. Anyhow, I jumped like a scalded cat."

He paused and smiled. "She seemed mighty happy when I flashed my badge, I'll tell you that. Anyway, I quick asked her what had happened, and when she told me, I advised her to stay in the car and lock it and roll up the windows. I also told her to watch the entrance to the park. I went back to my Chevy and put in a call—it's my wife's car, really, but I had a phone put in it a couple months ago—and then I came back over to the lady. I'm not sure exactly what I thought I was going to do about the mugger—I can't see too well, you guys know that, that's why I'm flying a desk now. But whatever it was that I was going to do didn't get done anyway, because then the backup started arriving—Atkinson and Carter, at first, then Rodgers and his partner, a new guy named Sims.

"I kept a close watch on the fence the whole time, especially after what she had told me. No one had come out since I heard the scream, so I knew that whoever the attacker was, he was still in the park. I kept on watching the entrance gate while Atkinson and Carter went in to check things out, and that's when they found the body. Rodgers' car got there next, and he took Ms. Fernandez downtown while Sims and I stayed at the gate. In the next ten minutes or so they rounded up the only three people in the park—they're in the holding rooms downstairs. I gave Sims a ride back here with me, afterward." Gustavsen paused again, and adjusted his glasses. "If you ask me," he added, "my money's on the Mexican dude."

When Gustavsen had finished his account, Lando Cash leaned back and studied the ceiling tiles. Meeker watched him closely, trying to gauge his reaction, but as usual his face was unreadable.

Finally Cash leveled his gaze at Detective Riley. "Tell me about the victim," he said.

Riley raised his eyebrows and his shoulders at the same time, then let them fall. "Like the Chief said, he was a high roller in this town. The commissioner'll want some fast answers, and the mayor too. I'll tell you this, though—Gordy's right. We got only three suspects. One of those three is the killer. Nobody got out past our men at the gate, and that's the only way out of that place. The cliffs aren't only steep, they overhang, so there's no way—"

"The victim," Cash said again, patiently.

"Sorry. His name's Alton Weathers—"

Cash blinked. Detective Riley noticed, and stopped short.

"You know him?" Riley asked.

"I remember him. Go ahead."

"Well, anyhow," Riley continued, "he was big in one of the insurance companies, pillar of the community and all that. Sat on a lot of boards. Earlier last night, before the murder, he had attended a meeting of the Urban League, and then, at eleven, a roast of the mayor. Everybody hung around afterward, and Weathers left around two a.m., headed home. As far as we know, his only stop was at the park."

Riley paused, bummed a cigarette from Meeker, and took his time lighting it. The female detective gave them both a hard look, but said nothing. After half a minute's wait, Cash turned to Gustavsen and said, "What happened, exactly?"

Gordy Gustavsen looked up, his eyes enlarged to the size of quarters behind his thick glasses. "To Weathers, you mean? One blow from behind, to the left side of the head." He glanced at Lester Riley for confirmation.

"We know it was from the rear," Riley agreed, fanning his match out, "because the Fernandez woman saw enough to know the attacker was standing behind the guy. They were roughly the same height, she said, which is about the only clue we have in the way of size or appearance."

"I remember Weathers as about five-ten or so," Cash said.

Riley nodded. "About that." Anticipating the next question, he said, "All three suspects range from five-eight to six feet. No real help there."

Cash shifted a little in his seat. Meeker wondered whether the leg still gave him trouble.

"Any more on the murder weapon?" Cash asked.

Riley glanced at his boss and back again. "What do you know right now?"

"I was told it was a hammer."

"That it was," Riley said. "A regular claw hammer. That's from Fernandez too, she saw it clearly in the attacker's upraised hand. The coroner agrees, from the size and shape of the skull wound."

Cash frowned. "She didn't get a good look at the killer, but she did at the hammer?"

"They weren't much more than silhouettes, she told me. At the front edge of the pavilion, outlined against the bright lights. The pavilion, you see, is the only really lighted place in the park—the rest is always pretty dark, since the streetlights are outside in the street, where they're supposed to be. And, the whole thing happened fast. Bottom line: no ID of clothes, build, race, hair color, or anything else."

At that point Philip Meeker sat forward in his chair, crushed out his cigarette, exhaled a long plume of smoke, and made sure he had everyone's attention. "So here's the deal," he said to Lando. "From what we know now, Weathers stops at the park on the way home, goes up to the ATM, withdraws some cash—we know it was two hundred bucks, from the transaction record we found in the machine and the receipt in his wallet—and while he's counting it or whatever, the attacker comes up behind him and pops him once with a hammer, on the left side of the head. Skull is crushed, death is instantaneous. Weathers' ATM card was still hanging out of the machine when we found him." He shot a glance at Gordy Gustavsen and the other two detectives. "Right?"

All three nodded.

Cash pondered for a moment, then asked, "What else did you find? The money? The hammer?"

"Nothing but the body," Riley said. "The woman's scream scared him, we know that from what she told us, but it didn't scare him enough to make him leave the cash. We found no trace of the two hundred dollars, and we found no claw hammer."

Cash considered all this as he stared sightlessly at a point on the far wall of the room. "And we're sure nobody left the scene?" he asked at last.

"Positive. The woman said she had the entrance gate in view the whole time she was on the phone. There still wasn't a lot of light, of course, even outside the park, but at least everything outside was open and exposed, with no cover. And the only time she lost sight of the gate was the few seconds when she ran to her car, and by that time—though she didn't know it yet—Gordy was already approaching the scene, and would have spotted anyone moving about out there. In fact, he was so intent on watching the park entrance he was caught off guard by the headlights."

Riley took a long draw on his cigarette. "No, Mr. Cash, the only thing we *can* count on here is that nobody was seen leaving from the time Rosemary Fernandez screamed until the time the police came and secured the area, and after that the entrance was guarded nonstop."

"He's right, Lando," Meeker said. "The killer's one of the three suspects."

A long silence passed, during which Cash went back to studying the reports. Everyone else in the room exchanged looks but made no comment.

"Vending machines, you said," Cash murmured.

Riley blinked. "Beg pardon?"

Cash raised his head and looked at him. "You said the park pavilion had park benches, a water fountain, and vending machines. What kind?"

"Didn't you see them?"

"The lab team was working when we stopped by," Meeker cut in. "We couldn't get near the pavilion."

Lando looked amused. "My cousin is too kind," he said. "The reason we didn't go to the pavilion was that the sidewalk was under repair. To get there we'd have had to wade through the mud, and with my infirmity"—Cash held up his crutch a moment, then replaced it on the floor—"I would've bogged down." He looked at Riley and said again, "What kind of machines?"

The detective thought a minute. "Well, you know about the ATM. There's also a Coke machine, a snack machine for peanuts and candy and so on, and three smaller dispensers—one for stamps, one for gumballs, and one for ferry tickets."

Cash's eyes narrowed. "Ferry tickets?"

"It's pretty new. The dock for the Davis Island ferry's five miles down the coast. You can buy tickets at the park and miss the lines. In fact, you almost have to."

"Lines?" Cash asked. "The place must've grown. And if tickets are sold away from the dock, I'd have thought they'd be sold in a more affluent part of town. Davis Island used to be a haven for the very rich."

Riley shook his head. "Not anymore. There's a fancy amphitheater in one corner of the island for operas and ballets and such, but the rest is farmland and factories. Hundreds of blue-collars ferry out there and back every day. Morning rush hour's a madhouse at the dock."

Cash was quiet for a while, then asked, "What about the ATM?"

"What about it?"

"Well, does it dispense twenties only, or tens only, or combinations, or what? Are they new bills or old? Does it dispense anything but cash, like traveler's checks or coupons or gift certificates? We need to be sure what we're looking for."

Riley seemed embarrassed. Meeker stifled a smile; Lando made a practice of thinking of things no one else had even considered.

"Like the Chief said," Riley replied, "the receipt we found in the machine was for a two-hundred-dollar withdrawal. I don't know about all the rest."

Cash made a note. "I'll check it out," he said. "The fact that you found his withdrawal statement in the machine helps already. It means that it was the last transaction he did. Otherwise, he could have taken money out and turned around and deposited some again, for all we know. We have no idea how long he stood there before he was attacked."

Riley just nodded.

"You said he attended a meeting for the mayor just before the killing?" Cash asked.

"A roast," Meeker said, answering for Riley. "A fund-raiser, really. City elections are a month away."

"You're sure about the time that he left there?"

"I'm sure," Meeker said. "I saw him leave. I was at the roast too, representing the P.D. I sat at Weathers' table with him."

Lando Cash was quiet a moment, processing this new information. "From what I've read lately," he said, "I'd have thought the police wouldn't be too friendly to Mr. Weathers. Hasn't he been threatening to conduct a witch hunt? Trying to flush out past corruption in the department?"

"Not just threatening," Meeker answered. "He'd already started the investigation. But that's all the more reason to be friendly to him, at the moment."

Cash made no comment. Meeker wasn't surprised; Lando had never had any patience with department politics.

"How about personal effects?" Cash asked, changing the subject.

Riley cleared his throat and frowned. He seemed to be trying to regroup after the ATM question. "Of the victim, you mean?"

"Yes. What did Mr. Weathers have on him, exactly?"

Riley shrugged. "The usual. Pocketknife, comb, change, car keys, handkerchief. Wallet was there, contents intact. Thirteen dollars in fives and ones. Nothing obviously missing, except for the money from the ATM withdrawal. Like we said, the scream must have scared the killer off."

"But not enough to run for the only exit," Cash said thoughtfully.

"The scream came from the only exit," Riley pointed out. "We figure he ran for one of the cliffs instead, and threw the hammer over the edge, into the bay."

"The money too?"

"That's the assumption," Meeker said.

Cash was quiet a moment. "I don't know," he said. "The hammer, maybe. But the bills . . ." He scratched his temple with the eraser on his pencil. "When Phil and I stopped there before dawn, there was a pretty stiff wind already, blowing in off the water. I think it would have been hard for somebody to throw a handful of loose bills over the guardrail without the risk of scattering them all over the park. And you said you didn't find any."

A few seconds passed as everyone seemed to think that over.

"I still don't get the hammer," Riley said. "Why not use a gun, or a knife?"

"Maybe he was worried about noise," Cash replied. "Also, a hammer doesn't make as much of a mess as a gun—or a knife either. Or maybe it was just planned to look *un-planned.*"

〰️ "What do you mean?" Meeker asked.

"There was construction in progress. Maybe the killer wanted us to think the hammer had been left there by workers, and was chosen on impulse, at the last minute."

"But the construction was on the sidewalk," Riley said. "Not the building."

Cash shook his head. "The cement had to be framed, and that means hammers and nails." He paused and raised a hand. "Don't get me wrong: I still think the hammer came in—and probably left again—with the killer. But he might not have wanted us to think that."

A silence passed. Lester Riley ran a hand through his crewcut and put on a sour look. All this talk seemed to be irritating him; Meeker gave him a calm-down glance before turning his attention back to Lando.

"What about the suspects?" Cash asked, addressing the room in general.

Riley turned his scowl to the right. "You want to take that one, Pen?"

The third detective, Penny Wallace, sat up a little straighter in her seat. She appeared relieved to be asked to contribute something.

Wallace drew a long breath, let it out, and said, "The first of the three is a white guy, named"—she picked up a notebook and flipped pages—"Fenway. Donald Fenway. Early thirties, long bushy ponytail, looks like a young George Carlin. Two previous arrests, one for fraud and one for possession. He was found hiding in the bushes near the west cliff, wearing a gold chain and soccer shorts and a white sweatshirt two sizes too big for him, with a lot of blue smudges on the right sleeve. He also had a fanny pack full of low-grade cocaine, which is probably one reason he was hiding in the bushes. Said he was waiting to meet someone. If he's telling the truth, we figure the someone was his buyer—ten more minutes and he might have been clean. Anyhow, he said he'd been shooting pool over on Crawley Drive before going to the park."

"Go on," Cash said.

"Well, the second guy's a Mexican, twenty-five or so, with a list of priors as long as your arm. Jimmy Dominguez. Had on a bright yellow T-shirt, blue jeans, and a pair of Air Jordans. He said he liked to come to the park late at night, to watch the ocean."

Riley snorted. "To watch for a dealer, more likely."

"That's probably right," Wallace said. "Most of his record was drug-related. To his credit, he had nothing on him when he was found. What he *did* have, in the pocket of his jeans, was an Astra .357, with a four-inch barrel. Oh, and one more thing. He was loaded with cash. More than three thousand in his wallet, including a dozen or so brand-new twenties. Considering what we know about the victim and the ATM, we figure ten of those bills—well, you get my drift . . ."

Suddenly she stopped talking, lost in her own thoughts. Cash waited a moment, tapping his pencil on the tabletop, then glanced at his cousin. "Penny?" Meeker said.

The detective blinked and cleared her throat. "Just thinking about Dominguez. It occurred to me that he could have been the guy that Suspect Number One was waiting for, to cut a deal."

Cash seemed to consider that, then asked, "What about the third suspect?"

"Oh. Right." Penny Wallace frowned and flipped another page. "Number Three is a strange bird. Ernesto Lombardi, Italian, late fifties, dressed in a threadbare jogging suit. We found him huddled under a blanket against the north end of the fence. No wallet, no money, not much of anything except a fancy gold watch and a bottle of cheap wine. One really odd thing: He has a peg leg. Not a regular prosthesis, understand— this is a *peg* leg, like a pirate or something. Said he made it himself, in the Old Country. He used to be a carpenter." Wallace paused to make sure Cash got the full significance of that last word. "Said he comes to the park a lot lately, since he got the shakes too bad to work."

"I wonder if he had 'em too bad to swing one of his hammers," Gordon Gustavsen murmured.

Cash ignored this. Still looking at Detective Wallace, he said, "What about the watch?"

Wallace shook her head. "The victim still had his on. A Rolex President." She paused, then added, "Seems to me Mr. Lombardi is the only one of the three that has a really good reason for being at the park in the middle of the night."

No one but Cash seemed to know what she meant. He gave her a rare smile as Gustavsen asked, "Why is that?"

"He was dead drunk," she said. "It took us an hour to wake him up."

Cash picked up his pencil and doodled a while on his pad. Finally he asked Meeker, "How long can you hold them, do you think?"

"Long as it takes," Riley cut in, his voice too loud for the close quarters. "One of those three is the killer, and if the two who're innocent wind up suing the department, that's the way it goes."

"What about their attorneys?"

"We've been lucky there," Meeker said. "The white guy with the ponytail and the coke hasn't been able to get in touch with his lawyer yet, and won't accept anyone else. He's not talking, but at least his lawyer's not here doing the talking for him. Number Two got an attorney appointed for him, but the lawyer didn't bother to hang around—Two's the Mex with the gun in his pocket, remember, so we've got him on that anyway, like we got Fenway with his coke, and with this guy's priors we can keep him as long as we want. The third—the Italian— couldn't care less about his rights or his representation. He just seems glad to have a roof over his head."

"Okay. Anything else I should know?"

Meeker had a sudden thought, and shifted in his chair. "The second guy's lawyer—the one appointed by the state, who left? He was complaining that his client was questioned at the scene, before he was Mirandized."

"Questioned how?" Cash asked.

"Patrolman Carter, who had been briefed by the woman in the parking lot, asked him where the hammer was. Not smart, I know, but it's done now."

Cash shook his head. "Doesn't matter. Questions to ensure the safety of the public can be asked before the reading of rights. In this case, a hammer was the murder weapon. It's a technicality, but that kind of inquiry, at the crime scene, is legal and proper. Forget it." He looked at each of them in turn. "Anything else?"

None of them said a word.

"Okay," Cash said. "Here's what I need." He picked up his pad and glanced through the notes he had made. "First, I want a temporary place to work. This is fine here, if I could have it to myself, but I'd really like a separate office someplace with a phone and a computer and printer. Then I want to see all the personal effects, and I want to visit each of the suspects, even if they won't talk. Where are they being held?"

"Three rooms on the second floor," Meeker said.

Cash thought a moment. "Do you still have that long meeting room on the ground level, south side of the building? The one with the little frosted windows near the ceiling?"

When the others nodded Cash said, "It used to have several sliding doors so it could be sectioned off into four smaller rooms—"

"Still does," Meeker said, puzzled.

"I'd like to have the walls put up and locked in place, and have the suspects moved there for a while. To the back three of those four rooms. Is that possible?"

Everyone looked at each other. "I suppose so," Meeker said. "There's nothing in there except some folding tables and chairs—"

"And the lights for all four rooms are controlled from one place, aren't they?" Cash asked.

"That's right—the front section. What's all this about, Lando?"

"I'll tell you later. Could you have all that done by"—Cash checked his watch—"nine o'clock, say?" Meeker glanced at Riley, who made a note and nodded.

Apparently satisfied, Cash picked up his crutch and stood. The others rose also, with a loud scraping of chairs. All four were watching Cash closely, as if he were about to wave his hand and produce a rabbit or something. After a moment Cash noticed the looks on their faces.

"That's it, guys. If you'll get me an office, and maybe some coffee, I'll get started."

Immediately Meeker said, to the others, "Okay, people. Nobody leaves the premises. We're all sleepy, but there'll be plenty of time for that later. Gordy, you get Lando's quarters squared away and then come to my office. Riley'll take care of the holding rooms. Penny, you stick with me."

Meeker hesitated, then turned to face his cousin. "When do you think you'll, ah . . . know something?" The other three were already heading for the door.

"Let's meet at eleven," Cash said. "We'll take it from

129

there."

***

Almost three hours had passed; it was just after eleven. Those who had attended the initial briefing sat in a tight semi-circle facing the desk in Cash's temporary office. All of them were staring at Cash, who was staring at an open file folder and notepad on the desktop. Rain was still falling outside, drumming tonelessly on the roof. Both Meeker and Riley held coffee cups, but no one was smoking; the room was tiny. After a long silence Cash raised his head and studied each of their faces before speaking.

"You all wanted to know when I had some . . . thoughts on the case. Here they are." He glanced at a notepad, rubbed his eyes a moment, and looked in turn at each of the four. His tiredness was beginning to show.

"I thought the first guy, Fenway, was the most likely of the three," he began. "At least it started out that way." He paused, watching their faces. "Remember the blue smudges on the sleeve of his sweatshirt? That was chalk dust. He was telling the truth about the pool hall."

Detective Gustavsen frowned. "Why is that important?"

"It's important because the smudges are on his right sleeve. I finally figured it out: because the shirt was too large, the sleeves were too long—while I met with him, he kept pulling them up, almost to the elbows. As soon as one slid down, he pulled it up again."

All the officers exchanged glances. "So?" Gustavsen said.

"So think about it. The victim at Hardison Park was killed by a blow to the left side of the head, and the attacker was standing behind him at the time. Correct?"

"Thus a left-handed killer," Riley said helpfully.

"Correct again. So if the chalk smudges on Fenway's sweatshirt are on the right sleeve, that means he chalked his cue with his left hand, since that's the only hand he could use to pull up his right sleeve."

A silence passed. "It sounds to me," Riley said, "like that proves he was left-handed."

Cash shook his head. "Wrong. In high school, I used to shoot pool for my lunch money. Chances are, if he chalked his cue with his left hand, he held the butt of the cue with his right."

"Wait a minute," Penny Wallace said. "I saw him too. I saw him light a cigarette in the interrogation room, and he struck the match with his left hand."

Cash shrugged. "He might wipe his butt with his left hand too, for all I know. But when it comes to using power—whether a cue stick or hammer, probably—he'd use his right."

"So what are you saying?" Gustavsen asked. "Number One's not the killer?"

"Hold on," Cash said. "Consider the second suspect. The Mexican." He hesitated a moment, collecting his thoughts. "You were right, Officer Wallace, he had a pocketful of cash, some of them crisp new twenties, grouped together. I agree that they probably came out of an ATM." He stopped long enough for Wallace to nod. "The trouble is, they didn't come out of the one at Hardison Park. That one used twenties, all right, but didn't use new bills, and according to the bank, it never has. It's stocked with older currency, what they call 'teller-quality bills.'" Cash looked around at their faces for a minute, then added, "It's easy to crumple up new bills until they look used. It's hard to do it the other way around. And if Number Two—Dominguez—didn't get those bills from the victim, then he got them somewhere else, before coming there. Stolen? Maybe. But if he already had three grand in his wallet it seems less likely he'd be as anxious to steal Weathers' two hundred."

"I'd say that's a pretty big 'if,' Lando," Meeker said.

"You're right, it is—by itself. But there's more." Cash

shifted his weight in the chair again, and winced a little. "For one thing, why use a hammer when you have a gun? Like we said, a hammer has its advantages, but Hardison Park's pretty remote, not many people around to hear a shot at two-twenty in the morning." He paused. "Another thing: As you know, he was wearing a bright yellow T-shirt—and it's not just bright, it's practically neon. I know the light wasn't good at the park, but that T-shirt would've stuck out like Madonna at a Boy Scout camporee." Cash leaned forward and checked reactions, as if to make sure everyone was following this. "If the Fernandez woman saw the attack, even for an instant, she'd have had to be blind not to see the T-shirt—and I feel the same about Number One's long ponytail.

"One last thing: Lombardi had on a watch, but neither of the others did. If the murder was committed by One or Two, why would they take the victim's money and not his Rolex, which was worth fifty times that?"

Cash sighed, rubbed his eyes a moment, and glanced again at Wallace. "And I think your comment about the drug deal is right on, by the way. I couldn't nail anything down, but there's a very good chance Dominguez was there to meet Fenway, and vice versa."

"And if they *were* there for a business deal," Wallace said, continuing the thought, "they weren't there to kill Alton Weathers. Right?"

"Not unless it really was an afterthought," Cash agreed. "And again, the type of murder weapon makes me think the attack was planned in advance. The only problem with the hammer would have been concealing it, especially in Dominguez's case, with his tight jeans. The wallet and the gun probably took up all the slack he had in there."

"The same with Fenway's soccer shorts," Wallace said.

Gordon Gustavsen's face, behind his thick glasses, was an

odd mixture of fascination and frustration. "So Two's not the one either?" he asked.

"Just hold on," Cash said again. "Now. Number Three. Lombardi. The strange thing about Three is his peg leg. I imagine he gets around on it pretty well, but there's one thing that bothers me. The ground at the park was soaking wet from yesterday's and last night's rain, and Phil and I poked around in the mud a bit at the crime scene. We didn't see many footprints—that's being examined now, in the light of day, but I think we would've noticed a hole made by a peg leg. In fact . . ."

Cash turned to a blank page in his notepad, paused a moment, then looked at Gordon Gustavsen. "Borrow your pen?" he asked. Gustavsen unclipped a ballpoint from his shirt pocket and slid it across the desk; Cash quickly sketched a map of the park.

". . . in fact," he continued, showing the others the sketch, "I think it was probably too wet for Number Three to have gone to the pavilion at all without getting completely bogged down, and damn sure too wet for him to have made it all the way to one of the cliffs and throw the hammer over and then get back to where the officers say he was found, by the front fence."

Detective Riley blinked suddenly. "The peg leg," he said, brightening. "What if it was hollow? The hammer, and the stolen money too, could have been hidden inside it. That could be why neither was found."

"A good point," Cash said. "I thought of that. But the leg's solid. I made a comment about the workmanship, since I have a bum leg of my own, and he let me take a look." He tossed the pen back to Gustavsen, who caught it and returned it to his pocket. "But the idea's still valid—if the hammer and money weren't disposed of inside the park, they probably came out the same way the hammer got there: in the possession of the killer."

"But no one came out," Riley said, frustrated again. "And

you just implied Number Three didn't do it."

"Well, it would also be hard to hide a hammer in a jogging suit," Wallace chimed in. She was clearly intrigued by the whole business, a fact which Meeker thought seemed to annoy Riley. Cash just held up a hand. "Bear with me a little longer, folks." After a moment he said, "The thing that's worried me the most about this case is something no one has even mentioned yet: Why would the killer pick the particular spot that he did to make the attack? After all, he could have struck anywhere on the path or in the parking lot—there were a lot more bushes beside the path than around the pavilion. Why make his move in the one place in the whole park that was really brightly lit?"

Another long, heavy silence. Everyone present sat and looked at each other.

"Well, I'll tell you, but first let me tell you another tale. As I suggested earlier, and with your chief's permission, I stopped in to see each of the suspects for a minute. I introduced myself only as a police officer, and gave each of them a form to sign, regarding the return of their personal belongings."

Riley frowned. "But . . . there is no such form."

"There is now. I designed one this morning, on WordPerfect, and printed three copies. The form stated, among other things, that one dollar of a suspect's pocket money would be used to contribute to the Police Widows' Retirement Fund unless the suspect checked a box saying not to. Each of them caught that—the first two even said a few choice words on the subject before checking the box that said no. Number Three said yes, by the way, and told me he thought the fund sounded like a great idea."

"What's your point?" Riley asked.

"The point is," Cash said, "that those three rooms were mostly dark. I had turned off all the lights from the front room before the three suspects were brought in, and taped the switches down. I told them there'd been a power outage, in the storm. All the rooms were lit only by the sunlight through the frosted glass windows near the ceiling, which isn't much on a rainy day like this. And even though I could hardly see anything in there, *every one* of the suspects could see well enough to catch the statements about the contribution, and say something about it, and check a box."

Detective Riley shook his head. "I'm still lost."

"The park was dark, Riley. With only the pavilion and the dim glow of the streetlights, visibility was probably pretty close to what it was in those rooms—kind of a late twilight." Cash paused. "I think the killer attacked Alton Weathers near the pavilion, and the ATM, because that was the only place where he could see what the hell he was doing."

"Then . . . you're saying—"

"I'm saying his eyes were bad." Very slowly, Cash turned to look at Gordon Gustavsen.

It seemed to take Gustavsen a moment to catch on. When he did, his eyes went even wider behind his glasses. "Just what are you suggest—"

"There's more," Cash said. "You told me you'd gone out looking for Pepto-Bismol. After what I saw in my little experiment, I came back and checked the availability of twenty-four-hour pharmacies in your area. And do you know what I found, Officer Gustavsen? There are seven of them, counting all-night supermarkets, within a mile of your house. *Seven.* Why, I asked myself, would a man want to drive five miles out of his way to a drugstore when there's one at the end of his block?"

Gustavsen's face was a fiery red now. "I can't believe what I'm hearing," he whispered, through clenched teeth. "If you're accusing me of something, you'll need better reasons than—"

"I'm not accusing you of anything yet," Cash said. "But

those are the kinds of things that start me wondering."

There was another stretch of silence, during which the two stared at each other. Meeker sat and watched them, and Riley and Wallace appeared to be holding their breaths.

"And what did you decide?" Gustavsen said tightly.

"I decided I'd better find out for certain." Without taking his eyes off Gustavsen's face, Cash turned his head slightly and called over his shoulder: "You there, Sergeant?"

The office door suddenly opened, and a young patrolman walked in, looking embarrassed. In his hand was a plastic evidence bag. "The contents were taken from Detective Gustavsen's private car, sir, ten minutes ago. It was under the driver's seat. Brinkley and Dabbs are witnesses."

Cash took the bag from him, nodded, and turned to the others as the sergeant left.

Inside the clear bag were three items: a cluster of twenty-dollar bills, two concert tickets, and a Craftsman claw hammer. The bills were used and wrinkled, the hammer bloodstained.

A stunned silence enveloped the room. Every eye was fixed on Gordon Gustavsen, who stared blankly at the package. His face had gone pale.

"You were right, Wallace, about the weapon," Cash said. "It left the park the same way it came in—inside the pocket of the person who brought it." He turned to speak directly to Gustavsen. "You must have had it with you, along with the money, when you were surprised by Ms. Fernandez's headlights. Then, when you told her to wait in the car while you went back to your car to place the call for help, you stowed this under the seat. You gave Officer Sims a ride back later, so there was no chance to get rid of it, but that didn't worry you, did it? It's your personal car, not a cruiser, and there was no reason to think it might be searched."

"And it shouldn't have been searched," Gustavsen said

loudly. He nodded toward the evidence bag. "You can't use that, you know. Not in a trial."

"Oh yes I can." Without looking down, Cash removed a document from a drawer and laid it on the desktop. "Judge Clarkson's an old friend. He signed the warrant an hour ago. Our helpful young sergeant ran it over for me." He paused and added, "We can also examine the insides of your pockets. I imagine there are some matching bloodstains there, from the hammer."

Gustavsen lowered his head to stare at his lap. After what seemed a long time he murmured, "I caught it with my left hand."

No one said a word. Wallace and Riley exchanged a puzzled look.

"That's why you asked me for my pen, wasn't it," Gustavsen said, raising his eyes to meet Cash's. "So you could throw it back to me."

Cash didn't reply. Somewhere in the building, a door slammed. The silence dragged out.

Meeker, not knowing whether to watch Cash or Gustavsen, asked no one in particular, "But why? What possible motive could there be—"

"If I had to guess," Cash said, "it was about Weathers' pledge to expose corruption in the department. The investigation is supposed to be focused on bribes and kickbacks that took place years ago, when people like you and me, Phil, were on the streets." Cash shot a questioning look at Gustavsen, who sagged further into his seat. Along with the color, all the fight seemed to have drained from his face.

"He was onto me," Gustavsen muttered.

"Gordy," Meeker said, "I should caution you here that you might want a lawyer to—"

"He was onto me," Gordy said again. "He had called, a

week ago. He was toying with me. He told me he had the goods on me, and a couple others too . . ."

His voice trailed off, and he was quiet for a long moment. Then he sighed and said, "My attorney's Hamilton Pinello. Could I call him, please?"

***

It was late afternoon of the same day. The breeze was cool and damp as Phil Meeker's patrol car pulled into the gravel driveway at Cash's old homeplace, several miles outside town. The rain had stopped again, hours ago. Behind them, in the west, the sky was clearing a bit, and from his place in the passenger seat Lando Cash was watching the sunset in the same mirror that had shown him the sunrise fourteen hours earlier.

"We're square now," Cash said, after a pause.

Meeker, who had switched off the motor, turned to look at him. Cash was sitting as still as a stone, gazing through the windshield at the house and the small pond at the bottom of the hill. "What?" Meeker asked.

"You know what I mean."

"No," Meeker said. "I don't."

For a full minute Cash sat and watched the gathering darkness. Meeker watched his cousin's profile. Neither of them spoke.

Finally Cash broke the silence. "Why was he there, Phil?"

Meeker frowned. The question had been quietly spoken, almost casual.

"Who?" he asked.

"Gordon Gustavsen," Cash said. "We know now that it wasn't coincidence. He was at the park because Alton Weathers was there. But how did he *know*?"

Meeker pondered that for a moment, still frowning. "I guess Gordy followed him there, in his car."

Keeping his gaze straight ahead, Cash shook his head.

"Not with *his* eyesight, he didn't. Not at night. He was there already, waiting."

Meeker shrugged. "I dunno, then. What difference does it make—"

"At about the time Ms. Fernandez turned her back long enough to run to her car and get inside it, Gordy must have come out through the gate," Cash said, still speaking to the windshield. "When her headlights caught him it scared him. He was telling the truth about that. But he was walking *away* from the park, not toward it."

Meeker's frown deepened. "That makes sense," he said. "But who cares? It's over now. Why are you—"

"What do you make of the tickets, Phil?" Cash said.

"Tickets?"

"The two tickets we found in the bag in Gordy's car. They were for admission to a symphony concert at the Davis Island amphitheater this morning. Pretty high-brow affair." Cash paused and rubbed the stubble on his chin. "Maybe it's just me, but Gordy Gustavsen doesn't look like a guy who'd enjoy that kind of thing."

Meeker shrugged. "Maybe they weren't his," he said. "Maybe they belonged to Weathers. The money did."

"I considered that. But when I checked with Weathers' office, his secretary said, tearfully, that she knew nothing about any plans to attend a concert. Weathers' calendar showed that he was to be in this morning, at work."

Meeker said nothing, waiting.

"So I figured, maybe Weathers bought the tickets last night sometime, before the meetings but too late to let his office know. Just out of curiosity, I decided to call the outfit that sells them—the fancier the affair, the fancier the ticket office, usually, and the fancier the office, the more likely they are to keep good records. And sure enough, they had. A young lady named

Yvonne looked up the numbers on the two tickets and found the name of the buyer."

Still Meeker made no reply. Very slowly, for the first time since the car had stopped, Cash turned his head to look at him.

"You bought those tickets, Phil. Now isn't that a kick? Those two concert tickets were sold to you, Philip Meeker, at three-forty yesterday afternoon."

Their eyes held for a moment. Finally Meeker turned away. He shrugged again, and this time he was the one speaking to the windshield. "So I did," he said. "I knew he and his wife liked the symphony, and since I knew I'd be sitting at his table at the benefit last night, well, I decided to buy them to give to him. Which I did, quietly, during a break. It's no big thing, Lando—the department does that sometimes, to those with . . . well . . . influence."

"Why didn't you say so, earlier?" Cash asked.

Meeker sighed. "Sometimes it's done, like I said, but it's frowned upon. You know that. Besides, I didn't think it was important."

Cash was quiet a moment. "What makes it important," he said, "is that Gordy took them off Weathers' body, and put them in the bag with the hammer and the money."

Meeker stared at him again. "I don't follow you."

"Why," Cash said, as if asking himself, "would someone who has just been caught in the act, so to speak—someone who has just committed a murder and thinks he might have been seen doing it—why would that someone, who is in a bit of a hurry at the moment, take the time to search his victim's wallet, to find and remove a pair of *concert* tickets?"

"I have no idea," Meeker said faintly. Outside, the wind gusted, and rainwater from the branches of an oak spattered the windshield.

"Then I'll tell you why, Phil. I think he did it because he

was told to. I think those were his specific instructions." Cash paused for a beat, watching his cousin closely. "After all, those tickets weren't for a downtown performance in the civic center, or the municipal auditorium. They were for Davis Island. For a nine a.m. performance this morning—a *weekday* morning. And if those tickets were received unexpectedly, late last night, they were essentially worthless, unless that particular concert-lover had one additional item in his possession." He paused. "You know what that is, Phil?"

Meeker just stared at him.

"Ferry tickets," Cash said. "Detective Riley told me himself, at the meeting this morning, that anyone who planned to ride the boat to the island better have a ticket beforehand or he might not get aboard." Frowning, Cash rubbed a fingernail along the smooth wood of his crutch. "And the only place to buy after-hours ferry tickets was, lo and behold, the vending machine at Hardison Park."

A long, deep silence passed. It was almost full dark in the car now.

"I think you told that to Alton Weathers, Philip. I think you just happened to mention, after presenting him with the gift of the two symphony tickets, that he might want to swing by the park on his way home—it would be miles out of his way the next morning—to buy tickets for the ferry, so his prissy wife wouldn't have to stand in line at the dock with a bunch of migrant workers. And then, I think you called Gustavsen, probably from a pay phone outside the roast—probably disguising your voice—and told him Weathers would be stopping by the park, alone, sometime between two and three a.m. Just in case he wanted to know."

Phil Meeker's face was as white as a lump of chalk in the darkness. He sat very still, waiting.

"As things turned out, of course," Cash continued,

"Weathers did in fact go to the park, right on schedule. The only wrinkle was that he decided to use the ATM first—he was low on cash, too—before getting to the ferry ticket machine beside it. That, of course, wasn't important; you didn't care whether the body, when it was found, had ferry tickets on it or not. Your concern was the *concert* tickets. And even that wasn't a really big deal—after all, who would ever think to trace them back to you? But it was a loose end, and no detective likes loose ends, and this was one that could easily be tied off and forgotten, with a little foresight. All you had to do was tell Gordy, in the phone call you made to him, to search the body for a pair of symphony tickets, and to remove them." Cash paused, watching his cousin's face. "One thing about Gordy, he follows orders, doesn't he? Even when he doesn't know who's giving them."

More silence. The only sound was the ticking of the cruiser's cooling engine, and the occasional rumble of a car passing by on the dirt road.

Meeker said nothing at all. He had lowered his head and was staring down at his hands, which were loosely—almost lifelessly—holding the bottom of the steering wheel.

"When Butch Carrigan and I were here, on the force," Cash said, "we were in a different section from you, and from Gustavsen too. I never even knew Gordy at all, except by sight, probably you didn't either. The two of you would have moved in different circles." He paused for a bit, studying the rubber tip of his crutch. "But even now, obviously, you're in a position to hear things that he wouldn't. Certainly you knew about Weathers' investigation. I think you also knew Gordy was already targeted, and found a way—a phone message, maybe, or a note in his desk drawer—to tell him about it. And I think you were afraid *you* wouldn't be far behind." Cash sighed heavily. "Butch and I spent a lot of time on the streets ourselves back then, Phil. I know a lot of things can happen in the bars and dark alleys over the years . . . and sometimes the wrong people find out about them, later. I think you did some of those things, like Gordy did, and you were at risk of being discovered. I think you figured that if you weren't already on Weathers' list, you would be soon. That part, of course, Gordy *didn't* know." Cash stopped a moment, and said, in a quieter voice, "And I think you decided to let Gordy take care of things for the both of you."

Meeker continued to stare at his hands. The expression on his face was totally neutral, as if he were in a trance.

"What I find hardest to take," Cash went on, "is that you called me in. You knew Gordy killed Weathers, but you couldn't reveal that without revealing your part in it too. So you called me, knowing I'd find some way to identify the killer. You got me to do it for you."

Finally Meeker looked up, and met his cousin's gaze. His face was still unreadable. "You can't prove this, Lando. You're good, but you're reaching. You can't prove a word of it."

Slowly Cash nodded. "You're right. The only way to do that would be to go deeper into the investigation Weathers had started, to find the names of the other cops on his suspect list. I won't do that. Besides, you've got enough to worry about, I think. Gordy's no mental giant, but it may be that he'll put two and two together one day. Maybe he'll finally place the voice that called him last night. Who knows?"

Cash paused, unsnapped his seatbelt, and put one hand on the handle of the door. "My suggestion to you is this: If you can find a way to get that investigation stopped—and that should be simple, with Weathers out of the picture—then get it stopped. You'll be in the clear." Still Cash hesitated, his hand resting on the doorhandle. "But I meant what I said earlier, Phil. Now we're square, you and me. You helped my dad when he needed it years ago, when I wasn't here to help him myself, and I've owed you for that for a long time. Now we're even.

Understand?"

Meeker cleared his throat. A trickle of sweat had run down his cheek and neck and into his collar. "I understand," he murmured.

"And don't call me again, Phil. I won't help you again."

"No," Meeker said.

Cash stared at him for a long moment, then without another word climbed out of the car, wrestled himself upright, shut the door, and made his way tiredly up the path toward the house.

In the dripping woods beside the road, crickets had begun to sing.

***

Cash watched from the kitchen window as Meeker's cruiser drove away. Afterward, he popped open a can of Coors and sat down on the sofa in the den. As he sipped his beer he looked around thoughtfully at the room. It bore little resemblance to the place he remembered as a child. It was redecorated and smartly furnished now, cheery and bright and attractive. His mother had sold it years ago, after his father's death, to friends of the family, who were now on their annual vacation to Hawaii. When Cash had called them and asked permission to drive over and fish in the pond while they were gone, they had invited him to stay in the house as well. He had only arrived yesterday.

After ten minutes he reached for his crutch, rose to his feet, tossed the empty can into the garbage, and retrieved his briefcase from the bedroom. From the case he removed a black address book, which he held open in his lap as he keyed in a number on the den telephone. It rang several times before he heard the click of an answering machine.

"Hello," the voice said. "This is the Carrigan residence. We can't come to the phone right now, but if you'll leave your name and—"

Cash waited for the beep, then said, "Butch, this is Lando. Just wanted you to know everything's settled. I'm here, but there was nothing to be done. Someone took care of it for us. It's a long story, I'll call you when I get home."

He hung up, regarded the phone for a moment, then stood and began to pack his gear. Funny the way things turn out sometimes, he thought as he limped with his bags out to the rental car in the garage.

He hadn't even had to take the sniper rifle out of the trunk.

John M. Floyd

GUARDIAN ANGEL

Angela Potts was always the first to see trouble coming.

A retired schoolteacher, she pictured herself as a lone sailor stationed on the bow, watching for rocks and icebergs in the fog. In reality, her lookout point was the wooden swing on her front porch. From there she monitored the usually calm seas of her hometown, alert for any sign of a threat.

The impending danger, in this case, was a man named Vernon Rollins. He had pulled his red sports car into her driveway five days ago, a glitter in his eye and a briefcase in his hand. The mere sight of him set off so many internal alarm bells she could almost hear her ears ringing.

"Financial planning's my field," he said, grinning at her from the porch steps. "May I sit down?"

Angela—Angel to her friends—informed him that the only sitting he would do here was in his carseat, on the way off her property. After he drove away she marched straight to the telephone and issued a warning to her neighbors.

It did no good. The next morning at the beauty parlor, Mary McCall and Bertha Woods were bubbling with news of the sexy fellow in the fancy car. An investment counselor, they called him, but they were much more interested in the color of his eyes and the brilliance of his smile. Angela was appalled.

"He could be a murderer," she told them.

"A what?" Mary said.

"He's probably checking us out, toying with us. Who knows?"

"What I know," Bertha said, "is you're watching too much TV."

"I'll remember you said that, Bert, when they're dragging the creek for your body."

"The creek's not deep enough to hide *my* body," Bertha said, which was true enough.

Two days later, when Angela ran into Kate Farrell at Wal-Mart, the situation had worsened. The dashing Mr. Rollins had taken Kate and the two Taylor sisters out to dinner.

"Sounds like close quarters," Angela said, remembering his little car.

"It was," Kate replied, with a wink.

Angela rolled her eyes. Would they never learn?

In desperation she phoned Sheriff Chunky Jones, a lazy but pleasant young man she had taught in the fifth grade.

"He's up to no good," Angela said. "I can spot these guys."

"I remember," the sheriff said dryly. He was referring, she knew, to her allegation last year that the new Baptist minister was embezzling funds. When no one would listen to her, she finally barged into the church study one morning and caught him not with his hand in the till but in the arms of the mayor's wife.

"I was right about him, Chunky. He was guilty as sin."

"He was guilty *of* sin," the sheriff corrected. "But not of a crime."

"Tell that to the mayor."

"Look, Ms. Potts—"

"This Rollins is planning something, believe me."

The sheriff sighed into the phone. "Why do you think so?"

"Would you trust someone," she asked, "who has blond hair and black eyebrows?"

"My wife has blond hair and black eyebrows."

Angela chose not to reply, and as a result was left alone in her mission. Undaunted, she continued to man her porch swing by day and her unlighted bedroom window by night, watchful and waiting.

And finally it happened.

One stormy evening she spotted a car parked in the trees behind Nell and Lizzie Taylor's house. She also noticed their rear windows were dark. That was odd: The Taylor sisters always stayed up late.

And then she saw him—a tall blond man, dragging a lumpy sack across their backyard.

Angela snatched up the phone and dialed the Taylors' number. No answer.

She went back to the window. A flash of lightning revealed Vernon Rollins loading the body-sized sack into the trunk of his car. Then he drove away.

That was enough for Angela.

"He's *what?*" Sheriff Jones said, into the phone.

"You heard me—he's killed one of the Taylors!" Quickly she described the car, and what she'd just seen.

It took her five minutes to run down the hill in the rain to their back door, and another minute to get her trembling key into the lock. Angela always kept a spare, since Lizzie Taylor often locked herself out. Inside, Angela switched on the light and found a window broken. "Nell?" she called. "Lizzie?"

Again, no answer. Then she heard something move behind her. She yelped and spun around—

And saw both sisters standing in their back doorway.

"Angel?" Nell said. They were as wet as she was. "What's going on?"

Angela just stared. "You're alive . . ."

"We've been downtown. Mr. Rollins suggested a movie—"

"He was here," Angela said, pointing. "While you were gone. He had a big sack—"

"Those were clothes, for Goodwill." Nell shrugged out of her raincoat. "He said he'd deliver them, if we left them in the toolshed."

"But . . . the window—"

"I broke that Tuesday," Lizzie said. "Locked myself out again, and you and Nell were both gone."

"But he parked out back—"

"So did we. Our driveway's being repaved, remember?"

Angela felt sick. What had she *done*? Dazedly she dialed the sheriff as Lizzie walked past her into the den.

"I'm at the Taylors', Chunky," she said, when she was patched through. "About Mr. Rollins—"

"Don't worry, we got him, Ms. Potts."

"No, you don't understand. That sack wasn't—"

"We know. We just opened it."

Suddenly she and Nell heard a piercing scream. Angela almost dropped the phone; Nell dashed from the room.

"Chunky," Angela blurted, "come quick. It's Lizzie—"

"I heard her," the sheriff said. "I expect she just noticed their gold clock's missing."

"Their clock?"

"And their silver and jewelry and Persian rug, among other things. It's all right here, in Rollins' sack."

"What!?"

"You were right, Ms. Potts. You just got your sins wrong again. He isn't a murderer—"

"He's a burglar," Angela said to herself. She looked up as both sisters ran wide-eyed into the room.

"Somebody's stolen everything," Nell shouted. "Call Mr. Rollins, he'll know what to do!"

Angela just sighed.

It was a lost cause . . .

A GATHERING OF ANGELS

Sheriff Chunky Jones poured a cup of coffee, propped his feet up on his desk, and decided to let someone else answer the ringing phone. He needed a break.

It didn't last long.

"It's Angel Potts," Sally called, from the outer office. "She says she and Betty Fenwick are at Riverside Park, and they need you to come quick."

The sheriff groaned. Distress calls from Angela Potts were almost always false alarms. He put down his coffee and reached for the telephone.

"Ms. Potts?"

"She already hung up, Sheriff," Sally said.

He picked up his hat and sunglasses. "You better radio Fred, have him meet me there. He might as well get used to this."

Ten minutes later Sheriff Jones and his deputy arrived at the park. They found Betty Fenwick and Angela Potts at a picnic table fifty yards from what looked like a circus tent. Betty was sitting at the table; Angela was standing on it.

She looked down at the sheriff. "About time you got here. You stop for lunch on the way?"

"Ms. Potts, what are you doing up there?"

"I'm keeping watch." She let Fred help her down. "You the new deputy?" she asked.

"Fred Prewitt, ma'am."

"Call me Angel. I never liked Angela, and Chunky's the only one calls me Ms. Potts, because I taught him in grade school."

"You plan to tell us what happened?" the sheriff asked.

"What happened was, somebody stole Betty's purse. She set it down on the table for a second, to help me with my bow—"

"Your bow?"

"On the belt of my dress—see? It won't stay tied. Anyhow, when we turned around again, her purse was gone. It has her billfold in it, credit cards, cell phone . . ."

Betty Fenwick, who hadn't spoken a word, just nodded.

"And neither of you saw anyone?"

"No," Angela said. And then her eyes narrowed. "But he's still here."

"How do you know that?"

"Because I've been watching, that's how."

"But there are people all over the place."

"Not carrying Betty's purse. It was big, and bright red— I've been watching for it, or for a bag big enough to hold it." Angela pointed at the tent. "Whoever has it, he must be in there."

"He?"

"Or she. And I know what you're thinking—I've checked the only two trash cans for the purse, and there are no restrooms close enough to hide in."

"What about the other side of the tent?"

"There's a pond there, he couldn't have gone that way. And those two flaps on this side, front and back, are the only ways in or out. He's in that tent, all right. With the evidence."

The sheriff studied her a moment, remembering her history of misguided notions.

"Not this time," she said, reading his mind. "Believe me, Chunky, he's in there."

He looked again at the oversized tent. "What is it, anyway? A church revival?"

"School program. At least a hundred people."

Sheriff Jones nodded, still studying the tent. "Okay, Ms. Potts, you can take Ms. Fenwick on home. Fred and me will handle this—"

"Fred and I," she said. "And forget that—I'm staying."

"What?"

"I'm staying here. Bets, you go on home and lie down, I'll call you later." After Betty Fenwick had wandered off, Angela said, "I have a plan."

"I was afraid of that."

"You'll never catch him, in that crowd. What you should do is—"

"Ms. Potts, you need to just let Fred and I—"

"Fred and me."

Sheriff Jones closed his eyes, pinched the bridge of his nose. "Fred, give us a minute, okay?" He waited until his deputy had moved away, then turned to Angela. "Ms. Potts, I wish you wouldn't correct my grammar all the time, I'm not your student any more. And don't call me Chunky in public— my name's Charles."

"Oh, hush up. Do you want my help or not?"

"Well, actually—"

"What you should do," she said, "is go in through the

front of the tent there, let everybody see you, and then leave again." When he didn't move, she said, "Hurry up, time's wastin'."

***

With a long sigh the sheriff trudged over to the tent, ducked through the front flap, and took off his sunglasses. To his left was a stage where kids dressed as white-robed angels were outnumbered by a group of red devils. Just like real life, he thought sadly. To the right was the audience, seated in rows of folding chairs. The heat was oppressive. The sheriff looked around a moment more, then left.

He found Angela up on the table again, watching the back flap of the tent. Just as he was about to say something, her eyes widened. "There he is!" she said. The sheriff turned to see a man holding a blue coat leave the tent. Within seconds the two lawmen had him cornered. And sure enough, underneath the coat was Ms. Fenwick's red purse, with contents intact.

"How'd you know it was him?" the sheriff asked Angela, as Fred took the robber away. "You told me you didn't see any-one."

"I didn't."

"Was it the coat, then? I mean, it *is* too hot to carry a coat—"

"Well, mostly it was because of when he left."

"Excuse me?"

"I called him," she said.

"You what?!"

"I called Betty's cell phone, while you were gone."

"And he answered?"

"Of course he didn't answer. I just let it keep ringing."

"Couldn't he have turned it off?"

"I doubt he could find it, with all the junk she keeps in her purse. Meanwhile, everybody around him was probably ready to strangle him. He was attracting attention, which was the last thing he wanted."

"So he left," the sheriff said.

Angela nodded. "Out the back way, because he'd seen you up front."

Sheriff Jones couldn't help smiling. "Not bad," he admitted. "Not bad at all."

She grinned. "So I helped?"

"You helped. In fact . . . we made a good team, you and me."

She seemed about to speak, then stopped.

"What is it?"

"You and I," she said.

HENRY'S FORD

Angela Potts was waiting outside the restroom at Roscoe's Cafe when the sheriff came out.

"At last," she said.

"Ms. Potts? What are you doing here?"

"Your job, is what I'm doing." Angela pointed to the front door. "The bank's being robbed."

"*What?*"

"You heard me. Hurry up."

Sheriff Chunky Jones, whose nickname was partially due to his fondness for Roscoe's donuts, followed her out onto the sidewalk. As they watched, two old ladies came out of the bank across the street, smiling and chatting.

"Sure looks like a crime scene to me," the sheriff agreed.

Angela snorted. "It will be. He'll come out soon, with the bank's money, and you can arrest him."

"Arrest who?"

"Whoever stole Henry McBride's car and drove it here,

that's who. It was double-parked there by the bank, with the motor running."

"Where is it now?"

She gave him a guilty look.

"Ms. Potts . . . ?"

"Well, first I tried to find you—Roscoe told me you were in the bathroom—and meanwhile I spotted your deputy—"

"You mean Earl?"

"So I asked him to drive Henry's car over to my house."

"You what?!"

"Don't look at me like that," she said. "It was the getaway car. The robber can't get away without his getaway car."

"But why would Earl—"

"Earl never knows whose car's whose. I told him it was mine, and I was having trouble with the gears. And the keys were already in it, so . . ."

Sheriff Jones sighed and rubbed his forehead. "Let me get this straight—you think the bank's about to be robbed, so you send my deputy away from the scene?"

"He's old as Methuselah, Chunky. I was afraid he might get hurt."

"But . . . what makes you think the car was stolen in the first place?"

"Because the owner didn't drive it here."

"How do you know that?"

"Henry would never leave the motor running. You know how frugal he and Maude are. He'd squeeze a buffalo nickel till its tail stood up."

The sheriff frowned. "You sure it's Henry's? Green Ford, two-door?"

"Yep."

"Maybe someone borrowed it."

Angela held up her cell phone. "I called the McBrides'

house, to check that. No answer."

"So?"

"So maybe the thief did something to 'em. Maude's already sick with the flu." Angela's scolding look reminded the sheriff of thirty years ago, when she was his schoolteacher. "Well? You gonna do anything, or not?"

"Ms. Potts," he said patiently, "we've been through this before, you and me—"

"You and I."

"—and I know you mean well, but—"

"But you think I'm crazy."

"No, I just—"

"Like a fox, Chunky. I'm crazy like a fox."

"Well, I can't arrest somebody just because—"

"You can if you catch him with the bank's money. That's what he'll have, when he comes through that door."

At that moment, a clean-cut young man with a briefcase walked out of the bank. Angela and the sheriff fell silent. They watched him approach the curb, stop, and blink. He seemed lost.

"Oh, yeah, he looks dangerous," the sheriff said. With a sigh he crossed the street and said to the stranger, "Help you, sir?" Angela hurried after him, eyes narrowed.

The man saw them and smiled. "I hope so. I seem to have misplaced my uncle's car."

"Your uncle?"

"I'm Jake McBride. My aunt and uncle live about ten miles west—"

"I know them," the sheriff said.

"Well, I'm visiting them, from New York. Drove down Friday. They asked me today to come pick up some checks they'd ordered." He saw the look on Angela's face. "Is there a problem?"

Sheriff Jones studied him. He was definitely a McBride. "Well, the thing is, we just tried to phone your uncle's house, and got no answer. Any ideas?"

McBride scratched his head. "Aunt Maude's probably inside—she has the flu—but Uncle Henry said if she's sleeping he might turn the phone's ringer down and go fish in the pond awhile."

"The pond?"

"The one behind the house."

Sheriff Jones nodded, then remembered Angela. "Excuse me—Jake McBride, Angela Potts."

"Potts?" The stranger grinned. "Angel Potts? Aunt Maude showed me your get-well card. She said, 'Angel's not just a nickname, it's a perfect description of her.'" He took her hand. "I agree."

Angela blushed. Her stern look vanished. "I think . . . well, we might owe you an apology, Mr. McBride—"

"Jake."

Her blush deepened.

"Mr. McBride," the sheriff said, "the car was in the way, so my deputy moved it down the street. Let's step over to my office, I'll get him on the radio." As they left, he said, "Stay here, Ms. Potts."

Fifteen minutes later the sheriff returned alone. He found Angela sitting on a bench by the sidewalk.

"Chunky," she said, "I'm sorry about that. But I really thought—"

"You were right," he said.

"What?"

"Jake McBride's under arrest. I had Sally call the McBrides' neighbors—they drove over to check, and found Henry and Maude tied and gagged. Henry said his nephew came there today, and forced them to sign documents authorizing the withdrawal of their life's savings. That briefcase didn't have the bank's money in it, it had the McBrides'. He's wanted in three states, up North."

Angela was, for once, speechless.

"I knew something was wrong when he mentioned the pond," he said. "Henry drained it a month ago."

"Well, I'll be," she murmured.

"And the briefcase. If you're picking up an order of checks, why bring a briefcase?"

"Or a stolen car," she said. "I guess he figured we wouldn't notice one with local plates."

The sheriff grinned. "You did."

A minute later Deputy Earl Wood appeared. "Here's your car keys, Angel," he said. "I left it in your driveway. And you're right, that clutch needs adjusting."

She took the keys, thought a moment, then handed them to the sheriff. He saw the mischievous glint in her eye.

"I don't like Fords anyhow," she said. "Give it to Henry McBride for me, for his birthday."

She winked at the sheriff and left.

"That's one crazy lady," Earl said, watching her walk away.

Sheriff Jones smiled. "Like a fox, Earl."

LADIES' DAY

"You have a visitor, Sheriff," the intercom said.

Sheriff Jones looked up as Angela Potts marched into his office and plopped into a chair. Her jaw was set, her purse held in a deathgrip.

"Have a seat, Ms. Potts."

"Don't be cute, Chunky. This is serious."

Before the sheriff could reply, the intercom on his desk said, "Want some coffee, Angel?"

"No, thanks, Sally." To the sheriff Angela said, with a nod toward the intercom, "What's this?"

He shrugged. "Sally's cousin Felix got it on sale. A wireless. He installed it himself, last week."

"No OFF button?" Angela said, studying it.

"No need. Sally knows everything I do anyway." Which was true. "If you're interested, I also have a new pager. From the mayor."

"What I'm interested in, is yesterday's burglary."

161

"Ms. Newman's house?"

"I think there's a connection."

"Why?"

"Two break-ins on two Thursdays, a week apart?"

"So?"

"It was the same time of day, Chunky." She watched him as that sank in. "Around three o'clock."

"That doesn't prove—"

"Thursday is Ladies' Day. They meet to play chickenfoot. Both victims were there."

"Chickenfoot?"

"It's like dominoes. Nine players."

"And they meet every week?"

"At the church, from two to four. I think the thief knew these women live alone, and that their houses'd be empty then."

The sheriff leaned back in his chair, which groaned dangerously. Charles Jones wasn't nicknamed Chunky for nothing.

Angela's voice interrupted his thoughts. "So what's your plan, other than stress-testing that chair?"

He closed both eyes and massaged his forehead, which sometimes eased the effects of Potts-induced headaches. This time it didn't work.

"My deputies are canvassing neighbors. I'm also waiting for a fingerprint report. Okay?"

Angela said nothing.

The sheriff sighed. "You have a suggestion?"

"Stake 'em out."

"Stake who out?"

She rolled her eyes. "I just told you, nine women play chickenfoot every Thursday. Two of their houses were robbed. Next week, post somebody at the others."

"Seven houses?"

"I never managed to teach you much English, Chunky. I

guess you did better at math."

"I did well enough to know a sheriff and two deputies can't be seven places at once."

"Borrow somebody, then."

"From where?"

Before she could invent an answer to that, he held up his hand. "Look. Let's check for witnesses, and hear back from the prints. Okay?"

Angela stood up. "This is a waste of time."

"Tell you what," he said wearily. "Until we catch this guy, ask the other seven to stay home on Ladies' Day."

She blinked. "And miss playing chickenfoot?"

"Right."

She looked as if he'd asked her to run naked down Main Street. "They won't do it."

"Why not?"

"They just won't." Speaking to the intercom, she said, "Sally, your aunt Nell's in this group. Would she miss a chickenfoot game, if asked to?"

"Nope."

"Why not?" he said.

"She just wouldn't."

Sheriff Jones didn't actually see Angela leave. He had his eyes closed again, and was massaging his forehead.

***

The next Thursday at noon Angela phoned him in his office.

"I have an idea."

"Surprise, surprise," he mumbled.

"Anything from the neighbors?"

"No."

"And the fingerprints?"

"Inconclusive. Her grandkids had touched everything."

163

"So you got nothing," Angela said.

Her tone irritated him as much on the phone as in person. "What's your idea, Ms. Potts?"

She hesitated. "Sally's out of town, right?"

"Right."

"Anybody in your waiting room?"

He glanced through the open door. "No."

"I don't want anyone else to hear this," she said. "Here's my idea. I've spoken to six of the seven other chickenfoot ladies. One has strep throat, and one has family at her house, so it'll be occupied while she's at the game this afternoon. That leaves four."

"Go on," the sheriff said.

"I think you and your deputies should watch three houses: Kate Farrell's, Betty Fenwick's, and Nell Tate's. That only leaves Martha Dooley's house unguarded."

"But she's the richest widow in town."

"She also lives on a crowded street, with more security. This guy would know that. That's the one house he won't try."

The sheriff pondered that. It made sense.

"Okay. From two to four, we'll watch those three residences. Farrell's, Fenwick's, Tate's." He paused. "But I'm not optimistic."

"I am," she said.

***

At three o'clock that afternoon, as Sheriff Jones sat hidden in the shadows near the Fenwick house, his cell phone rang. It was Angela Potts.

"We got him, Chunky. He's handcuffed and sitting in Deputy Wood's cruiser."

The sheriff blinked. "*What?* The guy came to the house Earl was watching?"

"Well—not exactly. We're at Martha Dooley's house. Both

your deputies and I were here, and caught him red-handed."

"Dooley's? But that's—"

"I had to lie to you, Chunky. You know that new intercom of yours, on your desk?"

"What about it?"

"You said Sally's cousin Felix bought and installed it. That got me thinking. I mean, it's wireless—what's to install?"

Sheriff Jones frowned, listening.

"And whoever did this knew the ladies. And Sally's aunt—"

"Is also Felix's?" he said.

"Right. So I decided this morning to check Felix's car. His parking lot's near your office."

"And?"

"Guess what I found in his glove compartment."

The sheriff blinked. Suddenly he understood.

"An intercom," he said.

"Just like yours and Sally's. He didn't buy two, he bought three. He heard your every move." Angela paused. "So I made up that mumbojumbo about one unguarded house, and called you—"

"Knowing Felix would be listening."

"I made sure he would be. I called him first, and asked if he'd seen you around. I said I had something urgent to tell you."

Sheriff Jones found himself grinning. "Not bad. I take it Sally didn't know about the third intercom?"

"Just Felix."

A thought struck him. "Wait—you found it in his glove-box?"

"Terrible thing, the way people leave their cars unlocked."

"But—"

"Don't worry. Anybody asks, I'll say Sally'd borrowed my sunglasses—which is true—and I was looking for them."

"In her cousin's car?"

"Was that his? I can't see much in the glare without my sunglasses."

The sheriff chuckled. "Ms. Potts, you've saved the day. I owe you."

"I don't want your new intercom, if that's what you're thinking."

"How about my pager?" he said.

FAMILY BUSINESS

When Sheriff Chunky Jones arrived at the hospital, he found Angela Potts waiting for him outside a patient's room on the second floor. She was frowning and tapping her foot the way she did thirty years ago, when her fifth-grade students were late for class. Sheriff Jones remembered it well.

"What are you doing here, Ms. Potts?"

"Your deputy called me, to comfort Janie Tate," Angela said. "She's inside, with her husband."

"I didn't think you liked her."

"I don't. Janie tends to keep other people's casserole dishes, after the church socials."

The sheriff looked past her. A handprinted card on the closed door said RONALD TATE.

"What happened, exactly? I heard Ron shot somebody, then had a heart attack."

"Other way around," Angela said. "He had chest pains and fell off his riding mower, in his back pasture. He was too far off to call for help, but he had his rifle—"

"He what?"

"Ron said he straps it over his shoulder while he mows, to shoot snakes with. You know how bad they've been this year."

"So he fired his rifle to attract help?"

"Not exactly. He was afraid no one'd hear the shots. Both his wife and his neighbor are half deaf."

"You mean his cousin?" the sheriff said. "Bud?"

"Right, Bud Tate. From where Ron was lying, Bud's house was the only one in sight."

"Go on."

"Well, Bud's guest bedroom window was dark, and Ron knew Bud never goes there—but he thought Bud might hear the glass break."

"So Ron put a bullet through Bud Tate's window."

"Right. Except he also put a bullet through Bud Tate."

"I thought you said Bud never goes there."

"Well, he won't be going there again," she said.

"Bud's dead?"

"Yep. And there's more. Guess who found the body?"

"Why don't you tell me, Ms. Potts?"

"Janie Tate. She'd walked over to Bud's about that time, couldn't get him to answer the door, and went inside."

"Uninvited?"

"Well, Bud is her husband's cousin—and business partner."

"Go on," the sheriff said.

"Janie said Bud had given them some homemade biscuits early that morning—Ron had eaten one for breakfast. She was bringing Bud a peach pie in return."

"So she strolls in, pie in hand, and finds the body?"

"She finds more than that. She finds biscuit dough, in a bowl on the kitchen counter. And white powder beside it."

"White powder?"

"Looked like sugar," Angela said, "but she knew that didn't make sense. Bud was diabetic, and so's Ron."

"Janie noticed this before she found Bud's body?"

"After. She called nine-one-one from the kitchen phone, and saw the powder then. She's a pharmacist, you know."

"Wait—where was Ron? Still lying in the pasture?"

"Yep. The paramedics spotted him through the broken window. They left Bud where he was—dead—and rescued Ron."

"And the white powder?"

"Janie told them, and they brought it in for testing."

"I take it it wasn't sugar."

"It was arsenic trioxide. Causes cardiac arrest. Bud must've put it in the biscuits thinking both Ron and Janie would eat some. Turned out, Ron did and Janie didn't. And Bud Tate, instead of inheriting his partner's half of Tate Construction, got shot dead by accident."

The sheriff frowned. "Who figured all this out?"

"Janie."

"One more thing—why was Bud at his guest bedroom window, in the dark, when Ron fired the gun?"

"I guess he was watching his victim. He probably just didn't see Ron aiming at him."

Sheriff Jones took off his hat and scratched his head. "What a story."

"Well, go ask them yourself—the doc said Ron's doing fine. I'm going to see your deputy."

"At the crime scene?"

"Just a friendly visit."

The sheriff sighed. "You been watching *Dragnet* again?"

"*Cops*," she said.

***

Twenty minutes later Angela was back. She found Sheriff

169

Jones in Ron Tate's hospital room, getting ready to leave.

"Hello again, Angel," Janie said. "Sheriff, you know this lady taught all my nephews, on the Bennett side?"

"But no Tates," Angela said.

Janie sighed. "Yes, I regret Ron and I had no children."

"And poor Bud was a bachelor."

Janie and Ron exchanged a glance.

"Now that he's dead," Angela added, "I guess the whole company's yours."

Ron frowned from his bed. "What are you saying, Angel?"

"Why'd you turn on the lamp in Bud's guest bedroom, Janie?"

Janie blinked. "What? I didn't. I told you, it was dark in—"

"Deputy Prewitt found your fingerprints on the switch."

Janie Tate gasped.

"Bud didn't poison those biscuits, Janie. Did he?"

Both the Tates' faces had gone pale. Scowling, Sheriff Jones said, "Ms. Potts, what are you—"

"Hush, Chunky. Here's what I think, Janie: You know poisons, and have access to them—Bud didn't. You doctored some biscuit dough and planted it in Bud's kitchen as evidence—without telling him—while Ron got into position with his mower and rifle. Then you led Bud to his guest bedroom, told him to look out the window, and turned on the light so Ron could shoot him. Afterward, you called nine-one-one, and let the paramedics find Ron lying out back, faking a coronary. He survives the 'poisoning' because no one was poisoned, the shooting's an unfortunate accident, and you two own the company free and clear."

The Tates were sweating now.

"Bud was making bad deals," Janie blurted. "We had to do something—"

"Shut up, Janie," Ron said. "Sheriff, I want my lawyer."

Sheriff Jones, whose mouth was hanging open, closed it with a snap. "Fine. Ah, excuse us a minute." He guided Angela out into the hallway.

"Prewitt dusted for prints?" he asked her.

"Not exactly."

"Can you even *get* a print off a lamp switch?"

"Probably not."

The sheriff groaned. "Then what are you—"

"I recognized my bowl, Chunky."

"You what?"

"The bowl that held the biscuit dough in Bud's kitchen wasn't his, it was mine. Janie Tate 'borrowed' it, a year ago."

Sheriff Jones stared. "You mean—"

"You heard her, in there. They're guilty as Satan."

He studied Angela a moment, then sighed and nodded. "I agree. But tell me—"

"What?"

"Where'd you learn this kind of thing?" he said. "From me?"

She grinned. "*Perry Mason.*"

John M. Floyd

A STITCH IN TIME

Sheriff Charles Jones was saying goodbye to the warden on the prison steps when he saw Angela Potts. She and several other women were in conference with a guard at the front gate. As usual, Angela seemed to be doing most of the talking.

The sheriff turned away, but wasn't quick enough. Angela spotted him.

"Chunky!" she called. "I need to talk to you."

The warden raised an eyebrow. "Chunky?"

"An old nickname," the sheriff said, looking pained. "She taught me in grade school. Keep me posted, okay?"

When he came through the gate Angela pulled him aside and said, "What's going on? They won't let us in."

"This your church group?"

"Sewing circle. Every month we bring things we've made to give to the inmates. Shirts, coats, sweaters—"

"Not today," he said. "There might've been a breakout."

Angela blinked. "Someone escaped?"

"Possibly. The headcount was two short, and a guard thinks he saw someone run into the woods over there. The warden's sent out search parties."

"They know who it was?"

"Not yet. They'll fax me names and photos when they—"

The sheriff stopped. Angela's eyes had narrowed, which he took as bad news. It meant she was thinking.

She turned to look west, toward town. A quarter mile away, a white motor home was parked beside the road.

"What is it?" Sheriff Jones asked.

"That R.V. stopped there a minute ago."

He studied it a moment. "So?"

"Afterward, I saw somebody walk up to it."

"You're thinking someone flagged them down?"

"Why not?" she said.

"Well, there were two escapees, not one. And that's west—the guard saw somebody running east."

"They could've split up. They always do, in the movies."

"Oh. Well then, it must be true."

"Don't you sass me, Chunky Jones."

"Be reasonable, Ms. Potts. Whoever's in that R.V. probably just stopped to use the john."

"In the woods? Why do that? Those things have nicer bathrooms than the one in my house."

"Maybe they're just resting."

"On a muddy shoulder? There's a picnic area two miles back."

The sheriff groaned. Just a typical conversation with Angela Potts. And he'd left his headache pills at home.

"Look, Ms. Potts, catching criminals is my job, not yours. You and these ladies go—"

"Where I'm going, is to check out that R.V."

He sighed. "I'll check it, I'm leaving anyway." He turned

and headed for the car marked COUNTY SHERIFF.

"Bertha?" Angela shouted to her sewing group. "You girls go on back to town. I'll ride with the sheriff."

***

Two minutes later she stood in the chilly wind beside the motor home while Sheriff Jones rapped on the door. The vehicle looked new, with Michigan plates.

The door opened. Staring down at them was a pale man in a sweatsuit, a brown woolen scarf, and a Tigers baseball cap. "Help you folks?" he said.

The sheriff asked to come inside, and Angela followed him. The three of them stood together in the tiny kitchen.

Sheriff Jones took out a notepad and pen. "Your name, sir?"

"Wayne Sills."

"I see you're from Michigan. Your occupation?"

"I'm a farmer. Why?"

"And your destination?"

"The Gulf Coast. To visit relatives." Sills frowned. "Is something wrong?"

"You're traveling alone?"

"Yes, I'm a widower—two years now."

The sheriff gave Ms. Potts a hard look and asked, "Why'd you stop here, Mr. Sills?"

"I saw somebody running across the field there." Sills stooped and pointed out the south window. "I even got out to help, but the guy never slowed down."

Sheriff Jones wrote down a description of the fleeing man and thanked Sills for his time. With a nod to Angela, the sheriff turned to leave.

"You going through Jackson later?" he heard her ask.

Sills nodded. "I-55, then Highway 49."

"You'll have a long detour," Angela said. "Interstate's

under construction."

"That so?"

She took the sheriff's notepad. "Better draw you a map."

"Ms. Potts," the sheriff said, "we need to go."

"It'll only take a second." She turned away to use the countertop as a writing desk.

The two men chatted idly about the unseasonable weather. Sills said he thought the South was supposed to be warm.

At last Angela finished, tore off a sheet, handed it over. "That should help," she said. The rest of the pad she gave back to the sheriff.

Sheriff Jones glanced at it and froze. He looked up at Sills, who was studying his new map, then down again.

The note on the top sheet said, in Angela's schoolteacher script:

IF I CALL OUT TO HIM, DRAW YOUR GUN AND CUFF HIM, QUICK. TRUST ME.

Before the sheriff could overcome his shock, he heard Angela say, "Mind if I use your bathroom?"

Sills hesitated, then said, "First door on your right."

Angela marched away, leaving the sheriff to ponder the note.

What in the world was the crazy woman up to now?

But there was no time to speculate. Seconds later he heard her call out, "Mr. Sills, I think something's wrong with your toilet."

Sills, of course, turned as predicted. And when he did, Sheriff Jones muttered a prayer, pulled his service revolver, and barked a command. Sills was handcuffed without argument.

"Ms. Potts?" the sheriff shouted. "I hope you know what you're doing."

"I do," she called. "And I think you better come back here."

***

The couple Angela had found tied up in the back bedroom

of the R.V. turned out to be Mr. and Mrs. Wayne T. Sills, from Niles, Michigan. Terrified but unhurt, they told a chilling story. As they were driving along, some guy in coveralls had run out of the woods waving his arms. They stopped and let him aboard. In short order he bound and gagged them and changed into Wayne's clothes. He had probably been preparing to drive away just about the time the sheriff arrived.

"How'd you know?" Sheriff Jones asked Angela, as the imposter was led away. He had already revealed the destination of the other escapee, who would be picked up shortly.

"I didn't," she said, "till I found the others, in the back."

"Yes you did. You knew. Was it his skin?"

"It was pale," she agreed, "for a farmer. But that wasn't the tipoff."

"What was?"

"His scarf." She pointed to the retreating prisoner. "The brown wool scarf."

"What about it?"

She smiled.

"I made it," she said.

THE BOMB SQUAD

"Lights," Becker said, looking up through the windshield. "We got lights on the top floor."

The driver, Ed Timmons, leaned forward over the steering wheel, took a quick look, and sat back again, his eyes on the road. "Oh God," he said, and swallowed. "It's really him, isn't it?"

Sergeant Tom Becker was already punching numbers into his cell phone. "I hope so," he lied. What Becker really hoped, as he waited for the security guard to answer the phone, was that there was a cleaning crew up there, or someone working late. But from what the guard had told him moments earlier, there was little chance of that. Unlike the other threats and tipoffs that had flooded the police switchboards since the bomber's latest attack, this one looked as if it might be the real thing. An anonymous call had come in to headquarters only minutes ago, delivered in a voice that was as clear and chilling as its message:

His next target's Remington Tower, top floor. He's there now.

Becker was leaning forward for another look at the building in question when he heard Ralph Hendrix, the security guard in the Remington lobby, pick up the phone.

"Mr. Hendrix?" Becker said. "Me again. You did say everybody on thirty-two had signed out already, right? And nobody's signed back in?" Becker paused, rubbing a hand through his crewcut as he listened. "Well, somebody's up there now, we just saw the lights come on." Another wait, and a weary nod. "Right. Well, what it means is, we don't have as much time as we'd hoped. And we're still a ways away."

Becker had a sudden thought, and turned to ask the driver, "Who were those guys who called in a minute ago, from the East Side?"

Timmons frowned, most of his attention on the road. "Spellman, I think he said. Spellman and Rice."

Becker turned back to the phone. "Two men from one of the other stations are close by," he told the guard. "They should be there soon. Officers Spellman and Rice—" He stopped. "They are? Good, put one of 'em on."

As he waited, Becker glanced again at Timmons, who was cursing softly as he weaved their cruiser through the late-night traffic. They had at least another twenty blocks to go. The building loomed ahead of them, a black monolith topped with a single row of lights.

Becker heard a new voice come on the phone.

"Rice?" he said. "My name's Becker, from Metro. Here's what I want you to—" Becker broke off then, and spent the next thirty seconds listening and nodding. Finally he said, "Right. Sounds good to me. We'll be there inside ten minutes." He started to break the connection, then added, "One more thing. Are you both in uniform? Yeah, us too. We don't need to be shooting each other." With that, Becker clicked the phone off and sagged back in his seat. His head had begun to throb.

"I take it he outranks you," Timmons said, swerving to pass a white limo.

"Don't know and don't care," Becker answered. "The important thing is, he's got a plan, which is more than I had." He sighed and took his pistol from its holster. As he checked its load he saw Timmons glance at him, and was reminded of a scene from *Bullitt*, when the driver of the car Steve McQueen was chasing turned to watch his passenger stuff shells into a shotgun. It occurred to Becker that Timmons looked a lot more scared than the guy in the movie.

"Rice said he and Spellman were just down the street when they heard the call," Becker explained. "He's already studied the floor layout and talked with the guard. Apparently there are two elevators on the east end of the building and stairwells east and west. The top floor—the one that's lit up—is thirty-two. He and Spellman want to take one of the elevators to thirty-one, send it back down, and go up the stairs to the top floor. They'll lock the stairwell door there, then go back down to thirty-one, down the hallway to the west end of the building, go *back* up to thirty-two, and wait outside that stairwell door until we call them. They don't have a cell phone, but they're taking one of the guard's radios and a set of keys to the offices."

Timmons seemed to think that over. "Four people," he said, "from two different stations. We don't know them, they don't know us, and none of us know what we might find up there . . ." He shook his head. "You sure we can go in this way, without more backup?"

"The only thing we can't do," Becker said, holstering his piece, "is let this jerk plant his bomb and get away again. Okay?"

Timmons said nothing. His face was grim, his eyes locked

on the street ahead.

"It's a smart plan, Eddie," Becker said. "This'll save time. Spellman and Rice'll be in place outside the door on the other end of the hallway by the time we get there. We can go in from both sides."

Though he still didn't reply, Timmons seemed to accept that, and Becker turned again to stare out the window. He found himself wondering why in the hell this had to happen now, on his last night of crossover duty. Becker's normal job was at a desk at headquarters, where the only danger was getting poisoned by the coffee. To make matters worse, this was the night of the Commissioner's roast, which meant a big chunk of their workforce was ten miles away, fidgeting in their chairs in the Hilton ballroom. The backup Becker had requested might take awhile.

"I heard you ask dispatch about the tipoff," Timmons said, interrupting his thoughts. "What'd they tell you?"

"Not much," Becker replied. "Male caller, sounded young, sounded white, thumping noises in the background."

"Thumping?"

"That's what they said. We'll listen to it, afterward."

"I hope so," Timmons said with a worried look.

Becker was pondering that comment when the car screeched to a stop in front of the Remington Building. In the blink of an eye, both he and Timmons were out of the cruiser and heading for the door, where they were met by an overweight guard in a rumpled tan uniform. His nametag said R. HENDRIX; his face said he was scared half to death. Smart man, Becker thought.

"The other two guys should be in place soon," the guard told them as they crossed the echoing lobby. He sounded out of breath. "They sent the elevator back down two minutes ago."

The floor plan was still spread out on Hendrix's desk, near

the elevator. While Timmons wrung his hands, Becker studied the layout, stopping every few seconds to fire questions at the guard.

"Any other exits?" he asked.

"Just the elevator and the two sets of stairs."

"Roof access?"

"Only from the stairwells."

"Outside fire escapes?"

"No. The windows don't open. If you go out you go down."

"What about lights?"

"On that floor? One switch, near the elevator. Controls the hallway and all the offices." When Becker looked surprised, Hendrix added, "I knew a guy who worked up there, years ago. The offices used to be a bunch of open cubicles, with partitions. The wiring never got changed."

"Well," Becker said. "At least nobody'll be hiding in the shadows." He chewed his lip a moment, his mind working. "What about noise, this time of night?" he asked.

The guard frowned. "Pardon?"

"How noisy is it, on thirty-two? Fans, generators, piped-in music?"

"Just the air-conditioning. It's a big unit."

"It's loud?"

"Kind of a rumble. You know."

Becker thought that over. "Can it be turned off, from up there?"

"Don't think so. Another throwback to earlier times. Some of the top floors used to have older computer gear that had to stay cool. It's controlled centrally, from somewhere."

"Okay." Becker stared at the plans, still thinking. "Right now I need you here, Mr. Hendrix, but later I may phone you to go find the A/C and switch it off. Understood?"

As the guard nodded agreement, Timmons cleared his throat. "Excuse me, Sarge," he said, his voice shaky, "but it seems to me . . . well, we might *want* a little noise up there, while we're poking around. If we can't hear him, maybe he won't hear us."

Becker glanced up from the floor plan. "That's not what I'm talking about. We might need to listen for sounds that he wouldn't."

"What *kind* of sounds?"

Instead of answering, Becker turned to the guard. "Where's your other set of keys?"

Hendrix held out a ring of about fifty. "Office numbers are written on 'em."

"No master key?"

"Not any more. All the locks were changed last week, after some folks left the firm."

"What *kind* of sounds?" Timmons asked again.

Becker looked him in the eye as he clipped the keyring to his belt. "Ticking sounds," he said.

Their gazes held for a second longer, then Becker scribbled a number on a desk pad and handed it to the guard. "Use your phone to contact me, but only if you have to. And when you see us reach thirty-two"—he pointed to the floor indicator above the elevator doors—"call Spellman and Rice on their radio. Tell them to wait five seconds, then go in. Timmons and I'll enter from this end of the hall. I'll send our elevator back down, and you hold it here, along with the other one. Okay?"

Becker waited for Hendrix to nod, then turned and headed for the elevator. Timmons followed, his face pale.

"Good luck," the guard called, as the doors closed behind them.

***

Inside the elevator, Becker checked his gear. Service

revolver, cell phone, cuffs, flashlight. The light was probably unnecessary, tonight, but he was glad he had it along. He wished he had a shotgun.

He glanced at his partner, who still looked a little green around the gills. "You okay?" Becker said.

Timmons swallowed and kept his eyes straight ahead, staring at nothing. "What do you think it would feel like?" he asked.

Becker regarded him a moment. Timmons was leaning back against the wall of the elevator car, beads of sweat glistening on his cheeks and forehead. "What would what feel like?"

"The explosion," Timmons said. "I've heard that when it happens you don't feel, or hear, a thing. You think that's true?"

Becker shook his head. "We're not going to get blown up, Eddie. Not tonight, anyway." He raised his eyes and looked at the floor numbers on the display panel as the car rose. "For one thing, our experts say this guy—if it's really him—is careful. He works slow. And since we know he's been here less than fifteen minutes—we saw the lights come on ourselves, remember—he probably hasn't had time to arm and plant anything yet." Becker paused, watching the numbers change. They were at the nineteenth floor and climbing.

"The second thing is, even if he *has* already hidden it, we've got at least eight hours to find the damn thing. This dude's ego is huge; he'll go for max headlines and max casualties. No way he'd set it to blow before the morning crowds arrive for work." Becker took a breath and let it out slowly, still watching the display. Twenty-seven . . . twenty-eight . . . twenty-nine . . .

"So if you want to worry about something, Eddie my man, worry about getting shot. Better yet, worry about *me* getting shot."

As Becker spoke the words, the elevator car slowed. The

red number 32 appeared on the display, and stayed there. Becker heard a DING, then a moment of total silence.

The doors opened.

***

The top floor was one long, narrow hallway with office doors lining both sides. Guns drawn, Becker and Timmons stepped out into the corridor. Becker held the elevator car until he saw the two uniformed figures at the far end of the hall, more than a hundred yards away; then he leaned back into the elevator, pressed "1," and came out again as the doors sighed shut. He heard the car start its long trip back down. Timmons acknowledged the two colleagues with an upraised hand, and Becker saw one of the figures bend down to lock the stairwell door on their end.

Well, that's that, Becker thought. All the exits were now sealed.

He took a moment to look around. From where he stood he had a clear view of everything in the hallway; all the lights were in fact on, there were no obstructing objects like file cabinets or water coolers or potted palms, and the only break in the corridor was at this end, where it widened a bit to include a reception area with desk, computer, and telephone. There was literally no place to hide. Whoever else was here—if he was here at all—had to be inside one of the offices.

Okay, Becker thought. Here goes. Another glance down the hall told him the other cops were already unlocking office doors and venturing inside. Signaling Timmons to stand by, Becker unclipped the ring from his belt, found the key to the first office on his right—3201—and turned it in the lock. The door swung open.

Becker crept inside. The office was large and cluttered. Plenty of hiding places *here*, he decided. While Timmons stayed put just inside the open door, Becker did a quick search.

Nobody home. Before leaving, he took a look through the tall window at the end of the room. At first he was puzzled: The entire city block below him, just behind and to the north of the building, was pitch black—no lights, no people, no anything. Then he saw the perimeter lighting, and the chain-link fence, and, as he looked more carefully, the deep pit with heavy equipment parked at the bottom. Construction site.

Satisfied, Becker turned and went back to the hallway. "One down," he whispered as he moved past his partner. He actually doubted whether Timmons had heard him; the guard, as it turned out, had been right about the air-conditioning. It made a deep, steady rumble that seemed to come from everywhere at once, with an occasional knock or rattle thrown in. Becker couldn't imagine having to listen to it all day long. If it did come down to a search for the device, the bomb squad would definitely have to get the A/C shut off first.

Slowly they worked their way down the corridor, checking rooms on both their left and right; 3202 was a restroom and 3203 contained only a copier and a fax machine, the rest were offices. Ten minutes after starting out, while they were searching room 3208, the air-conditioning cut off—or at least cycled down, Becker figured. The resulting silence was even more unsettling than the noise had been.

That was when they heard the shots.

Two of them, one right after the other. Then, a second later, the crash of breaking glass. The sounds had come from the other end of the hall.

Both Timmons and Becker froze for an instant, then eased out into the hallway. Resisting the impulse to hurry, Becker flattened himself against a wall and waited for several seconds, his heart pounding and his gun sweaty in his hand. Finally he nodded to Timmons, who was trying to make himself small on the other side of the corridor. They both moved forward.

As they approached the west end of the floor, Becker saw that the five farthest office doors were open. He assumed that whatever it was that had happened, had happened behind the nearest door, since the other team would have started its search at the stairwell and come this way. Having heard no more noises, he and Timmons stopped just outside 3246, cocked their revolvers, and waited a moment.

If one of the cops had just been trigger-happy and then knocked over a lamp, Becker said to himself, we're all going to feel like fools.

Oddly enough, when he followed his gun around the corner and into the open doorway, the first thing he saw was a broken lamp, lying in the middle of the room—but beyond that was a broken window, and on the floor beside the window was the sprawled body of a policeman. Off to the right, on the far side of a wooden desk, a second cop was looking through an open briefcase. He jerked upright when he saw Becker and Timmons, then all three relaxed.

Becker lowered his gun, his mind racing with a combination of relief and confusion.

Where was the suspect?

As he stood there dumbfounded, Timmons brushed past him to check on the fallen officer.

"He's dead," said the second man, who had immediately resumed his search of the briefcase. Becker studied him a moment. The man's shirttail was out, his hat was off, and his blue nametag said SPELLMAN in white block letters. He continued with the briefcase for several seconds, then closed the lid and pushed it away in frustration. "The bomb's here somewhere," he added. "We surprised him."

As Timmons rose from the body, Becker walked to it, knelt, and looked at the nametag above the shirt pocket: Rice. Though he hadn't known the man, Becker still felt a lump in his throat. He had, after all, spoken to him on the phone twenty minutes ago. After a pause Becker waved his gunbarrel at the window. "That where he went?"

Spellman nodded. Though his voice had been fairly steady, his face was ashen, his hands trembling.

Becker and Timmons exchanged glances, then Becker rose to his feet, holstered his pistol, and looked through the broken window. There was no construction site on *this* side of the building; when he leaned out the window he looked down on a lighted city street. Thirty-two floors below, a crumpled figure lay on the sidewalk, surrounded by a growing crowd. For a second it looked as if the body might be wearing tennis clothes. Becker quickly dismissed that thought, blaming his poor eyesight. It was night, after all, and the sidewalk was a long way down.

When Becker turned again to face the room, he saw Timmons helping Spellman to a chair. Watching them, Becker took out his cell phone and called Hendrix in the lobby. He told him the situation, then put the phone away and approached Officer Spellman. The man's eyes were glassy and vacant.

"What happened?" Becker asked him, as gently as he could. He was vaguely aware that the air-conditioner had come on again.

"He killed Rice," Spellman said, in a monotone. "He killed him, then took a shot at me. I jumped behind the desk there."

"You sure you're not hit?"

Spellman blinked, then ran a hand over his chest and stomach in a gesture that would have been comical under other circumstances. "I don't think so."

"No struggle?"

"No time."

"What happened next?" Becker said.

Spellman motioned with a lift of his chin. "He went through the window."

Becker frowned. "Isn't that safety glass?" he asked, studying the jagged hole.

"Beats me. He just put his head down and rammed through." Spellman swallowed and said, "I never saw anything like it."

"Okay, you just rest a minute." Becker picked up the cell phone and punched numbers. "Hendrix? Free up one of the elevators, we got a man coming down. Any sign of the bomb squad?" He listened for several seconds. "Well, when they do, send 'em up, quick. And see if you can kill that A/C, we got a search to do here."

He signed off and turned to Officer Spellman. "You go on down to the lobby, sport. I'll tell your people you did good."

The cop nodded dazedly, but made no move to get up.

"You need some help?" Timmons asked him.

Spellman blinked, then focused on him and said, in a faint voice: "No. No, I can make it. Thanks, guys." He rose unsteadily to his feet, took a breath, and made his way out the door. Moments later, Becker heard the elevator chime at the other end of the hall.

"What about the body?" Timmons asked.

Together they turned to look at Officer Rice, lying dead on the floor ten feet away.

"He'll get a hero's burial," Becker said. "But right now we got work to do."

Both of them took a deep breath and directed their attention to the office. It was pretty much in order except for the floor on the left-hand side of the room, which was strewn with books and boxes apparently taken from a line of storage bins and shelves along that wall. It was clear that the two other cops had indeed interrupted the bomber as he was preparing a place to plant the device.

"Spellman was right," Timmons murmured, looking at the items scattered about on the carpet. "The bomb's here, somewhere."

Becker nodded agreement. But something was nagging at him, something at the back of his mind.

"We should have a while, though," Timmons was saying. A drop of perspiration ran into his eye, and he brushed it away with the back of his hand. "Like you said, it'd be set for the morning rush hour, right?"

Even as Timmons spoke the words, Becker noticed the lamp again. The lamp worried him. If there had been no struggle, why was it broken? Had the suspect knocked it over in his dive through the window?

The cell phone rang. Timmons waited for Becker to answer it, and when he didn't, answered it himself.

Becker was still staring at the fallen lamp. Not only was it broken, it was unplugged. Unplugged and lying in the middle of the floor. Becker frowned and concentrated, letting his eyes sweep the room. The open bins, the cluttered shelves, the carpet, the window, the walls—

"It's the Chief, Sarge," Timmons said.

Becker's gaze stopped on two small holes in the wall just above the baseboard, beside the window. He walked over and examined them. They were bulletholes, spaced no more than an inch apart.

Bulletholes?

"Sarge," Timmons said again. "The Chief wants to talk to—"

Becker squeezed his eyes shut, searching his memory. Whatever was nagging at him had been there since they first entered the room and found the dead officer. And something else, too, something Spellman had told them . . .

Then it hit him. His eyes snapped open.

The shirttail. There hadn't been a struggle, yet Spellman's shirttail was all the way out, and his hat missing. It was as if he had not yet finished dressing. And the body on the sidewalk, decked out in what looked like tennis whites—

My God, Becker thought.

Without even looking at Timmons, Becker reached out and snatched the phone from his hand. "Chief?" he said.

"What the hell's going on up there?" Chief Wellborn demanded. He was outside; Becker could hear traffic noises in the background. "I got a dead body on the sidewalk, and the guard here says there's another one up—"

"Let me speak to him," Becker snapped.

The Chief, who was not accustomed to being interrupted, said, "Now just a minute, Sergeant—"

"The security guard," Becker shouted, his face red. "Put him *on!*"

After a short pause, the guard's voice came on the line.

"Mr. Hendrix, this is Tom Becker. I want you to look at the dead man's face."

"Look at his . . . I can't. His arm's in the way—"

"Then move his arm! Look at his face, and tell me if you recognize him."

A long silence passed.

"Hendrix?"

Still no reply. But Becker could hear him breathing into the phone.

"Mr. *Hendrix?*"

"I see him," the guard answered, in a strange voice. "I see his face now . . ."

"It's one of the two cops, isn't it," Becker said.

He heard the guard swallow. "Yessir, it is. It's the other one, the one who didn't talk to you on the phone. Spellman."

Hendrix paused, then mumbled, "Why's he in his underwear? There's a pile of clothes laying way over there, bundled up and tied with a pants leg—"

"Mr. Hendrix, listen to me a minute." Becker eyes were shut again as he spoke. "The man I told you was coming down in the elevator. Did you see him get off?"

The guard hesitated. "I didn't see him, no, but I'm sure he's down by now. By the way, I got a maintenance guy working on cutting off the A/C, and there's a bunch of cops on the way up to you right now."

"The bomb squad?"

"No, just cops. From all over."

"Oh, great," Becker murmured. "Put the Chief back on."

When the phone had been handed over, Becker said, "Chief, we got some trouble here. The body in front of you is a cop from an East Side station. The bomber shot him and his partner too, and got away. We need to get the explosives team up here on the double, and we need to put out a call to all units, with the following description . . ."

He spoke a moment more, listened, nodded, and signed off. Then he turned to Ed Timmons, who looked a bit like a business student who had just wandered by mistake into a class on quantum physics.

"He changed clothes," Becker explained. "After they surprised him, he put Spellman's uniform on and threw him out the window."

Timmons swallowed. "So . . . he shot both of them?"

"Looks that way." Becker's eyes were roaming the room again, clicking off each item even as he spoke. "Except I imagine he shot Rice first, then swapped clothes with Spellman *before* shooting him. That's why there was no blood on the uniform."

"But . . . we heard the shots. They were close together—"

Becker pointed to the two bulletholes in the wall. "Those were the shots we heard. I figure he used a silencer to kill the partners, then used Spellman's gun to put two rounds into that baseboard later, just so we *would* hear them, to back up his story. Then he used the floor lamp to smash the window and threw Spellman's body out."

Timmons still looked lost. "To back up his story? Why'd he need a story? How did he know about you and me at all?"

"I imagine he got that out of Spellman, during the change of clothes. There'd have been plenty of time."

Timmons thought that over, then said, "Okay. Okay, if that's what happened . . . then there's still plenty of time for us too, right? We have till morning to find it. That's what you said."

"I know what I said."

"Then why do you look so worried?" Timmons' face had gone very still. "If that's true, why do you keep wanting the bomb squad to hurry up and get here?"

Becker turned to look at him. "Because there's a chance I'm wrong."

Timmons' eyes widened. "What do you mean, wrong?"

"The lights," Becker said. "That's been bothering me from the start. Why would he announce himself that way, turning on all the lights? Why not just use a flashlight? Was he arrogant? Was he careless?"

"Maybe he's just stupid."

"No. I don't think so. Arrogant, maybe. Insane, probably. But careless, or stupid? No."

"Then what's the answer?" Timmons asked. "Why the lights?"

"What do *you* think?"

Timmons pondered that for a moment. He seemed to be having trouble getting his breath. "To get us here in a hurry?"

"That's what I'm thinking, now."

"But why?"

Becker just shook his head. "I don't know," he admitted. "But I think it means we better find that thing, just as quick as we can."

As he spoke, the air-conditioning sputtered and bumped one final time, and then clicked off. "At last," Becker said.

Timmons had already begun looking through the litter on the floor and in the shelves, and Becker was crossing the room to join him when another thought struck him.

The briefcase.

He turned to look at it, recalling the way the man in Spellman's uniform had it open, its contents hidden from their view, when he and Timmons arrived on the scene. Becker felt a sudden chill ripple down his spine.

Had that been an act? Had the suspect just been going though the motions, pretending to search the case in order to convince them that he was who he appeared to be? Or had he been doing something else entirely?

Like setting a timer.

No, Becker thought, his mind racing. He wouldn't have waited that late to set it, even if he *had* been surprised by Rice and Spellman. The scattered contents of the shelves was a good indication that at the time he was interrupted he had been about to *hide* the bomb, not arm it. That surely would've been done by then.

But what *had* he been doing with the briefcase?

On impulse, Becker approached the desk. As Timmons turned to watch him in the eerie stillness of the now-silent room, Becker took a deep breath, held it, and placed his ear against the side of the case.

It was ticking.

Becker's heart lurched.

John M. Floyd

The bomb was in the briefcase.

And at that moment, it all came together. The truth hit him like a slap in the face.

The bomber hadn't been setting the bomb's timer; he'd been *re*-setting it.

Keeping his head down and motionless, Becker raised his eyes to meet his partner's. He opened his mouth to tell Timmons to alert the others, to warn them away, but it was too late. Even now, Becker could hear the footsteps of a dozen cops in the corridor. And all of them, he realized, were about to be killed. He, and Timmons, and the men in the hall, and heaven knew how many more in the street below.

Because they were out of time.

Becker knew it; he could feel it in his bones. The bomber had already been gone for almost ten minutes, and the timer wouldn't have been reset for a minute more than the man thought it would take him to fake his grief and get out of the building. He would want all the witnesses to go up with the blast.

And at the very instant that all this was flashing though Becker's mind, one of the policemen stuck his head through the doorway and looked in at him and Timmons.

"You guys the bomb squad?" the man asked.

Becker straightened up, his heart pounding in his chest. "We are now," he said quietly. In the same tone of voice he said, with a glance at the new cop, "Get away from that door. All of you, lie down in the hall and *stay there!*" To Timmons, whose face showed that he knew, Becker murmured, "Be ready. You'll have to get the window."

Timmons hesitated, then understood. He stepped back as Becker drew his pistol and fired through the open doorway, four shots, POWPOWPOWPOW, his bullets shredding the lock on the door across the hall. Timmons was already moving, dashing out and across the hallway, lowering his shoulder and crashing through the ruined door of 3245. At the same moment, his ears ringing, Becker dropped his gun, picked the briefcase up by the handle, and ran after him. As Becker passed through the doorway and crossed the hall he had a glimpse of a corridor full of cops, all of them lying on the floor and staring up at him with wide, frightened eyes.

Not as frightened as I am, he thought.

In the office across the hall Timmons had snatched up a heavy chair and slammed it through the window as Becker charged in through the open door. Now the window was open as well, a gaping hole in the center of the glass. While Timmons dived out of the way Becker flung the briefcase as hard as he could out and through the jagged hole and into space. It spun away into the black night like an oversized frisbee.

Becker didn't stop to watch its descent into the construction pit behind the building. He hit the floor three feet from his partner and folded both arms over his head, waiting.

Four seconds passed. Five . . . six . . . seven . . .

The explosion rocked the building, and blew out what was left of the office window. It also, though they did not yet know it, blew out all the other windows on that side of Remington Tower. Most of the cops in the hallway, some of them hardened veterans, cried out like kids in a thunderstorm.

When the rumble finally died down, Ed Timmons raised his head, brushed a dusting of glass fragments from his hair, and stared into Becker's eyes.

"I was half right," Timmons said. "I didn't feel a thing."

***

Two hours later both of them were still in the building. They had been debriefed in the lobby by both the Chief and their captain, and had spoken at various times to the mayor, the police commissioner, three TV reporters, two journalists, and a pair of constipated-looking agents from the FBI. What little feedback they had received so far indicated that there were, incredibly, no reported casualties and no serious damage to the building itself. Most of the force of the blast had been absorbed, as Becker had hoped it would be, by the earthen and stone walls of the thirty-foot-deep pit.

To the casual observer, however, the scene was one of a first-class disaster. Policemen and city officials and newspeople were everywhere, and Becker was amazed at the sheer number of firemen the city had been able to produce on short notice. Outside, especially in the streets immediately surrounding the building and the construction site, was a blinking logjam of squad cars and ambulances and television vans. Inside, at least in the area immediately surrounding officers Becker and Timmons, things had—for the moment—actually quieted down a bit. It was the first time since the explosion that the two men had a chance to say much to each other.

"Well," Timmons observed, his eyes twinkling. "Looks like you saved the day."

Becker gave him a glum look. "Two cops dead and nobody in custody, I'd say the day wasn't all that saved."

"Not according to the Chief. He's saying you're a hero. And me, too." He paused, then added, "I like the me part."

Becker couldn't help smiling. "Well, if the governor calls, *you* can talk to him."

A silence passed. Becker could still hear the sound of sirens outside, though he couldn't for the life of him think of a practical reason for it at this point, two hours after the fact. He finally decided the sirens were going simply because big things had been happening, and it was a shame to have a siren and let it go to waste on a night like this.

"He was setting it, wasn't he," Timmons said. "When we came in, I mean."

Becker nodded tiredly. "Changing the settings, most likely. To give him time to get away."

Timmons thought about that awhile. "So we were just lucky," he said.

"That's right."

After another silence, Timmons said, "At least we stopped him, Sarge. At least it didn't go off tomorrow morning, like you said it might, and kill a thousand people."

Becker shook his head. "I was wrong about that, Eddie. He never intended it to go off tomorrow morning."

"But . . . what you said made sense. Max casualties—"

"Oh, he wanted casualties all right. He was just after a different kind."

Timmons just stared at him, waiting.

"You saw me go over there and use that phone a while ago, right? To call in?"

Timmons nodded.

"I called the dispatcher," Becker told him. "I got to thinking about what you had said in the car, about the tipoff call. So I asked the guy at dispatch to replay the tape of the call, while I listened in." Becker paused long enough to touch a finger to the bandage over his left eye. He had taken a few minor cuts from the explosion.

"Remember the thumping noise they had said they heard in the background?" Becker continued. "Well, as it turned out, I recognized it. It was a kind of a rough hum, with a whump and a rattle thrown in every now and then."

Timmons looked a little puzzled, then blinked. "The air-conditioner," he said.

Becker nodded.

"You mean . . . the call came from *here*?"

"More than that."

Timmons frowned again. After a moment his face cleared.

"It was him," he said, in an awed voice. "He was the one who called . . ."

"He had to be. It came from here, and he was here."

"*Why?*"

"He was reeling us in, like we said before. First he called to tip us off, then he waited a bit and turned on the lights to make sure we got the message. He knew the bulk of the force was out of pocket tonight, at the roast, and he knew that meant it'd take the police longer to get here, and also longer, probably, to locate the bomb once we *did* get here. The idea of hiding it in the briefcase, by the way, was a nice touch."

"I still don't follow you," Timmons said.

"I think he knew we'd think we had plenty of time to look for it. I think he set it, the first time, not for the morning rush but for right about now, give or take an hour, so he'd get as many cops as he could. Maybe even the bomb squad itself."

Timmons looked thoughtful. "And then we showed up."

"Right. And he figured he'd better move the schedule up a bit, and reset it to give himself just enough time to get clear."

Timmons considered for a moment, then shrugged. "Okay, so we saved a dozen people instead of a thousand. I'm not picky."

Becker barely heard him. He realized he was about as tired as he had ever been in his life. As he looked around the lobby, he caught a glimpse of Ralph Hendrix talking into three microphones at the same time.

After a pause Timmons spoke up again. "That brings up one more question," he said. "Why'd he get surprised in the first place? If he'd done all this planning, why'd he take so long to do what he was doing?"

Becker sighed. "I've been puzzling over that," he agreed. "I think what happened was, he hid somewhere in the building until after everyone left, then went up the stairs to thirty-two and made the tipoff call from the secretary's desk. Then he waited a bit, then cut the lights on and went down to a random office, where he planned to hide the briefcase and then get out again, fast, before the cavalry arrived. Which he could have—should have—been able to do, with no problem."

"Except . . . ?"

"Except for the keys."

Once again, Timmons just stared at him.

"Hendrix told us all the locks had recently been changed, remember? I don't think the bomber knew that. I figure he had a master key that was old, and would no longer work. When he found that out, it was too late—he was reduced to having to pick the lock, which took him a while. Meantime, enter Timmons and Becker."

"And Spellman and Rice," Timmons said.

"Yeah."

Both of them fell silent. After a moment Timmons asked, frowning, "Why 3246?"

"What?"

"Why'd he pick that particular office? He was in a hurry, right? If he had a master key, and he could pick any room he wanted, and he was in a hurry, why pick one at the opposite end of the hall from the phone and the light switch?"

Becker frowned too. That hadn't occurred to him. "Go on," he said.

"I don't think he had a master key," Timmons said, his brow furrowed. "You were right about the lock-change delaying him, but I think he had an *office* key. I think he had a key just for room 3246."

"You mean he had an accomplice?" Becker could see his point. "That's possible. We could check and see whose office that is—"

"Whose it was," Timmons corrected. "Our theory is that

John M. Floyd

the key didn't work, remember? I'll bet we'll find that whoever *used* to be in 3246 was one of the people Hendrix said left the firm."

Slowly Becker nodded, then turned to stare at his partner. "Not bad, Eddie. Not bad at all."

Timmons shrugged, looking embarrassed. "Well, we better have a *few* leads, right? I realize we've got a description and prints, which is more than we had before, but he did get away. And if he's gone to ground . . ."

Becker nodded. "Then he could still be hard for you to catch."

"You mean for *us* to catch."

"No, I mean you, Eddie." Becker sighed. "I'm getting too old for this. Come tomorrow, I'll be back to being a desk sergeant, and—"

"Nobody'll have to catch him, gentlemen," a voice behind them said. They both turned to look at Chief Wellborn, who had walked up without their noticing him. "One of the firemen just found this, out back." He held out a hand, and what they saw in his palm was a blue police nametag. It was blackened and warped, with almost an inch missing off one end, but the lettering on it was perfectly clear.

"Spellman," Timmons murmured.

The Chief nodded. "Your suspect ran, but he ran the wrong way. He must've gone out back, and climbed down into the construction site, thinking he'd sit out the show at a safe distance and still have a good view, I guess. The body—what was left of it—was found hidden behind a bulldozer in a back corner of the pit." The Chief shook his head. "Talk about bad decisions . . ."

Becker swallowed, his eyes still riveted to the nameplate. He couldn't quite believe it. The bomber was dead, killed by his own bomb. Maybe there *was* justice in the world, after all.

Later, after the Chief had left them to report this latest news to the media, Becker stood up, ran a hand through his hair, and stretched. "Hold the fort, partner," he said. "I need to get some air."

"Not yet," Timmons said, nodding toward the other side of the lobby. A young fellow in a business suit was hurrying toward them with a cell phone, his eyes fixed on Tom Becker. He looked excited.

"You Sergeant Becker?" the young man whispered, as he drew closer.

"That's me," Becker whispered back.

The young man thrust the phone at him, holding it with both hands like a sword. "It's the governor," he hissed.

Becker turned to look at Timmons.

"Eddie?" he said. "It's for you."

He was still smiling as he walked out the door.

MURPHY'S LAWYER

"Anyone see you?" Murphy asked.

The man with the ferret eyes looked bored. At least until he fastened them on Murphy. Then he just looked suspicious. "I came through the park, like you said. Nobody saw me."

"Good." Murphy spread a sheet of paper out on the coffee table between them. "I have a few questions."

"You didn't say anything about questions, on the phone."

"What I said on the phone, Mr. Diggs, was that I could make you a wealthy man. I think that entitles me to a few questions."

"I'm already a wealthy man," Diggs said.

"That mean you're not interested?"

This time Diggs didn't reply. Outside the den window, an October wind moaned in the trees. A siren wailed.

Looking down again, Murphy said, "You are the attorney who recently sued Dahlmeyer Chemical for twenty million dollars, is that correct?"

"You know I am."

"And your client was Billy Longstreet?"

"The family of Billy Longstreet, yes."

"And you were with him at the time of his death?"

The ferret eyes narrowed. "What is this, Mr. Murphy?"

"Bear with me, please. You were with him?"

"Yes."

"Just the two of you?"

"Yes."

"And why was that?"

"I was representing him in a lawsuit. Billy was showing me the place in the plant where he was injured, two months earlier."

Murphy scanned his notes. "His right leg had gone through a metal catwalk and into a vat of acid, it says here. Burns to the foot and ankle."

"That's right."

"And what happened the next time, when you were with him?"

Diggs shifted in his chair. "He fell in. I almost did, too. He was demonstrating the accident, lost his balance, and tumbled into the tank."

"And afterward you filed, for the family, a wrongful death suit for twenty million."

Diggs shrugged. "That's standard procedure. The catwalk was faulty. Even if the fatal accident hadn't happened, the company would have paid dearly for his previous injury."

"And he'd have been alive to enjoy the money," Murphy said.

Diggs's face darkened. "Are you going to tell me what this is all about?"

Murphy folded the paper and put it away. "I should first tell you what I do for a living." He looked the lawyer straight in the eye. "I'm an agricultural engineer, Mr. Diggs. I work for Dahlmeyer Chemical, in their research lab, and I often bring my work home. I have a lab of sorts myself, in the next room."

"And why should that interest me in the least?" Diggs said.

"I'll show you." From his shirt pocket Murphy produced a photograph of a small green bottle. It was unlabeled, and shaped like a bowling pin. "Recognize this?"

Diggs examined the photo. "It's a bottle of BreatheFree decongestant."

"Right," Murphy said. "That's what it looks like. But in this case, it's not. It's a container of Zenthrax 4, a pesticide used to mix boll weevil spray."

Diggs pondered that a moment. "You actually have some of this, at work?"

"I have some here, in the next room. Dahlmeyer makes and markets it."

"I don't understand. Why'd they choose that design?"

"Who knows? Point is, that's what the bottle looks like. And after reading about your little damage suit the other day, I got to thinking about a suit of my own."

Diggs studied him. 'Have you been damaged?"

Murphy smiled. "Not yet."

As the lawyer watched, Murphy rose and pushed open the door to the adjoining room. Visible through the doorway was a lighted laboratory worktable, a microscope, rows of bowls and bottles, and a videocamera on a metal tripod. The camera was aimed at the workarea.

"For documentation purposes, I sometimes videotape my lab procedures. Right now, I'm working with Zenthrax 4, to study its possible side effects on cotton and soybean plants."

"And?"

"And I happen to have a slight cold. Nothing bad, just

some coughing now and then—but it got me thinking, wouldn't it be a shame if I, in my congested and sometimes feverish state, happened to take a swig of Zenthrax one night, mistakenly believing it to be BreatheFree." Murphy stared off into space. "And even if I happened to take just enough to give me a stomachache—not actually kill me—I'd still have grounds to sue the company. After all, they should have known better than to design a container of poison that looks like a well-known, brand-name cold medicine. Wouldn't you agree?"

Murphy turned to Diggs, who looked a little more attentive than before.

"How would it work, exactly?" Diggs asked.

Murphy shrugged. "Easy as pie. I'd go into the next room, put on my lab coat and goggles, turn on the camera, and spend a few minutes doing routine work. After a while I'd start to cough a bit—I really do have a cold, as I said—and I'd distractedly pick up a bottle of Zenthrax and unscrew the cap. Humming to myself, I'd pour a dose of 'medicine' into the bottle cap, which is calibrated like a measuring cup, and raise it to my lips just as I wander out of camera range."

"What do you mean, out of range?"

"I want this realistic, Mr. Diggs, but I don't want to die. The plan would be to leave the room and come in here, while the videotape keeps rolling. Later, after the paramedics arrive to find me 'poisoned,' I would reveal that there was a taped record of my activities just before I took ill. When the investigators get around to examining the bottle they saw me pick up in the lab, they'll see that it does in fact contain a deadly pesticide."

"But . . . wouldn't the doctors be able to tell—" Diggs looked around. "We're alone here, right?"

Murphy nodded. "My wife's in Birmingham, visiting her mother."

"Wouldn't the doctors be able to tell you're faking?"

"That's the beauty of my plan." Murphy left the room, then returned carrying a plastic bottle cap. Inside the inverted cap was perhaps half an ounce of clear liquid. He set the cap down on the table in front of Diggs.

"This is plain tap water, with a few drops of Zenthrax added. Clear-colored, like the real thing. It'll taste funny, but it's not enough to hurt me, and it'll leave a trace of the chemical for the doctors to find in my system. It'll validate my claim."

Diggs thought that over. "When would all this take place?" he asked.

"Right now." Murphy tapped his watch with a fingernail. "Everything's set up."

Diggs blinked. "Now?!"

"Why not?"

"Well, for one thing, *I'm* here. Don't you want to do it alone?"

"I'm no fool, Mr. Diggs. After I drink that capful of water there, I plan to call nine-one-one. If I've misjudged the potency of those few drops, I may need *you* to call them."

"Me?" Diggs's already pasty face lost even more color. "Those calls are recorded. They might know, later, it wasn't your voice."

"Not if you mumble and groan a little. People calling for help never sound their best. Besides, I don't plan to need you—you're just insurance. Right after the call you'll leave anyway, and go back home through the park. This time of night nobody'll see you, and it'll take the ambulance at least twenty minutes to get here."

For a moment neither man said a word. Diggs seemed lost in his own thoughts.

"Well, that's the plan," Murphy said. "Are you with me?"

Diggs paused, then nodded. "I'm with you."

Murphy grinned. "Then observe the master at work." Without another word he rose from his chair and walked through the open doorway to the lab.

The whole thing took less than five minutes. With the camera taping away, Murphy acted his role well. After a suitable time at his worktable, he opened the green bottle and poured some of its contents into the cap. Unbottled, it looked like water. When he left the workarea and exited stage left, he really did appear to be about to drink the dose of "decongestant" in the bottle cap. Only when he was safely out of camera range did he lower the still-full container of poison from his lips.

In the den once more, he stood facing the lawyer, his face calm and confident.

"Done," he said. He put the capful of clear liquid down on the table and focused on the other one, which still sat in front of Diggs. "Hand me the watered-down version, would you?"

Diggs hesitated and looked past Murphy into the other room. "What about the tape?" he whispered.

"We'll let it run, just as it would if I'd really met with an accident."

"But our voices—"

"No problem. There's no audio."

"At least close the door, then."

"Good idea." Murphy walked to the lab door, pulled it shut, and returned.

Diggs handed him the bottle cap.

"Cheers," Murphy said. He tilted his head back and drank the contents.

"A robust flavor indeed, Higgins," he announced, smacking his lips.

Diggs wasn't amused. "Make the call," he said, with a glance at the phone.

John M. Floyd

"Not yet." Murphy set the empty cap down on the table beside the full one. "There's a strict timeline here. If that was really poison I just drank, it'd take at least five minutes to affect me. The tape running in there is timestamped, and the call to nine-one-one will be too. We have a few minutes to kill." He grinned. "What's your pleasure?"

"What?"

"I'd like a touch of alcohol on my breath for the paramedics' sake, and I don't like to indulge alone. I have Bud and I have Bud, by the way."

"Then I guess I'll take a Bud."

"Excellent choice." Murphy went to the kitchen doorway, then turned. He studied Diggs's face a moment.

"What is it?" Diggs said.

"Nothing." Murphy disappeared into the kitchen, puttered awhile, and reappeared with two open cans of beer. He gave one to Diggs and held the other up with a flourish.

"To your health," he said, "and my recovery." Both men drained half their cans and checked their watches. Neither had much to say for the next few minutes.

When the time was up, Murphy picked up the phone and made the call. In a choked, urgent voice he told his story—name and address included—and hung up. He looked pleased with himself.

"And that's that," he said. Another glance at his watch. "There's no great hurry, but you should probably be on your way. I'll call you later, from the hospital."

The lawyer didn't move.

"Is something wrong?" Murphy asked.

Diggs just sat there, watching him with a strange little gleam in his eye.

And then Murphy stiffened. He put one hand to his stomach, the other to his chest. He began to sway on his feet. Even as he stooped to grab the table edge for support, he saw the two bottle caps, one empty and the other full—

And his face cleared.

"You switched them," he whispered. "When I went to close the door." His eyes widened. "Why . . . ?"

Diggs rose from his chair. He took out a handkerchief and wiped the tabletop, his can of beer, and both the inverted caps. He also picked up the photograph of the bottle and put it in his pocket. "I'm an accomplished chess player, Mr. Murphy. To be good at it, as in life itself, you must think several moves ahead."

Breathing hard, Murphy sank first to his knees, then onto his side. Through sagging eyelids he watched Diggs carry the watered-down capful of liquid to the kitchen. Moments later the lawyer came back and walked to the outside door.

Murphy swallowed. "I think I understand," he said, wheezing. "This'll get you a bigger cut. You'll call my wife, tell her I phoned you when I realized I'd poisoned myself by accident, and tell her I told you about the tape. After I'm dead, you'll sue Dahlmeyer on her behalf. What'll you get, by the way—four million? Five?"

The lawyer turned and smiled, holding the doorknob with his handkerchief. "Seven, in Longstreet's case. He, like you, was worth much more dead than alive."

Murphy lay still now, his eyes squeezed shut. "You pushed him, didn't you?"

"He made it easy for me," Diggs said. "So did you. How could I resist?" With a final smile, he stepped through the door and into the night.

Behind him, on the den floor, Murphy counted to fifty before opening his eyes. He sat up and watched the door for another minute, then stood and looked out the window. Not a soul was in sight.

Taking his time, Murphy picked up the telephone and followed the cord to the corner behind the sofa, where he found the disconnected phone jack and plugged it into the wall. Armed now with a dial tone, he punched in a number and waited.

"Mr. Dahlmeyer? John Murphy here. Everything went fine." He paused, listening. "Yes sir, you were right. He killed Billy Longstreet, and tried to do the same to me." Absently Murphy unbuttoned his shirtfront and reached inside to touch the warm microcassette recorder strapped to his chest. "It's all on tape." Audio this time, he thought with a smile.

He listened a moment more, then said, "No sir, I didn't. I decided not to. He's alive and well." Murphy's gaze had settled on the beer can on Diggs's side of the table. "But it was tempting." Another pause. "That's right, about three minutes ago. They can pick him up in the park, if they hurry."

He was quiet for several seconds. "I appreciate that, Mr. Dahlmeyer. Glad I could help." With a sigh he hung up the phone and ran a hand through his hair.

Adrift in his thoughts, Murphy walked into the lab, switched off the camera, and picked up the green bottle from his worktable.

Zenthrax 4, he said to himself. At first, he had wondered whether such an obviously phony name would work. Apparently it had.

And the real thing worked too, he decided, as he tipped the bottle and took a swallow.

His cough *had* been better lately . . .

VITAL SIGNS

Tom Wilson stood alone in the hallway, staring at the number on the door in front of him. He knocked three times, softly, waited five seconds, then knocked twice more. The door opened immediately.

The uniformed police officer standing in the doorway was tall and wide and female, though Tom Wilson felt some uncertainty about that last adjective. The only thing really feminine about her was her name: Anne Marie Flowers. How a woman like this could have a name like that had always been a mystery to Tom. In point of fact, she had the disposition of a warthog and the physique of a sumo wrestler.

"You took long enough," she said. Her words, though delivered in a low voice, boomed and resonated as if they had been spoken into a barrel. "I thought this deaf school of yours was just around the corner."

"That's the school office," Tom said. "The classrooms are a block north." He looked warily past her into the apartment,

211

then back again. "Why'd you call me at work?"

"Just get in here." She leaned out the doorway and looked both ways as he squeezed in past her. Then she came back in, pushed the door shut, and locked it. Without another word she led him down a hallway and around a corner into the living room.

He looked around as he followed her, still wondering what the hell he was doing here. "Is this supposed to be your apartment—"

Tom Wilson stopped in his tracks.

On the far side of the living room, propped up against the wall, a man lay bleeding on the carpet.

For several seconds Tom was unable to speak. He stared at the unconscious man, then at Officer Flowers, then at the man again. "Who's that?"

"A suspect," she said. "Bank robbery."

"What . . . what happened?"

"He tried to shoot me. I shot him instead." As she spoke, Flowers moved a few steps closer to the injured man, hands on her hips. She studied him thoughtfully for a moment, as if he were a stain that she couldn't quite figure out how to get rid of.

Tom swallowed hard. "Is he . . . ah . . ."

Flowers shook her head. "No. Not yet. He will be soon, though."

The man groaned. Tom jumped, then leaned over and peered at his face. The eyes were shut, his breathing labored. Blood was everywhere.

"We have to get him to a hospital," Tom whispered.

"An ambulance is on the way. I called them just before I called you."

Tom turned and looked at her. "Why did you call me?" he asked again.

Flowers met his gaze, her eyes dark and flinty. "I want

you to ask him a question."

The man moaned again, a pitiful sound; his head lolled from side to side. Tom Wilson watched him, feeling helpless. Flowers had knelt over him, one hand braced on her knee and the other on the carpet as she stared down into the chalk-white face.

"What kind of question?" Tom asked her. "For that matter, why don't you ask him yourself?"

The big policewoman straightened up again, examining her hand to make sure it wasn't bloody. She wiped it absently on her thigh. "I tried," she said. "We've had some trouble communicating."

"I don't doubt it; you're the one who shot him."

Flowers turned and looked at Tom. "That's not what I mean," she said.

She continued to stare at him, saying nothing. Then, suddenly, Tom understood. He blinked once, then turned and gaped at the man on the floor.

"So he's the one," Tom said in a hushed voice.

"Yes. He's the one."

Wilson studied him, seeing the resemblance. For almost a week now, this man's face, captured on a bank security camera, had been making regular appearances on the nightly news. According to the reports, he had walked into the State Street branch of First Fidelity Bank last Monday, handed one of the tellers a note, and showed her a small square device with a red button mounted on its top. The note had instructed her that this was a holdup, and that the device in the man's hand was a remote transmitter to a bomb located just outside one of the lobby windows—a bomb big enough to destroy the bank and everyone in it. It also instructed her to empty her cash drawer— as well as those of the other tellers—into a large red duffel bag he had placed on the counter in front of her.

The teller had had no trouble recognizing the logic of this request. After a quick conference, she and two of her colleagues began to fill the bag with neat green bundles of cash. Several minutes into this procedure, an off-duty policeman had walked in, noticed the tension of the moment, spotted the potential thief—who was facing the other direction—and went into action.

First, the cop drew his revolver and shouted a warning. The robber never even looked around; his eyes were, at that point, going nervously back and forth between his wristwatch and a video camera mounted on the wall behind the teller line. So the cop shouted again, and fired his gun into the ceiling. Still no reaction. It was at that moment everyone in the bank first realized the man was deaf.

He was not, however, blind. An instant later he noticed the look on the teller's face, and—following her gaze—whirled around to look behind him. When he did, the policeman fired at him. Twice. The trouble was, neither bullet hit the robber; they hit the teller instead, one on either side of her chest. She was blown, quite literally, out of her shoes. The thief didn't hang around to see the crowd reaction; he grabbed his bag and dashed out the side door with almost eighty thousand dollars while the cop and everyone else in the bank stood and stared, thunderstruck, at the limp body of the teller, spreadeagled on the floor. And since no one saw the robber leave, no one saw which way he went, or how he left. By car, maybe? On foot? Nobody knew. He could have gotten away on a pogo stick and not a soul would have remembered.

Within an hour of the shooting, the entire city police force was looking for a deaf-mute with a transmitting device and a red bag full of money. The area around the bank was searched; no bomb was found. Eventually someone thought of the security camera, reviewed the tape, and found they had a good picture. When all was said and done, it didn't matter much; they still couldn't seem to find him. He was a face with no name. He had disappeared.

And now here he was—lying in a pool of blood on the floor of Officer Anne Flowers' living room.

Tom Wilson blinked as the thought occurred to him. "Why here?" he murmured.

Flowers frowned at him. "What?"

"What's he doing here? At your place?"

"It's not my place. It just . . . fits a key I happen to have."

"That's no answer. Why is he here?"

"I brought him here."

"But why?"

Flowers hesitated. "He approached me on the street. Said he wanted to see the police commissioner—personally. It sounded fishy to me, and he looked dangerous. I brought him here instead." She paused. "Along the way, I recognized him, from the video. When I confronted him he pulled a gun, and I shot him."

Tom pondered that for a moment, then looked her straight in the eye. "And how did you know?" he asked.

"What?"

"If he couldn't hear or speak," Tom said patiently, "how did you know he wanted to see the commissioner?"

Another hesitation. Flowers stared down at her finger-nails, her face impassive. "He gave me a note," she said.

"May I see it?"

After a pause she reached into the blouse pocket of her uniform, produced a folded sheet of paper, and handed it to him. Her expression was as hard and cold as granite; this was obviously not a part of her planned agenda.

Tom scanned the note silently. The man had in fact asked to be taken to meet the commissioner, to whom he would deliver certain privileged information. The robbery, the note stated, had been a mistake, and had only been attempted at all because a huge sum of money had been needed to treat a wife stricken by cancer. But the stolen money, as things had turned out, was of no use: The wife had died that same morning. And now that she was gone his life was meaningless. His only wish now was to turn himself in and—

Tom blinked. He couldn't believe the final words of the message. He read them again, then raised his head and looked at Officer Flowers.

"He wants to give the money back," he said.

The policewoman stared back at him, saying nothing.

A light came on in Tom's head. He nodded slowly. "That's what you need me for, isn't it. You want me to ask him where the money is."

"That's right," she said. "And time's running out."

Tom Wilson glanced again at the man on the floor. She's right about that, he thought; if this guy lives till the ambulance arrives it'll be a miracle.

"But what makes you think he'll tell me?"

"Two reasons," she said. "First,"—she held up her hand and wiggled her fingers—"you teach at a deaf school. You speak his language. Second, I gave him a note of my own." She grinned smugly. "I told him you work for the commissioner's office."

Tom was quiet a moment, looking down at the robber. And thinking.

Thinking the way he had learned to think since meeting Officer Anne Flowers, five years ago.

"Isn't it interesting," he said, "that a man returning stolen money—a man who wants to give himself up—would pull a gun on the cop he's surrendering to."

Flowers said nothing.

"It's also interesting," Tom continued, looking at the stomach wound, "that he should be shot in a place that wouldn't kill him right away, but would almost certainly kill him in a short time."

Still no reply. The only sound in the room was the ragged breathing of the injured man.

"There's no ambulance on the way," Tom said. "Is there."

Silence.

"And when you find out where the money is . . . I doubt you'll be taking any witnesses with you to retrieve it. Right again?"

This time Flowers raised her head to stare at him, and the look in her eyes made a chill move slowly up his back.

"You listen to me, Wilson. You're here because I need you here, and when I need you the next time I'll call you again, and you'll come. The way I see it, you don't have a choice." She paused, her eyes blazing. "Now get over there and limber up those talking fingers and ask him where that stolen money is. Because if he dies before you find that out, you just might die with him. Is that clear?"

Tom Wilson stared back at her, trying to appear calm and unruffled. It was hard to do; his pulse was pounding like a drum inside his head. He had almost overstepped this time, and he knew it. Flowers was dangerous even under the best of circumstances, and this was about as far away from that as you could get.

And she was dead right, too: He didn't have a choice. All she had to do was reopen the investigation into the old Hawkins case, and Tom Wilson would be done for. Both of them knew that. It didn't really matter that he hadn't approved of, nor profited from, the scandal; he had been involved, and that was enough. And Flowers had the evidence to prove it. For five years now she had held it over his head, and though she had never demanded cash—she knew he had none—she often summoned him to handle her dirty work.

And there wasn't a thing he could do about it.

Her message clear, Flowers' eyes shifted from Tom Wilson to the dying man. "Go ahead," she ordered. "Wake him up and get some dialogue going before he croaks. Besides, he's bleeding all over the carpet."

Tom regarded her in silence for several seconds. "You know, Flowers," he said, "I think maybe it's a mistake to assign women to police work. They're just too tenderhearted."

Their eyes met again, just for an instant; then he turned away and knelt beside the man on the floor. The face was even whiter now, the breathing more labored. Gently Tom touched a hand to the sweaty forehead. The eyes flickered. After a second or two they opened to tiny slits, and focused on Tom's face. Then, suddenly, they opened wide.

He probably thinks I'm a doctor, Tom thought guiltily.

"Go on," Flowers said, from behind him. "Ask."

Holding the man's gaze, Wilson raised his right hand and signed the message: "My name is"—Tom hesitated—"Jack Tyler. I was sent by the police commissioner."

Immediately the man's eyes lit up. He nodded weakly.

God, how I hate myself for this, Tom thought.

Very, very slowly, the man raised his own hand, bloody and trembling.

He began to sign.

Tom Wilson watched the moving fingers, then nodded and responded with another message. A question. When he finished, he took a small pad of paper from his back pocket and held it ready. This time, as the dying man began signing again, Tom scribbled on the pad, taking notes.

Three minutes later it was over. The man's hands dropped onto his stomach, a shudder moved through his body, and his head sagged to one side. The eyes remained open, gazing sight-lessly at the wall.

"Well?" Flowers said.

Tom stood up and sighed. "He's dead."

"I can see that," she snapped. "What did he say?"

Tom stared down at the body a moment longer, then turned to face her. He was bone-tired.

"The money's still in its bag, in the trunk of a car—a green Buick—in the garage of a house on the West Side. The keys to the car and house are in his right pants pocket." Tom tore a sheet out of the notepad and handed it to her. "Here's the address—and some things to watch out for."

It took a moment for that to sink in. Flowers, who was holding the paper as if it was the Star of India, glanced up at him. "What do you mean, to watch out for?"

"The house itself is empty, he told me, but the car's tied to an alarm—and there are neighbors around."

"An alarm?"

"It's wired to the car's door locks." He leaned over and pointed to the page in her hand. "You want to open the trunk from the back; don't try to open one of the doors and spring it from the inside. If you do, you'll have a lot of company."

The policewoman nodded, scanning the page. "Anything else?"

He didn't reply immediately, and she looked up at him from the slip of paper, waiting.

"This is wrong, Flowers," he said. "This is dead wrong. You've done things like this before, I know; I've helped you with some of them. But this is the worst. There was never any gun, we both know that. You've killed a man in cold blood, a man trying to make amends. And you did it for nothing but greed."

Flowers' face hardened. "Don't you get holier-than-thou

with me, Wilson." She jabbed a finger at the corpse on the floor. "This guy was a thief, good intentions or not. A woman was killed during that holdup, and dozens of others threatened with a bomb—"

"That teller was killed by a cop, not by him. And there was no bomb—I asked him about that. He said the 'triggering device' was an old computer joystick he found in the garbage."

"Whatever," Flowers said. She had tucked the piece of notepaper into her pocket and was looking around the room, taking stock. After a moment she remembered the keys, and bent over to fish them out of the dead man's trouser pocket. She clipped them onto her own keychain, checked her surroundings again, and turned to Tom.

"I'm leaving now," she said. "And so are you. You never came here, you never met me today, and you never saw this man, living or dead." She paused, pulling on her gloves. "I don't care where you go when you leave, as long as it's nowhere near this car he told you about. I'll be taking care of that myself, very shortly. Understood?"

Perfectly, Tom thought. He left in a hurry, and didn't breathe easier until he was halfway down the block.

Finally he relaxed a bit. He walked past the school and continued walking, adrift in his thoughts. When he reached his car he got in and drove north, away from town. Ten minutes later he turned off the highway and onto a side road that wound its way into the hills that bordered the city. The trees were in full autumn color here; a million fallen leaves carpeted the roadway.

The sky was a brilliant blue. His was the only car in sight—he was totally alone on a quiet and peaceful country lane. Slowly, Tom felt the tension drain away. He parked on a hilltop beneath a towering oak, cut the engine, and got out.

Behind the oak was an old stone fence, and beyond that,

spread out in the valley below, was the gray sprawl of the city. Tom leaned comfortably against the fence, his forearms draped over its top, staring down at the town and thinking. Mostly he thought of Anne Marie Flowers, and the man lying dead on the floor of the apartment. He thought of the look on the dying man's face in the moments just before his death, and the look on Flowers' face in the moments just after, when she realized that her plan had worked after all, and that she would soon be rich, and that no one would ever know.

Tom Wilson sighed, long and deep.

Finally he reached into his pocket and took out a second page of notepaper, a page he hadn't shown to Officer Flowers. Glancing down at it now and then, he walked along the stone wall for ten or twelve yards, then stopped. On the far side of the wall, and flush against it, was a thick head-high growth of briers and brambles. He bent over, studied the ground, checked his notes, and counted up three stones from the bottom of the fence. Keeping his eyes on that spot, he tucked the note into his pocket again and felt along the edges of the stone. It was loose.

Thirty seconds later he had it out; the hole it left in the wall was roughly a foot square. The heavy red duffel bag was right where the man had said it would be, in a hollowed-out nest in the brambles just on the other side of the hole. Tom pulled it through easily and replaced the stone.

As he walked back to the car with the bag, he heard something. He stopped and frowned, listening hard. Nothing moved on the hilltop. After a moment he smiled.

That was one of the strange things about the crisp, cool air of autumn, he thought. Distant noises come through crystal clear, as if they were just around the corner.

Even the sound of a bomb in a car trunk, eight miles away.

John M. Floyd

ONE LESS THING

Patty Boatman had seen better days. Her marriage was on shaky ground, her company was downsizing, and—insult to injury—she was running a fever.

And now this.

Patty stood beside a display case in Farrell's Jewelers, watching the wall mirror behind it. Her gloved hands were in her overcoat pockets, her head bowed as if she were studying the merchandise. What she was studying were the faces of the other customers.

A moment ago, outside in the mall, she thought she had seen Joe Dollerhyde.

She prayed she was mistaken. Dollerhyde's face belonged to the dark, to bars and alleys and seedy hotels. The lights and gaiety of a shopping mall would probably burn him to a crisp, like Count Dracula.

Still, Patty's defenses were up. She had ducked into the first bolthole she saw, and was keeping a careful watch.

What would her husband think? she wondered. Absent from her job, wandering aimlessly, afraid of everything, her work, her future, their future . . . she was even afraid of herself.

Especially herself.

The arrival of the beachfront casinos had supposedly been a good thing for the city, for the economy. But it hadn't been good for Patty Boatman. In six months she'd lost thirty thousand dollars, a loss she and Glenn couldn't afford. She'd covered some of it with salary advances, and insurance policies Glenn didn't know about. The rest had come from Joe Dollerhyde.

She had heard about Dollerhyde for years. It was easy enough to find him, and almost as easy to borrow the money. Paying it back wasn't, but she had done it, mostly by pawning her mother's silver. Glenn didn't know about that either.

But now, at least, she was out of debt. In trouble at work and at home, but out of debt. As Forrest Gump would have said, One less thing.

And then, tragedy. Four hours ago, Joe Dollerhyde had taken payment—and told her she was five thousand short. "We agreed on fifteen," she said, stunned. He shook his head. "Twenty. You're five short."

Distraught, she fled his office. She decided she'd tell Glenn everything, and beg forgiveness. He'd know what to do. But instead of finding Glenn at home she'd found his note: FLYING TO MIAMI, COULDN'T REACH YOU AT WORK. WILL CALL TONIGHT.

And now here she was, alone and sweating in her overcoat in a crowded store, watching for Dollerhyde's face.

Had he actually followed her here?

If so, she seemed to have lost him. With a sigh she dropped her gaze to the display case. Inside were bracelets, necklaces, watches of all kinds. One, a man's wristwatch with inlaid diamonds, gleamed up at her—

But it wasn't inside the glass. It was lying on top, probably left there by a harried saleslady.

The watch drew Patty's hand like a magnet. Holding it in her gloved palm, she pictured a life in which she could afford something like this, for Glenn. The pricetag said: $26,000.

Suddenly she sneezed, her left hand covering her nose while her right held the watch. Seconds later she opened her eyes—and stared at Joe Dollerhyde's face in the mirror.

She almost cried out. That crooked grin, that soulless gaze . . .

"You don't look so good," he said.

"Leave me alone." She swallowed, her head throbbing. "I paid you what I owe you."

"Another five grand, is what you owe me." He tilted his head. "Move away from the mirror."

When she did, he crowded in beside her in front of one of the cases. "Maybe," he said, leering, "we can work something out."

She fought down the bile in her throat. "Maybe I'll just scream for the cops."

His smile widened. His left hip pressed against her; even through both their topcoats, she could feel his body heat. "What'll you tell 'em?"

"That you're harassing me. With your record, they'd lock you up forever."

"I'll say you made the first move. Offering favors, for a loan. How would your husband like that?"

Patty's heart sank. If only she'd told Glenn . . .

And then she had an idea.

The answer was right there, hidden in her fist.

"You'll get your money," she said. "Today."

"How?"

"Trust me." He crowded her even more, and suddenly she

pushed away from him, jammed her hands into her pockets. "But for it to work, I need to go now."

"We'll go together."

"No." She glanced down at her coat, drawing his gaze.

Puzzled, he stared at her baggy overcoat, then at her face, then at the jewels glittering in their cases. He blinked. "No. Surely you didn't—"

"Why do you think I'm here?" She raised her chin. "I'll do what I have to."

He studied her a long moment, then nodded. His eyes swept the crowded store. "Okay. North parking lot, fifteen minutes," he said. "If you make it."

"I'll make it." She turned and headed toward the door. She knew he wouldn't follow—at least not right away.

Patty felt her mouth go dry. She wished she'd studied the watch more closely. Were they fitted with sensors, to trigger an exit alarm? Not that it mattered. She didn't have the five thousand, so this was her only chance. As she walked she kept her hands in her pockets and her eyes on the mall, just beyond the door.

And then she was through it and out into the crowd. She turned only once to look back. Joe Dollerhyde was standing where she'd left him, watching her.

She rounded a corner and stopped there, her heart pounding. She sagged backward against the wall—and waited.

It didn't take long. Four minutes later, an alarm blared. Security guards sprinted past, in the direction of the jewelry store. She heard loud voices, and the grunts and curses of a struggle.

She didn't have to look around the corner; she knew what had happened. She'd caused it.

Finally she stopped trembling, and even smiled a little. She might still have career and marital troubles, and a sinus infection too, but Joe Dollerhyde was no longer a threat. A $26,000 theft—a felony in anyone's book—would lock him away for a long, long time.

And it was his own fault. He shouldn't have pressed so close against her, in the store.

His coat had big pockets too.

SAVING MRS. HAPWELL

"What I can't figure out," Nate said, as he lay in the dirt behind a clump of cactus near Rosie Hapwell's house, "is why you married that idiot in the first place."

Before Rosie could reply, another bullet whined off a rock three feet away. Both of them ducked their heads and crawled to the dry wash where Nate had left his horse.

When they were safely out of sight she said, breathing hard, "I had to, that's why."

"You what?"

"How else was I gonna get out of Lizard Flats?" She pulled off one of her shoes, turned it over, and poured out a stream of sand and dirt. "You was in jail at the time, if I recall."

Nate pondered that awhile, then said, "Well, I'm here now."

Rosie's face softened. "I know you are, honey. It's a noble thing, too, after all these years, that you rode out here to see me in my exact hour of need, to save my life."

"Well, I rode out here to see you, that's true. Can't say I knew your life was in danger, though."

She scowled. "It weren't, until about ten minutes ago. He just went crazy, is what he did."

As if to emphasize that statement, two more shots rang out from the porch of the house thirty yards away. Nate's horse, Blue, tied to a dead tree at the bottom of the wash, whinnied and pulled against its reins. After a moment Nate seemed to remember he had a gun of his own, and on impulse he raised his head above the rim of the gully and took a potshot at the house. Just as he was aiming for a second shot, the gun jumped from his hand as if it were alive.

Nate slid back down beside Rosie, his eyes wide.

"Did you see what he did? That fool shot my gun right out of my hand!"

"A lucky shot," she said, lacing her shoe up again. "Earl can't hit the side of a barn."

"He hit my *gun*, Rosie!"

"Nathan, he's got glasses *this thick*. It was lucky, that's all. He can't see us down here, and he can't hit us unless he comes closer."

"I'm comin' closer!" a deep voice shouted, from the direction of the house. "I intend to kill you, Rosie, and if that's Nate Callahan I saw out there with you, I'll kill him too."

Nate and Rosie looked at each other a moment. The situation, it seemed, was about to get worse.

"Let's get outta here," he said.

"How do we do that?"

"On old Blue, that's how. He's standing right there."

"Both of us?"

"Sure, both of us."

"You told me in your letters he won't let a woman ride him."

Nate's face fell. "That's right. He won't."

"I'm comin' to kill ya!" Earl Hapwell shouted.

"Well, we better do something," Nate said.

Rosie thought a moment. "You go, Nathan. You done proved your love and your bravery. You ride off and save your self."

"I can't do that," he said. Suddenly he brightened. "I know. I'll send Blue off without us. Since Earl can't see good, he'll think we're getting away. When he chases the horse, we'll run off the other way."

"Oh, honey," Rosie purred. She was overcome with emotion. "You'd really stay here with me and die?"

"Maybe we won't die. I told you, he might think we rode off." Nate was untying his horse from the tree as he spoke.

"Yeah, and he might not, too. He might come right down here and shoot us."

"Well, it's our only chance." Nate turned Blue loose and slapped him on the rump. He went charging off, and Nate and Rosie huddled in the shadows to wait.

A minute passed. Nothing happened.

"Did he go after your horse?" Rosie asked.

Nate listened. "I don't think so."

"That means he'll come kill us, then."

"I expect so," Nate said. He thought hard for several seconds. "How far does this gully go?"

"It plays out right around that corner," she said, pointing, "and the other end curves back toward the house. The only way out is west, toward the flats, and if we do that he'll see us. He can't see good, but if he sees us at all he'll chase us, and then we're dead."

For the first time, Nate looked really glum. "I think we're dead anyway."

They were both quiet a moment.

"You know," Rosie said, "this is really romantic, you stayin' here to die with me and all."

Nate just went on looking glum.

"In fact, it's crazy," she said suddenly. "Listen to me, Nathan. You can still save your self. There might be time for you to get your horse back here and ride off."

"How would I do that, even if I wanted to?" he asked.

"Didn't you write me once that Blue will come runnin' when his owner whistles?"

"That was his other owner. Not me."

"He won't come when *you* whistle?"

"I can't whistle."

Rosie nodded sadly. "Me neither. Never learned how."

They fell silent again. Just as they were beginning to think Earl Hapwell might have forgotten all about them, he appeared at the edge of the wash, ten feet away. He had his rifle, and he looked mad.

"Gotcha," he said. "You two better say yore prayers."

"Wait a minute, Earl," Nate said, standing up with both hands in the air. "What do you want to kill us for?"

Earl gave that some thought, then admitted, "I don't really want to kill *you*, Nate. If you can find yore horse, you can go on and leave. It's her I'm set on killin'."

"But why, Earl?"

His face darkened. "Cause she did an unforgivable thing, that's why."

That stopped Nate for a second or two. He had never heard Earl say a five-syllable word before. In fact, Nate didn't think he'd ever heard *any*one say a five-syllable word. He got the meaning, though.

"What'd she do that was so bad?" he asked.

Earl frowned a moment, as if reliving the horrible deed, then said, "I told you to get yore horse and leave, Nate. I mean it."

"Not till you tell me what she did that's so bad you want to shoot her. If it's bad enough, I'll leave."

"You swear?" Earl asked him.

"I swear."

Earl hesitated, then said, "She turned off my football game."

Nate blinked. "She what?"

"She turned off my ballgame. Then she throwed away the knob."

It was suddenly very quiet in the gully.

"Was it halftime?" Nate asked.

"Nope. Fourth quarter."

"Was it a one-sided game?"

"Ten to nine," Earl said.

Another silence. Earl stared at his wife and his wife stared at Nate and Nate stared at the ground in front of him, deep in thought.

Finally he looked up at Earl.

"Can you whistle?" Nate asked.

John M. Floyd

THE BLUE WOLF

Jason Plumm lay on the beach for three hours before he was found.

His rescuer was a four-foot-tall native islander named No Sin Kahano, who was working in a field of sugar cane with a machete as long as he was when he saw the body lying on the sand just above the waterline. No Sin, a man unusual in both name and appearance, was typical in his dislike for manual labor: He promptly dropped his knife and trotted down the hill to investigate. He was also, as Jason Plumm would later discover, typical in his choice of employer. He worked for Colonel Hanson McDade, who owned everything and everyone on the island.

It took the small man five minutes to drag Plumm's limp body to the shade of a clump of mango trees, ten to retrieve a battered pickup truck and load him inside, and another ten to drive the bumpy jungle road to the Colonel's estate. Once there, the truck's horn attracted enough servants to help carry the groggy and sunburned American into the Main House and put him to bed.

Plumm recovered quickly. He was awake and coherent by midafternoon, and around six o'clock he was brought supper in bed by his host, a smiling and gracious Colonel McDade. The two men hit it off right away; the Colonel was grateful to have a visitor from his homeland and Plumm was grateful to be alive. Their conversation stretched far into the night.

Plumm's sailboat, he said, had been blown off course in a storm several days ago. Lost and desperate, he had headed north, hoping he would eventually hit one of the Marquesas Islands. He didn't. On his third day at sea he encountered another storm, and this time he capsized. He had no idea how long he had been in the water—he just swam aimlessly until he could go no further. The next thing he remembered was waking up in one of the Colonel's upstairs bedrooms, under the watchful eye of No Sin and the household staff.

Colonel McDade listened closely to the account, and when it was done he told his own story. This was a private island, he said, small and fertile and almost entirely self-sufficient. Its human population was less than fifty souls, its crops were sugar cane and pineapple, and its coordinates were largely unknown. Simply stated, the island was unnamed and uncharted. To all but a very few, it did not exist. "It's better that way, really," the Colonel said. "For the animals."

Plumm looked at him and frowned. "The animals?"

"Sugar cane and pineapple aren't all we raise here," McDade said with a smile. Over the course of the past three years, it turned out, Hanson McDade had established quite a facility—a kind of specialty zoo, stocked with unusual examples of wildlife from all over the world. Through the Colonel's determined efforts—and at tremendous expense of time and money—animals from the farthest reaches of the globe had been captured and transported (under the supervision of McDade's men and in the secret holds of his supply vessels) to this tiny and remote location. As a result, at least one representative of almost every rare or endangered species on earth could be found right here on the island.

"I have them all," Colonel McDade said, unable to conceal his satisfaction. "Platypus, white rhino, sable antelope . . . this is their home now. And I can see and study them anytime I want."

The only drawback he had found to life on the island, he explained, was the isolation. There were no telephones here, no radios, no telegraph, no airstrip. By choice and by design, the island was cut off from the rest of the world. Only then, the Colonel reasoned, could he have the freedom to run his facility the way he wanted it. So far, it had worked out well. Most of his employees were Polynesian natives, well trained and well paid, and all of them understood and accepted the circumstances that went along with the job and location. The island's one and only lifeline to civilization was the Colonel's supply boat from Papeete, which came once a month. And it was due again, McDade informed his visitor, less than a week from now. "You're here for at least five days, I'm afraid, like it or not," the Colonel said.

Somewhere in the house a clock chimed the hour. With a sigh the Colonel rose to his feet, then wished his new houseguest a pleasant night's sleep. When Plumm restated his thanks for the hospitality, his host responded by issuing an invitation—and one word of caution. The invitation was that Jason Plumm was welcome to remain here on the island as long as he liked; the restriction was that he must stay away from the walled compound directly behind the Main House. That was off limits.

"The tree of forbidden fruit?" Plumm asked, with a grin.

"Don't worry, Mr. Plumm—I am not God, and this is not

Eden." McDade considered this for a moment, amusement gleaming in his eyes. "Though I suppose I could be mistaken."

Both of them smiled and shook hands. After the Colonel had left, Jason Plumm sat in bed and stared at the door for a long time, reviewing in his mind the long story he had told his host.

Not a word of it was true.

***

Radar had been Plumm's biggest worry. A needless concern, as things had turned out, but he hadn't known that two days ago, on the chartered pleasure-boat out of Bora Bora. All he had known then, for certain, was that Colonel Hanson McDade ran a very expensive and secure operation, and he knew that if anyone was watching a monitor in an operations center somewhere on the island, the forty-foot Bayliner would make a sizable blip on his screen.

But no intercepting vessels had come out to challenge them, and in the darkness of last night he had slipped into the water two miles from shore, dressed only in his carefully tattered sweatshirt and jeans, and clutching a watertight plastic bag attached to a cord around his neck. As he started the long, easy breaststroke that would take him to the island he heard the boat turn and begin the long trip back to port. He had no worries about the crew—they were chosen by his own hand, and had been paid generously for their silence. His worries lay ahead.

The moonlit swim to the beach, however, proved to be easy going. Plumm was in good shape, except for a recent bout with the flu, and had been a champion swimmer in his college days. His newly-acquired sunburn was painful but necessary to his plan; if anything, the caress of the water felt good to it. When he reached the island he hid the plastic container in the grass beneath a palm tree and, when dawn came, stretched out on his stomach on the white sand a few yards above the water-line.

Plumm had seen No Sin long before the islander saw him, and had watched the little man from the corner of his eye for almost an hour before he was finally spotted and rescued.

And now here he was, safe inside the stronghold he had come all this way to conquer, with a fine meal in his stomach and a soft bed underneath him. A suitable end, he thought, to a trying journey . . . and a good beginning to what might be the most challenging assignment of his career.

For Jason Plumm was no frustrated businessman on sabbatical from his ex-wife and his job, as he had told Colonel McDade. He was an insurance investigator. In fact, he was probably the best insurance investigator in the business—and certainly the most sought-after. Again and again, using a formula that mixed equal portions of planning and ingenuity and daring, Plumm had broken cases that everyone else—including the police—had declared impossible to solve. Though his fees were high, his reputation was solid and his results were real. He was known as a man who could get the job done.

It was for that reason that Jason Plumm's name was the first one recommended in the aftermath of the sensational theft that had occurred almost three months ago. That same night, the St. Louis people had flown him in and made him an offer; the very next day he had begun the investigation that had eventually led him to this island, and this house.

He was smiling when he drifted off to sleep.

***

Plumm spent the following day "regaining his strength"—he was, he thought, a fine actor when he had to be—and getting the general feel of the place. Colonel McDade stayed near his bedside most of the morning, chatting about this and that and making sure his guest was receiving the best of care. At one point, the Colonel introduced him to Dr. Toshiro Sumoru, the resident veterinarian (and McDade's second-in-command). When Plumm jokingly asked Sumoru if he worked on people as well as animals, the sour-faced little man gave him a cold stare. Looking amused, the Colonel repeated the question in Japanese. Sumoru's only response was a curt shake of his head, once to the right and once to the left. His steely gaze never wavered.

"To effectively treat human patients," McDade explained, "Dr. Sumoru would need to acquire more advanced equipment."

"What he needs to acquire," Plumm said, "is a sense of humor."

The Colonel just chuckled. "Don't hold your breath," he said.

Around noon, when it was evident that Plumm was much improved, McDade led him on a tour of the Main House and the surrounding area. Once, when the two of them were crossing the vast green lawn that lay west of the house, Plumm got a distant look at the fenced compound the Colonel had mentioned the night before. Nothing was said about it this time, but Plumm caught McDade watching him closely until the tall wooden walls were out of view.

That afternoon both the Colonel and Dr. Sumoru were called away for several hours, after an employee reported that one of the Grevy zebras had been injured by damaged fencing. Since Plumm was left to his own devices, he decided to take the Colonel up on his suggestion to continue exploring the grounds.

Over the next few hours Jason Plumm wandered every part of the estate that was accessible and within walking distance. What he found was that Hanson McDade—retired Army hero, nature enthusiast, and only son of a Kansas millionaire—had created a world that far surpassed the information revealed by Plumm's prior research. For one thing, the island seemed larger and more primitive than he had thought. And the zoo itself—actually more of a wild animal park, like the one east of San Diego—was an absolute wonder. By the time Plumm returned to the Main House, he had seen koalas and anteaters and eagles and at least half a dozen varieties of deer and ante-lope. Many of the species he didn't even recognize.

But there was one animal he hadn't seen . . . and he thought he knew why.

***

That night Plumm began to make preparations. Silently he scouted the house, squirreling away the items he would need: a flashlight, spare batteries, gloves, a paper clip, a pocketknife, even an old pipetool he found in a desk drawer. By the time he and the Colonel met in the dining room for dinner, Plumm had everything he required, including a black poncho-style raincoat that had been hanging in the guestroom closet. With these resources in his possession and the details of the plan in his mind, he was ready to go.

At the stroke of midnight, long after the Colonel had left him—and after the last light had winked out in the block of workers' quarters visible from the windows of Plumm's bed-room—he gathered together his wares and his nerve and crept out onto the roof and the ladderlike rose trellis and down into the shrubbery beside the house. Within minutes he had made his way to the gate of the forbidden compound, and seconds later, using the paper clip and the pipetool the way he had used sim-ilar implements a hundred times before, he sprung the simple padlock that held it shut.

Inside the fenced area, the layout was exactly as he had hoped. In the shielded glare of his flashlight he saw a network of pathways flanked by barred cages. Only the first few were visible, but from what he knew of the size of the place, he estimated there were probably dozens of cages in all. Already, as he began inching his way along the dusty path, he was breathing easier: He had worried he might find that the interior of the compound was a huge open area where its occupants could roam free. If that had been the case, he might have gotten himself eaten before he had a chance to do any investigating.

Most of the cages, Plumm found as he moved among them, were empty. The ones that were not, he left strictly alone. At each enclosure he took a moment to check its contents with a sweep of the flashlight's beam—a giant rabbit here, an emu there, a black leopard across the way—then moved quietly on. Very quietly, as a matter of fact. The last thing he wanted was to start a chorus of roaring and bleating and screaming from the inmates of this bizarre prison. The truth was, none of them seemed very interested in him, and that suited him just fine.

When he finally found what he was seeking, it didn't happen the way he'd planned. He was crouched outside the last cage on the first row, playing his light along the darkness inside, when he heard a low, rumbling growl. Then, too suddenly for him to react, a shape came flying out of the shadows, rammed its snout through one of the gaps between the bars, and grabbed his hand in its teeth.

Actually it grabbed more glove than hand, and Plumm's cry of surprise made his attacker open its jaws and retreat. Plumm fell backward into the dirt, clutching his right hand. His assailant melted into the darkness, still growling with a sound like that of a poorly tuned outboard motor.

Inspecting his hand in the beam of the flashlight, Plumm saw with relief that the damage was slight: He had a red scratch on the bottom of his palm, where a flap of torn glove hung down from it like a sixth finger. Nothing serious. He was lucky, and he knew it: another inch and he'd have been buying a set of left-handed golf clubs when he got home.

Once more Plumm turned his attention to the cage, and when he trained the circle of light on the thing that had attacked him, his breath caught in his throat.

It was even more beautiful than he'd suspected.

Crouching ten feet away in the beam of the flashlight, baring its fangs and glaring at him with pure yellow-eyed hatred, was a full-grown timber wolf. Its head was held low to the ground, ears laid back, powerful shoulders hunched as if ready to spring again. Its bushy tail twitched like a tiger's as it tried to figure out exactly what it was that stood looking at it through the bars.

And what Plumm noticed at once was its coloring. Even in the harsh glare of the flashlight he could tell this was no ordinary wolf. Its coat was a beautiful bluish-white, the shade of a snowy mountain stream or a summer sky streaked with clouds.

The Siberian blue wolf.

There were only a handful of them left in the world, and only two in captivity. One was rumored to be at the palace of King Qasani of Bandar-Kalam; the other was at the famous St. Louis Zoo.

Except that the one from St. Louis was missing.

Plumm spent another moment gazing into the animal's eyes, then turned and crept back down the path to the gate. Carefully he relocked it, made his way to the trellis, climbed it to the roof, and crawled through his bedroom window. Moments later, in the bright lights of his locked bathroom, he saw that he had been right about the bite: It had hardly bled at all. He'd had paper cuts that were worse. He dabbed his hand with everything he could find in the medicine chest, then applied a Band-Aid. Walking back into the bedroom, he considered for the first time just how close a call he had had: If the wound had been serious—or even if the wolf had happened to snatch the glove off and pull it into the cage with him—

Plumm's master plan would have been finished before it started. As things stood now, he was right on target. He had located what he had come here to find; all he had to do now was secure the proof.

He'd take care of that tomorrow.

***

As things turned out, he had to wait a bit longer. Getting proof meant getting photographs, and to do that he had to retrieve the camera and film hidden beside the beach in the little plastic bag he'd brought ashore with him two days ago. His plan was to arrange a trip to his landing spot this morning, where he would elude his host long enough to find the hiding place and stuff the bag inside his shirt—but a sudden change in the weather kept all that from happening. The heavy rains began just after daybreak, and it was a storm such as Jason Plumm had never before seen. It lasted two days, and during that time no one ventured far from home.

When the skies finally cleared, Plumm moved quickly, approaching the Colonel with a casual but well-rehearsed request to visit the area where he had washed ashore. With McDade's permission, Plumm borrowed one of the trucks and made the trip alone; it took him half an hour to drive to the beach, locate the palm tree where he had hidden the watertight container, and return to base. That night, after dinner and a game of chess with Colonel McDade, who had spent the day checking on flood damage, Jason went to his room to prepare for another midnight foray into the mysterious fenced compound behind the house.

Armed now with a miniature camera and film—in addition to his set of makeshift tools and the flashlight—Plumm retraced the route he had taken three nights ago. This time the trip was quicker, since he knew the way; it took less than fifteen minutes to get down off the roof and through the gate and down the long pathway to the cage. Keeping well clear of the bars this time, he sat down in the dirt outside the cage, took out his camera, and aimed his flashlight.

The cage was empty.

Plumm blinked. He looked all around; nothing was there. The wolf was gone. On impulse he reached up and tried the door to the cage. It was unlocked. In a panic now, Jason rose to his feet, dashed inside, and searched every corner of the cage, as if the animal weren't gone at all, but had somehow become invisible.

"Where *is* he?" he wailed softly. He couldn't believe something like this had happened. He had been so close . . .

Frustrated, he made his way out of the compound and back to his room. What was going on? he kept asking himself. Only three nights had passed; what had happened? Why had they moved the wolf? Did they suspect something?

Did they suspect *him*?

Plumm swallowed. That was a sobering thought. Maybe he hadn't been so lucky that night in the compound after all. Maybe the Colonel or his helpers had found a drop of his blood on the ground, or on the bars, or his footprints outside the cage, and decided that Plumm had come to kill the wolf, or steal him . . .

But that would be stupid. What reason would anyone have to kill it, and if an animal were stolen in a place like this, what could the thief have to gain? It wasn't as if you could escape and run away. There was nowhere to run.

He just couldn't figure it out.

Long after he had returned to his room, and as he lay awake and confused in his bed, Plumm finally accepted the only possible answer: They had moved the wolf for reasons that had nothing to do with Jason Plumm. It was as simple as that. And it wasn't the end of the world, either—just a setback. It made his job harder, yes, but not impossible. The wolf was here, he knew that now; and if he found him once he could find him again. All he had to do was be patient.

But he wouldn't make tomorrow's boat.

***

The arrival of the supply boat was quite an event for the island. Almost every employee was present, either to help with the unloading or to chat with the crew or just to observe from the grassy ridge above the dock. As the Colonel had said earlier, this was the only lifeline to the outside world. That made it special. Even if all it brought was news, it would still have been welcome.

Plumm stood beside Colonel McDade at the foot of the dock, watching the proceedings like the others. McDade's foreman and a grim-faced Dr. Sumoru were supervising the transfer of goods. The morning was cool but humid.

"I'm glad you decided to stay a bit," the Colonel said, squinting at the boat.

"I don't have a lot to go back to," Plumm said. "No wife anymore, no kids, a crummy job . . . everybody thinks I'm dead by now anyway, I might as well stay a while longer and get my head on straight." He turned and looked the older man in the eye. "I appreciate the favor."

The Colonel regarded him a moment, smiling. "Just don't start beating me at Scrabble," he said.

***

The next two weeks passed quickly. Jason Plumm went out on horseback every day to look for the wolf, using his long-neglected engineering degree to help advise McDade and his men on the placement of culverts and the repair of storm-damaged roads. It was the perfect cover, he thought, since it allowed him to earn his keep but also afforded him open access to all corners of the island without having to constantly think up reasons for his absences. His interest-in-wildlife excuse had been wearing a little thin.

It was on one of these excursions that he finally saw the wolf. The animal was standing on a ridge fifty yards away when Plumm spotted him, and for a moment both man and beast remained completely still, each studying the other. Staring at him now, Plumm was reminded again of the quiet beauty of this rare and magnificent animal. The pale-blue coat rippled and shimmered in the afternoon sun, and even from this distance Plumm thought he could sense the intelligence—even recognition, perhaps?—in the small yellow eyes.

But he waited too long to act. Even as he reached for the camera in his pocket, the wolf turned and bolted into the brush. Cursing himself, Plumm urged his horse into a gallop, skirting the entire area in hopes of catching another glimpse of his target. It didn't work. Half an hour later he headed back toward the Main House, but for the first time in many days he felt encouraged. Certain types of animals were often restricted to specific parts of the island, and by now he knew most of the boundaries. Now that he had found the wolf's assigned area, all he had to do was concentrate on it alone, and keep his camera ready. Very shortly now, he would have what he needed.

It happened five days later, when he had stopped on the trail and was drinking from the canteen he took along on his outings. The wolf was above him on a shelf of rock, no more than twenty yards away, and outlined perfectly against the overcast sky. Moving with great care, Plumm raised the camera and shot a full roll of film. When he returned to base that afternoon, he knew he had what he required. The pictures he had just taken, when compared to the existing photos of the wolf before the theft had occurred, would be conclusive evidence—certainly enough to convict the Colonel and restore the prized animal to its owners. More importantly, the staggering insurance settlement would be prevented, and Plumm could collect his fee.

He smiled to himself as he loped his mount through the grassy meadows to the dirt road that led to the house. His job here was done.

All he had to do now was catch a boat.

***

A week later Plumm said his goodbyes to the staff, with a special thank-you to No Sin and those who had nursed him after his arrival. Under Dr. Sumoru's parting glare, he climbed into the passenger seat of the Colonel's Jeep for the ride to the dock.

It was a gorgeous day, the sky clear and the wind brisk through the open windows of the car. Several of the field workers and animal handlers waved as the Jeep passed them on the rutted road. Neither of its occupants waved in reply: Plumm was feeling a little under the weather—his flu symptoms had returned during the night, leaving him weak and feverish—and Colonel McDade was moody.

"I truly hate to see you go, Jason," he said. "It's been damn fine having a companion to talk to around here."

"We've had a few debates, haven't we?" Plumm agreed.

In the silence that followed, Plumm came to a decision. Partly because of his sluggish feeling and partly because they were about to part forever, he felt a very uncharacteristic pang of guilt at what he was about to do to this kind man who had befriended him for almost six weeks.

"Why is it, Colonel," Plumm asked, "that in all those talks we've had, you've never told me about the wolf?"

McDade fixed his passenger with a stare. Then his face softened and he turned again to face the road. "So you saw him," the Colonel said quietly.

"Yes. A week ago, up in the hills."

They rode on in silence for a moment. At last McDade explained, with a sigh: "I'm a little funny about my animals, Jason. When bad things happen to them it affects me deeply. I find it hard to even talk about."

Plumm frowned. "What kind of things? The wolf I saw seemed to be in the best of health."

"Oh, he is. None better." The Colonel paused. "We had a hard time with him at first, of course—the temperature and humidity here are far different from his previous home—but with time he has adjusted well. A magnificent animal."

Plumm felt, above the flush of his fever, a little twinge of satisfaction. *That* was why the wolf had been in the compound behind the house, he realized: It had had trouble becoming conditioned to the climate, and was being treated.

Plumm decided to press a little.

"Actually," he said, watching the older man from the corner of his eye, "I wouldn't have thought the weather in St. Louis would be that much different from here."

McDade frowned. "St. Louis?"

Then, slowly, the Colonel's face cleared. "Ah," he said. "I take it they are missing their Siberian wolf."

"That's right."

A silence passed. "My friend," the Colonel said, "I do not indulge my . . . hobby, shall we say . . . at the expense of others. I would not be so unfeeling, or so presumptuous, as to attempt to purchase a rare animal from a public zoo."

Despite his headache, Plumm kept his eyes on McDade's profile. "I wasn't referring to a purchase, Colonel."

For a moment it was very quiet in the car. Ahead, the dock moved into view, and McDade, expressionless, steered the vehicle onto a gravel pad near the water's edge. The supply boat had already begun unloading; the wooden platform was busy with golden-skinned workers moving carts and boxes.

Hanson McDade sat there awhile, studying the blue ocean beyond the boat, then cut the engine. Without looking at his passenger, he said, "You think I . . . abducted him. That's it, isn't it. You believe I had him stolen, and brought him here."

"What I think, Colonel," Plumm said, "is that you were a victim of your own obsession. I think you meant no harm."

"So you're a policeman, then?"

Plumm sighed. His headache was worse now, and it hurt to swallow. "Nothing so noble, I'm afraid. I was hired by the company that insured the animal. They hope to restore him to his owners, and reclaim their loss."

"And how is it," the Colonel asked, "that you suspected *me?*"

"I have contacts in Papeete. The men on your supply ship are not all quite so loyal as you believe."

McDade thought that over, then smiled. "Ah. Joe Pintana. I might have known. He remembered the delivery?"

"No, but he'd heard others talking. It's hard to transport an animal like that one without attracting attention. The odd color, you know."

The Colonel nodded tiredly. After a short silence, he blew out a sigh and turned to face the younger man. "The truth is, son, you've made a mistake. A rather large one, I'm afraid, but still only a mistake. You were trying to do your job, and I bear you no grudge because of it."

Plumm just stared at him. "What do you mean, a mistake?"

"The wolf you saw didn't come from St. Louis, Jason. He came from Bandar-Kalam. I bought him myself, a short time ago, from King Qasani."

Plumm blinked. "Qasani?"

"You don't have to take my word for it. I have the cancelled check, and both our banks can verify the transfer of funds. Besides that, I am familiar with the wolf at the St. Louis facility. I have pictures of him, which you are welcome to compare to the pictures I assume you took last week, when you saw my specimen." He paused. "Theirs is a smaller animal, and lighter in color."

Jason was stunned. "But . . . where could he be, if not here?"

"I have no idea."

"But I—"

Colonel McDade held up a hand, stopping Jason in mid-sentence. Their eyes remained locked for several seconds.

"I'm telling you the truth, my boy. I believe you know that now."

Plumm swallowed hard. He did indeed know it. As he had said a moment ago, he was no policeman—but he had dealt with criminals and cheats and liars for many years now, and he knew with a terrible certainty that the Colonel had spoken the truth. He could see it in the man's eyes, for one thing. Also, Plumm had neglected to follow up on the small inconsistencies he had noticed recently—things that hadn't seemed to matter at the time, like the wolf's larger size that night in the compound, and the slight difference in coloring last week. With a sinking feeling he realized that he had screwed up, and on a grand scale. For the first time in his long career, Jason Plumm had shot himself squarely in the foot.

Neither of them said anything for a while. Outside on the dock, the unloading had finished. Plumm sat there, slack-faced and staring, until the silence was broken by the droning of the boat's horn.

Plumm blinked and looked around, feeling dazed.

"They're ready to sail," the Colonel said.

It occurred to Plumm then, with the force of a punch in the stomach, that he couldn't leave. His bosses were waiting for an answer—no, not an answer, a *solution*—and even now they must be wondering what the hell was taking so long. Plumm had left them no word on where he was going or who he was after, and now that almost two months had passed they would be furious to learn that their star investigator had been off chasing shadows while the real trail grew as cold as a Canadian winter.

"What do I do now?" Plumm murmured.

The Colonel sighed. "That's your choice. But I meant what I said—I hold you no ill feelings. I like you, Jason Plumm, and I believe we could work well together."

Plumm turned to look at him.

"You've already done wonders assisting my men with their construction work," he continued. "And I desperately need an irrigation system for my outer fields, and bridges over the ravines north of the lake." He studied his passenger a moment. "You think you could handle that?"

Plumm swallowed and winced at the pain in his throat. "Are you . . . offering me a job?"

"That's the idea. There is one condition, at the request of Dr. Sumoru—but it's just a formality."

"What kind of condition?"

"You'll see."

Plumm thought a moment. "When would I start?"

"How does tomorrow sound?"

Plumm hesitated.

Could he just abandon his life and profession—at least for a while—and stay here, on the island?

The answer, of course, was another question: Why not? He loved the island, he enjoyed the work, the outdoors, the animals . . .

Why not, indeed?

Trying to keep from smiling, he raised his head and looked the Colonel in the eye. "I accept," he said.

"In that case, welcome to the family." McDade reached out and clasped Plumm's hand in his, then frowned with concern. "You're hot as fire, boy," he announced, studying Plumm's face. "I can't have a sick employee on my hands; let's get you back to the house and fix you up."

With a reassuring wink, the Colonel started the Jeep and pulled out of the lot. As they made the turn away from the coastline, they could see the supply boat heading slowly out of the bay that sheltered the landing. McDade waved through the window, and the boat's whistle blew.

"You'll come to love it here, Jason," he said. "It grows on you."

Plumm nodded, still a little overwhelmed by this turn of events. The movement made his neck ache; he was trying to rest his head against the seatback when he had a sudden thought.

"You never did tell me what happened," Plumm said.

"Excuse me?" McDade's eyes were fixed on the curving road.

"You said something about 'when bad things happen to your animals.' But then you agreed that the wolf I saw was in top shape."

McDade nodded. "Right. He is. I was talking about the other one."

Plumm raised his head. "What?"

"His brother. You see, I didn't just buy one wolf from Qasani. I bought two."

"You mean . . . there was a second wolf?"

The Colonel's eyes turned sad. "Even bigger and prettier than the one you saw. He was in isolation when you arrived, in the holding compound." He paused and sighed. "He died two days later."

"Died?" Plumm felt a cold tremor go through him. "Died . . . of what?"

"Rabies," the Colonel said. "One of the few things

Sumoru can't treat."

***

Jason Plumm woke up an hour later, flat on his back on a couch in the living room of the Main House. At first he didn't know where he was. Gradually he recognized the faces of Colonel McDade and Dr. Sumoru, and the memories came flooding in.

He was going to die, and he knew it.

"You fainted," the Colonel told him.

"The least of my troubles," Plumm murmured. And then, just as he was about to close his eyes again, he saw something in their faces. Miserably, he asked: "What?"

The Colonel and his vet exchanged glances. "I have a confession to make," McDade said. "As I told you earlier, we have no advanced medical resources here . . ."

"But?" Plumm said.

"But we do have a communications facility." McDade paused, studying Plumm's face. "If you're going to play at being a spy, you really shouldn't use your real name, you know. I checked out your story. Within an hour after our conversation that first night, I knew about the St. Louis theft, and your investigation into it. I also found out, later, about your little scouting expeditions, into the holding compound. No Sin followed you, both times."

Plumm swallowed, his mind racing. "So . . . you knew I was bitten?"

"I knew everything."

"Then why didn't you *tell* me? For God's sake, if the wolf was rabid . . . you could have *saved* me. I could have boarded the next boat, or you could have called for help—"

Another look passed between McDade and Sumoru. And this time Plumm thought he saw a flicker of amusement there.

They were *trying* to kill me, he thought feverishly. This

was their plan all along . . .

Even in his despair, he felt a warm rush of anger.

But then the Colonel said, his eyes narrowed: "Tell me, Jason: Did the wolf *look* sick, when he bit you? Staggering, maybe? Foaming at the mouth?"

Plumm blinked. "What?"

McDade smiled. "The holding pens were off-limits," he said, "because we were mating Chinese pandas there. Nothing else."

"What do you mean?"

The Colonel leaned forward, watching him. "There is no second wolf, Jason. There never was. And the one I got from Qasani isn't rabid."

Plumm's jaw dropped. "You mean . . . I don't have—"

"What you have is the flu. And hopefully not for long; we have work to do, you and I, on that irrigation system." Still grinning, McDade stood up, as if he were ready to go get started right now.

Plumm could only stare. "You . . . lied to me?"

The Colonel somehow managed to look both guilty and pleased at the same time. "There's been a lot of that going around."

"But . . . *why*? You scared me half to death—"

"I had to. If I wanted to hire you, that is."

Plumm just gaped at him.

"That," McDade explained, "was Dr. Sumoru's condition."

During the silence that followed, both of them turned and looked at the little veterinarian.

Sumoru shrugged. In perfect English, he said to Plumm, "I have been working on my sense of humor."

And, very slowly, all three of them smiled.

DELLA'S CELLAR

"Oh, no," Billy whispered.

He was standing in the tall grass at the top of the hill, his cane fishing pole in one hand and his baseball cap in the other, staring wide-eyed across the fields at the white wooden buildings of the Bloodworth farm. The problem was, the farm didn't look quite the same as it had five hours ago, when he and Jack McClellan had climbed this same hill, heading the other direction.

The reason was simple: The barn was gone.

Billy Kendrix felt sweat break out on his forehead; a chill rippled its way down his spine.

This can't be happening, he thought.

In fact, the barn was not completely gone—some of its blackened framework was still intact, charred and smoldering under the overcast sky. As he watched, too far away to hear anything, a roof beam cracked and toppled into the ashes.

Billy's mouth had gone dry as sandpaper. Dazedly he let

his cap and fishing pole drop to the ground. On legs that felt like chunks of stovewood, he began to trudge down the long hill toward the farm.

At two hundred yards he could smell the smoke; at a hundred he emerged from a clump of woods and saw Della Bloodworth sitting in a wooden swing near the back steps of the house, staring at the barn with her hands in her lap. Moments later she saw him approaching and walked out to meet him, smoothing her apron. Though he was only twelve years old and she didn't know him from Adam, she greeted him as solemnly as if he were the family minister.

"We've had a bit of excitement, I'm afraid," she said. Then, as she noticed his clothes: "Heavens, child. You're soaking wet."

Billy didn't really know how to respond to that. He was used to getting rained on now and then, during his wanderings. And the sudden shower that had caught him and Jack as they fished in Widow Lacey's pond an hour ago had obviously come through here too—water stood in the corn rows, and the rutted driveway was dotted with puddles. Just as obviously, it had come too late to be of any help to the barn.

Looking again at the charred remains, Billy spotted the man he had come to see. Amos Bloodworth, dressed in a straw hat and flannel shirt and overalls, was standing with his back to them, thirty yards away. He appeared to be studying the damage. But it was something else, something in the grass only a few feet from the old farmer's workboots, that caught Billy's attention.

It was a square pine door, mounted on iron hinges and set flat into the ground some twenty feet from the barn's nearest wall. Under that door, Billy knew, was the wood-bordered entrance to the storm cellar that tunneled underneath the barn.

Trembling now, Billy forced his gaze away from the trapdoor and focused on Mrs. Bloodworth. With a mighty effort he asked, even though he felt sure he already knew the answer, "What happened?"

The old woman sighed. "It started in the storm cellar. This morning, around seven o'clock."

Billy closed his eyes. His heart sank. He had hoped against hope that maybe, just maybe, his suspicions weren't true. But now he knew.

He opened his eyes to find the old lady staring at him. "I have to talk to Mr. Bloodworth," he said.

She studied him a moment, then turned and walked the short distance to where her husband was standing. Billy saw her speak to him, saw Amos Bloodworth look in his direction. And the weary, frustrated expression on the old man's face—coupled with the fearsome scowl Billy had heard so much about—almost made him lose his resolve. Somehow he kept his gaze level and his back straight as Amos looked him over.

The old man didn't come at once, though. He and his wife exchanged several more words, then he handed her something which she examined and tucked into the pocket of her apron. Finally they walked back to where Billy stood waiting.

"You got something to say to me?" Bloodworth asked.

Billy clasped both hands behind his back to keep them from shaking. "Yes, sir. I do."

Amos Bloodworth was quiet a moment, his eyes narrowed. "What's your name?" he said.

"Billy Kendrix."

"You're Will Kendrix's boy?"

When Billy nodded, the old man's face darkened.

"I'm not sure you're welcome here," he said, in a cold voice. "But since you're here anyway, you can tell your daddy I won't have time to listen to any more talk about water rights for his stock. Looks like I'll have my hands full, for a spell.

Understand?"

"Yessir."

A silence passed. Amos Bloodworth looked him up and down. "Well? If you have something to tell me, spit it out."

Billy swallowed. "I started the fire," he said.

The old man blinked. "What?"

"It was me," Billy said miserably. "I burned your barn down."

Amos and his wife exchanged a glance. At last he said, "I think you'd better explain that."

Billy swallowed again, hard. Tears had begun to well up in his eyes. "Jack McClellan and I walked through your woods this morning, a little before seven, on the way to Miz Lacey's pond. When we passed the edge of your yard we saw the trap-door to your cellar. Jack . . . well, he dared me to go inside. He knew how scared I was of you, and how much you and my dad don't like each other . . ." Billy paused, searching for the right words. "Anyway, he dared me, and I went in."

At that point, Billy happened to glance at Della Bloodworth, who looked almost as if she understood. She had undoubtedly heard the local talk about her and her mysterious husband. Probably because they were childless and kept to themselves, and possibly because of their strange last name, rumor had it that she was a witch and he a warlock, and that their unusual little hole in the ground was the site for all kinds of horrors, not excluding an occasional human sacrifice. In reality, of course, the tunnel was no more than a bomb shelter turned storm cellar turned storeroom—Billy knew that now—but to the local teen and preteen population, "Della's Cellar," as it had come to be called, was haunted.

"You went into our storm cellar?" Amos said, interrupting his thoughts.

Billy's shoulders sagged. "Yes, sir. I did."

The old man regarded him a moment, frowning. "How'd you get in? Through the hole in the barn floor?"

"Through the trapdoor, in the yard."

Amos and his wife exchanged another look. "That end of the tunnel—the trapdoor—was locked," he said.

Billy shook his head. "No, sir. It wasn't. I wish now that it had been."

"But I was down there myself, last week. I pushed up on it from inside. It wouldn't give an inch."

"From inside, it wouldn't have," Billy agreed. "There was a padlock in the ring, holding the doorlatch shut, but it wasn't all the way locked. I just took it off the ring and opened the latch and pulled open the door."

The old man seemed to think that over. "And then?"

"Jack and I went inside."

"How far inside?"

"Only a few steps. Six feet, maybe."

"And how did you see, in the dark?"

"I had a book of matches." Billy's face reddened, and again he felt hot tears in his eyes. "I struck one, to look around. Then we thought we heard something, and left." He paused. "I was sure the match was out . . ."

Amos Bloodworth stayed silent a moment, then cleared his throat. "Let me get this straight. You broke into our storm cellar—"

"It wasn't actually locked, Mr. Bloodworth."

"But you did remove the lock, and open the trapdoor, and go in to snoop around. Right?"

A single tear rolled down Billy's cheek. "Yes, sir."

"What then?"

Billy drew a long, ragged breath and let it out. "Like I said, we thought we heard something, farther back in the tunnel, toward the barn. We got scared, and climbed out. I let the door fall shut after us, but I couldn't find the padlock. It must be over there somewhere—"

"And then you ran away."

"Yessir."

The old man nodded, a stern look on his face. "And where is young McClellan, right now?"

"I don't know," Billy said. "He went home through town, to pick up some things for his mother. He wouldn't know yet about the fire."

For a full minute no one said a word. A damp breeze swept in from the hills to the west. A horsefly buzzed past. Somewhere far away, a dog barked.

Amos Bloodworth tucked both hands into the pockets of his overalls and looked Billy in the eye.

"Why did you tell me this?"

The question caught Billy by surprise. "Sir?"

"Nobody saw you here. I would never have known. Isn't that right?"

"I guess so."

"So why did you tell me?"

Billy mulled that over for a moment. "I don't know," he said. "I guess . . . I guess I know it's what my dad would have done."

A long silence passed. Amos studied the boy carefully, then turned and looked at the skeleton of the barn and then past it at the green fields that stretched away to the little creek and the town beyond. Watching the old man stare off into the distance, Billy felt about as guilty as a person could feel, and as sad as he had ever been in his short life.

Finally Amos Bloodworth turned to face him.

"Now I have something to tell *you*," he said. He took off his straw hat and knelt in the grass at Billy's feet. From a distance of eighteen inches or so, man and boy stared directly into each other's eyes.

"You didn't start the fire," Amos said.

Billy blinked. After a stunned pause he murmured, "But Mrs. Bloodworth told me—"

"That it started in the cellar? It did. But farther in, under the barn. The cat knocked over a lantern."

"The cat?" Billy felt a wave of relief rush through his body. He put out a hand to steady himself, and the old man gently took it in his own.

Holding Billy's small hand, Amos said, "It's a brave thing you did, a brave and noble thing, telling me this. Do you realize that?"

Billy tried to answer, but couldn't. His mind was whirling.

"I admire courage, Billy Kendrix. And honesty." The old man rose to his feet, put his hat on, and looked down at the boy. "I'd be pleased, in a week or so, if you'd come be our guest for supper," he said.

Billy just stared up at him.

"The missus makes a fine meatloaf," Amos added.

Another silence. Billy was vaguely aware that the sun had come out, and was warm on his shoulders.

"I'll take that as a yes," Amos said. He started to leave, then stopped and turned again to the young man. "Tell your daddy we'd be pleased to have him and your mother, too."

Then he walked away.

Billy gazed after him with wide eyes. At last he looked at Mrs. Bloodworth, who was still standing there, smiling.

"I don't understand," Billy said.

"You heard him. You earned his respect, for what you did. And for what your folks taught you."

"But what I did was . . . I did wrong, and then told the truth about it. That's all."

"No," she said. "That's actually not all." Della's face

crumpled and huge tears rolled down her cheeks. In one smooth motion she knelt the way her husband had done and swept the astonished boy into her arms, squeezing him so tight he could hardly breathe.

"What . . ." he croaked. "What is it?"

Finally she released him, but remained kneeling at eye level, holding him with one hand on each shoulder. She was still sniffling.

"How do you suppose the cat knocked over the lantern, child?" she asked. "What do you think a lit lantern was doing down there in the first place?"

"I don't know—"

"It was there because *he* was there. My Amos had gone down into that cellar this morning, down the stairs inside the barn, to look for me some mason jars. Around seven o'clock. That must have been the noise you and your friend heard."

She paused, the tears bright on her pale cheeks.

"What you didn't hear came later," she continued. "Amos said the cat had followed him, and knocked the lantern off the peg where he hung it, and some old sacks caught fire." The old woman stopped to wipe her eyes, then touched her palm to his cheek. "But the sacks—and the fire—were between my Amos and the stairs. He was trapped in the tunnel. He was suffocating there, while I sat in the kitchen, not suspecting a thing. The first I knew was when I saw him walking up the path to the house a while later, his face all smudged and his clothes smoking and the barn burning in the distance." She paused again. "He came very close to dying, down there in that cellar. And he would have, if not for you."

Billy just stared at her. Her blue eyes sparkled through the tears.

"What do you mean?" he asked, his voice hushed.

Without looking down, she reached into her apron pocket

and took out the object Amos had handed her. It was an open padlock, still wet from the grass.

"Something sent you here, Billy Kendrix," she said, still smiling. "How could you not be welcome?"

John M. Floyd

THE PULLMAN CASE

It was almost dark when Scott Varner arrived at the four-story apartment building on Hamilton. He knew it was the right address: Three police cars lined the curb. He found his older brother Mitch waiting at the top of the stairs on the second floor.

He also found a barrier of yellow crime-scene tape stretched across the far end of the corridor. Scott turned and studied his brother. "A locked-room mystery, you said."

Mitch nodded and spoke around the stem of the pipe in his mouth. "Looks that way. Thought you'd be interested."

"I'm interested," Scott said, unbuttoning his overcoat. "I'm also confused. I ran into McCain downstairs—he said the victim was shot through a window. Simple case of murder."

Mitch shook his head. "Nothing simple about it."

Before he could explain, a short man in a plaid sportcoat and glasses charged through the doorway of the apartment at the end of the hall. In his hand was an open folder of papers,

262

which he was reading as he walked. He ducked under the police tape and stopped in his tracks when he looked up and saw Scott standing there. His eyes widened behind the glasses.

Both brothers were used to this. Despite a two-year age difference, they looked almost like twins.

"Walter Biggins," Mitch said, "this is my brother Scott. He's a detective too."

The short man looked puzzled. "Here in town?"

"P.I.," Scott said.

Walter Biggins didn't seem to know how to reply to that. Instead he turned and said to Mitch, "I've been on the phone, Lieutenant. Lab says it was poison. I forget the name, but it was fast. Fifteen seconds max."

Mitch just nodded. He didn't look overly surprised.

"Vanderford's trying to reach the guy's wife. Friends say she's visiting relatives upstate, with her kid. And McCain and Parsons are checking out the woods across the street."

"Good." Mitch pointed his pipe at the sheaf of papers in Biggins's hand. "These the notes?"

"Notes, photos, sketches," Biggins said, handing them over. "I'm done except for typing it up."

Mitch was already scanning the documents. "I'll get 'em back to you." It was clearly a dismissal; Biggins nodded once to Scott and left.

The Varners watched him hurry down the stairs.

"I'm hurt," Scott said. "No one on the force remembers me."

"Biggins is new. And you weren't exactly famous."

"Sad but true." Scott peered at the papers, reading upside down. "Poison?"

"It was on the slug we found in his throat. I wondered about that. The wound was shallow—"

"Mitchell," Scott interrupted, "why, exactly, did you call me?"

The lieutenant looked up from the notes. "I told you. I've got a mystery on my hands. One of your few talents is that you can think logically. I need your advice."

Scott narrowed his eyes. "I know this is April Fool's Day," he said, "but this ain't funny."

"What do you mean?"

"What you've got here is a murder, Mitchell. The only mystery, seems to me, is finding whoever put a bullet—poisoned or not—through your victim's window."

Mitch nodded. "That's what I thought too. At first."

Scott heard the sound of voices in the lobby below, then the creak and slam of the front door. The other policemen had gone.

"Come on," Mitch said. "Something I want you to see."

***

The apartment was small but tidy—living room, kitchen, two bedrooms, bath. The broken window was in the living room. A padded green armchair faced the window from a distance of ten feet or so, and in the space between them, a few spots of blood mingled with the broken glass on the floor.

"He was found here," Mitch said, handing Scott the stack of notes. "Sitting dead in his chair with his shirt and shoes off, looking peaceful considering he'd been shot in the throat with a pellet."

"A pellet?"

"Like you and I used to shoot in that big air-rifle of Jake Mayhew's. Except this pellet had grooves filed into it, and was coated with poison."

Scott grunted and began studying the documents. Especially the photos of the body.

"Name's Howard Pullman," Mitch said. "Sheet metal worker, down by the river. Haven't found his wife yet, but we've talked to several friends." Mitch paused and struck a match with his fingernail. When his pipe was going to his satisfaction, he said, "Sad story. He was about to be laid off, and had told one of his pals his biggest worry was the fact his daughter's so sick. Juvenile arthritis, I think. Anyway, if he's let go, his family's medical coverage goes too. Also, he has a company life insurance policy, which he'd lose."

Scott was watching him now, the papers forgotten. "You saying what I think you're saying? He . . . set this up, somehow?"

"Just hear me out." Mitch walked to the broken window and looked down at the street. "Out there on the sidewalk below the window, we found a slingshot. A kid's cheap slingshot—plastic handle, long elastic sling. No prints. Inside the little pouch on the sling, though, were traces of the same thing we found on the pellet buried in his throat—which we know now, of course, is poison."

"The murder weapon," Scott murmured.

His brother took out his pipe and scowled at it. "What bothers me is, the only reasonable place that pellet could've come from, assuming it was fired using the slingshot, is that vacant lot there, across the street. There's a good angle to the window, and lots of bushes and trees for cover. But there are two problems. First, I'm not sure that slingshot was powerful enough to reach that far. Second, if it was shot from there, why'd the killer then cross a busy street, *toward* the building, and drop the weapon in plain sight on the sidewalk?"

Since no answer was expected here, Scott didn't try to provide one. He just listened.

"And another thing," Mitch said. "Pullman was found right there, in his armchair. Shirt and shoes off, like I told you, and his right sock. His shoes—lace-up workboots—had been neatly placed side by side, with the one sock tucked inside his right shoe."

He paused.

"And?" Scott prompted.

"And the shoes had bits of glass embedded in the soles."

For a moment neither of them spoke.

"I found it myself," Mitch said. "Haven't mentioned it to anybody else yet. I wanted your opinion."

Scott ran a hand through his hair. "Your lab team missed it?"

"What can I say? It's hard to get good help."

Scott sighed. "Well . . . we know he had to get from the window to the chair. Only a few steps, but maybe he picked up the bits of glass in his shoes then, after being shot, then sat down in a daze and took his shoes off. Maybe that's why only one sock was still on. The poison could've gotten him before he finished."

"I suppose. But that way there wouldn't have been any cuts on the bottom of his bare foot—and there were. Besides, I can't see the guy calmly sitting down and unlacing his shoes and taking them off and lining 'em up neat as you please if he's just been plugged in the neck. I don't even think he'd have had time to. If the poison was supposed to take less than fifteen seconds—"

"I see your point," Scott said. "The shoes must've been off already, before he was shot. But if they were, how'd they get glass in the soles, right?"

"Right."

Scott Varner backed up and leaned against the wall by the window, thinking. At last he blinked and looked at his brother. "When did Pullman arrive here at the apartment?"

Mitch tipped his head toward the papers in Scott's hand. "Around twelve-fifteen, maybe as early as twelve-ten. Lady who lives down the hall saw him come upstairs. Spoke to him, she said, but he didn't respond. He just marched down the hall and through his door and locked it behind him. He was found an hour or so later, at one-twenty."

"How?" Scott asked. "Someone hear the window break?"

Mitch smiled. "That'd clear up a few things, wouldn't it? No, nobody heard anything. The lady who'd seen him come in got to worrying about him, coming home unexpectedly and all—he never comes home at lunch, she said—and decided to check on him. She knocked on his door, and when he didn't answer she went back to her apartment, called him on the phone. He didn't answer that either. That's when she called the super and got him to unlock Pullman's door." He paused, then added, "She verified, by the way, that nobody entered or left his place between twelve-ten and one-twenty."

Again the Varner brothers fell silent. Mitch studied the smoke from his pipe and Scott studied the notes in the report.

Finally Scott turned to face the window. He bent over, squinted at the broken pane. A piece of glass the size of his hand had fallen inward and onto the floor, but one edge of a hole and its spiderweb cracks were clearly visible.

"So," he said, "the window might've already been broken when he walked in."

"That's what I figured, yeah. But how?"

For a long while Scott stood there, staring at the window and through it to the wooded lot across the street, two floors below. Still watching the hole, he backed up a step, moved forward again, crouched down, stood on tiptoe. Then he turned slowly to look across the living room at the wall opposite the window.

"Get me something to stand on," he said, his eyes fixed on the wall. He was gazing at a point just below the ceiling.

With a puzzled look, Mitch went into one of the other rooms to fetch a chair.

Scott continued to stare at the wall, where several cheaply framed pictures were hung in an erratic pattern. After a moment he stepped up on the chair, turned, and looked once again over his shoulder at the window. Then he reached up and lifted the top picture off its hook in the wall.

Underneath was what looked like a bullethole.

He handed the picture to Mitch, took out a pocketknife, and probed the hole in the Sheetrock. Seconds later he held a small lead pellet in his hand. "No poison on this one, I bet."

Mitch looked at the pellet for a long time. "So when was this done, you think?"

Scott shrugged. "Sometime before twelve-ten, I imagine. That way, the broken glass was already on the floor when Pullman came in. Thus the glass fragments in his shoe soles when he crossed the room." He stepped down from the chair. "I think, now, that Howard Pullman must've fired this pellet himself, though probably from a big, heavy pellet-gun like we used to use, instead of the slingshot. That way it'd be sure to reach, and would be more accurate."

Mitch nodded. Unlike BB guns, old-style pellet rifles were powerful. Scott figured his brother was remembering the two of them drilling holes in soup cans from twenty yards away.

"But something doesn't figure," Mitch said. "You can't just shoot a window out in broad daylight."

"Maybe you can," Scott said. "This is April the first."

"So?"

"I noticed a fire station a few doors down."

Mitch did a palms-up. "So . . ."

"So they probably blow a siren at noon on the first of every month. I know ours does, at home. And a whistle like that would be loud enough to drown out the pop of a pellet gun, not to mention the sound of a breaking windowpane." Scott scratched his chin. "You want my guess, Mr. Pullman knew that too, and chose that moment to fire his shot. Twelve o'clock on the nose."

"But—"

"He had to show that the window was broken from the outside, Mitchell. So he made the shot, ditched the gun, then circled way around somewhere and walked into the building. Then he climbed the stairs, came inside, locked the door, and— his one mistake—walked over the broken glass with his shoes on."

Mitch was watching his brother closely now, absorbed. "And then?"

"Then he got a picture, hung it on the wall to cover the pellet hole, took off his shirt, sat down in the chair, removed his shoes, arranged them just so, and took off his right sock."

Scott's mind was humming now, his eyes glazed. He was in his element.

"Okay," Mitch said. "Enlighten me. Why his right sock?"

Scott turned and focused on him. "Because he needed a bare foot for his slingshot."

"What!?"

"He took the poisoned pellet from his pocket, along with the slingshot. You said the sling was a long one, remember. He fitted the pellet into the pouch of the sling, wedged the pouch between the toes of his right foot"—Scott extended a leg and acted it out—"and then, with his hands, he held the handle up here, a few inches from his throat, stretching the elastic—"

"I get the picture," Mitch said.

"That's why the pellet had to be poisoned. He wasn't sure how hard it would hit him, or how far it'd go in. And that's why his shirt was off. In case he missed the soft skin of his throat a little."

Mitch pondered that for a moment. "But . . . after he shot himself—"

"He got up, probably used his shirt to wipe the slingshot clean of prints, then dropped it out through the hole in the window. He had to get rid of it—he was smart enough to know there might be signs of the poison on the pouch of the sling. Anyhow, that's when he got the glass in his bare foot, and the blood on the floor. Then he came back and collapsed in his chair. An hour later he's discovered by the landlord and the neighbor, they call you, and you call me." Scott spread his hands like a magician. "And I solve your case," he added, with a grin.

Mitch drew his brows together, thinking.

"The question now," Scott said at last, "is what are we going to do about it?"

Mitch blinked. "Do about it?"

Scott gave his brother a long, measuring look. "Mitchell," he said, "it's not like you to find new evidence, of any kind, and keep it to yourself. We both know that." Without breaking eye contact, Scott held up the report and tapped the top page with his finger. "I think, from the point when you found the glass in his shoe soles, you had doubts it was a murder. A locked-room mystery, you told me on the phone. You meant it, didn't you? And you hadn't told anyone else your suspicions because of one thing: If it wasn't murder it must have been suicide, and if it was suicide then this poor sucker's family wouldn't get a penny of his life insurance, employee or not. Right?"

Mitch Varner frowned, fiddled with his pipe, heaved a sigh. "Yeah, I had my doubts, I just couldn't figure it all out. And I kept thinking about . . . well, I kept thinking about what our ma could've done with some extra money if the old man had had sense enough to be insured when he flipped his truck that night." He glanced at Scott and shrugged. "You know?"

Scott didn't answer. Instead he said, "Let me ask you this. What if one of your men happens to find a pellet gun out there in the woods?"

Mitch shook his head. "They won't. They're done with

that now. Even if it did turn up, if Howard Pullman was as careful as I'm beginning to think he was, he'd have wiped it clean before he left it anywhere."

Scott gave that some thought. It grew very quiet in the room. It also grew cold; the wind was whistling in through the hole in the window.

"So what do you think?" Mitch asked.

Scott looked his brother in the eye, then handed him Walter Biggins's folder. "I think your man's written a thorough report. I can't come up with a single thing to add."

Mitch took the folder, waiting. He seemed to know something was coming.

"On second thought," Scott said, "I do need some surfacing compound. They should have some at the paint store on the corner."

"What?"

Smiling, Scott glanced at the little hole in the wall, just below the ceiling. "I'm the handy brother, remember? I can cover that over in two minutes flat."

John M. Floyd

NIGHT WORK

Jack Randall loved computers. He loved all kinds of computers, and the one in front of him now, encased in half a ton of ATM armor, wasn't much different from the one in his bedroom at home. Except that he was being paid to play with this one.

It was that thought, together with the drumming of rain on the roof of the little ATM shed, that kept him from hearing the car drive up outside. He did, however, hear the door open behind him, and felt the cold muzzle of the gun on the back of his neck.

"Hand over the money, kid," a voice said.

Jack swallowed. "I don't have any money." He pointed to the duffel bag on the floor beside him. It contained half a dozen narrow rolls of paper. "I just restock the printer, when it needs it, and change the bank's marketing message once a week."

"The keys, then. To the cash compartment."

"No keys either." Jack turned out his pockets as proof. "And I'm not a kid. I just got my driver's license—"

"So that was your junkheap we saw parked outside, huh?"

We? Jack thought. Sure enough, as a rough hand spun him around, he saw that there were two of them—the one with the gun was short and heavy, the other so tall his head almost touched the low ceiling. Neither was much older than Jack. Past them, just outside the half-open door, an empty Ford Taurus glistened in the rain.

The boy with the gun looked at the tall one and said, "I thought Kenny told you this guy could get us the money."

"Kenny?" Jack blinked. "Kenny Doomis?" He focused on the tall boy's face. "You must be Al. Kenny talks about you."

Al Doomis glared at his partner, then said to Jack, "He talks about you too, sport. He said you started out sweeping the floors around this thing, and now you help program it. That right?"

Jack just stared at him, sweating.

"Well," Doomis said, "if you don't have the money and you don't have the keys . . ." He reached into his pocket.

Jack held his breath.

Doomis took out a plastic ATM card. He tossed it to Jack and said, "Make this work."

Jack looked at it. "The name on this is Ralph Longmeyer."

"You expect me to use my own? Mr. Longmeyer was even kind enough to write his secret number on the back."

"I don't get it," Jack said, his mind spinning. "If you have a stolen card, why do you need me? Just put it in and get your cash."

"We tried that already. The account's overdrawn."

"Overdrawn?"

"It means—"

"I know what it means," Jack said. "You think I can make the machine give you money when the computer downtown says there's no money in the account?"

"The computer downtown won't know about it."

"How do you figure that?"

Once again, Doomis reached into his pocket.

Once again, Jack held his breath.

Doomis took out a pair of wirecutters. Keeping his eyes on Jack, he handed the pliers to his short partner, who bent over and cut the phone line to the ATM.

"I think you call that operating 'offline.' Am I right?"

"That's right," Jack said.

"So the machine can't check the account balance now, at the central computer. Right again?"

"The central computer'll check the phone line, though. And they'll probably send a repairman."

"All the way out here, in the rain, at night? I doubt they'll hurry."

That was true, and Jack knew it. "But you still can't get more than the daily cash limit."

"Then reset the limit. According to good old Kenny, you can program it to do that right here.' Smiling, Doomis nodded toward the computer keyboard on the ATM's back panel. "How many words a minute can you type, sweetheart?"

"It's not that simple," Jack said. "Even if I recode it, there's a hardware limit of twenty bills per transaction. Since the machine uses twenties, that's a four-hundred-dollar maximum."

"Not if you do enough transactions." Doomis seemed to remember something, and studied Jack's face a moment. "You said you change the marketing message, right?"

"The bank pays me to come type in a new one, every Monday."

"What is that, exactly?"

"It's an ad. A blurb customers see on the screen when they use the machine."

"Like what?"

"Like, 'Take advantage of our low rates on consumer loans.'"

Doomis grinned. "Our plan is to take advantage of a lot more than that."

"We're wasting time, Al," Shorty growled.

Jack kept his eyes on Doomis. "What *is* your plan, exactly? I mean, afterward?"

"Well, afterward, you're going for a little ride down the interstate with us, to Blue Lake."

Jack swallowed. "Because I know who you are?"

"That is a problem," Doomis agreed. He glanced at his watch. "Any more questions?"

"I guess not."

"Then get your programming hat on, Jackie boy. Put a bonus upon us."

***

The whole thing took less than an hour. With Doomis watching, Jack typed in the necessary commands and restarted the system. When that was done, Shorty took the stolen card around to the front of the ATM and went to work; he withdrew more than ten thousand dollars in twenties before Doomis called time. Laughing wildly, both stuffed the cash into their coat pockets while Jack went around back to the keyboard again to finish up. Then they all climbed into Doomis's red Ford and skidded out of the parking lot. The rain had ended, and the moon was out.

Jack spent a nervous twenty minutes in the back seat as they drove through town and turned onto the interstate. Three miles north of Blue Lake his luck changed: A state trooper pulled them over, and two minutes later five black-and-whites screeched onto the scene. Orders were shouted, guns pointed, hands raised. Jack Randall's ordeal was over.

Afterward, backlit by the flashing bubbles of eight police cruisers, a glum-faced and handcuffed Al Doomis asked one of the officers how they had known. Smirking, the patrolman nodded to a colleague, who produced his notepad and held a flashlight to the top page. Printed in the cop's hurried block letters were the words:

HELP!!! KIDNAPPED BY AL DOOMIS & PARTNER, RED FORD TAURUS LICENSE RDH673, I-55 SOUTH TO BLUE LAKE, 9:20 PM

"So it actually worked," Jack said. "You did read the screen."

"After we came to respond to your door-open alarm." The officer gave him a sly look. "I guess you forgot to lock it when you left, huh?"

Jack returned his grin, then sobered as he saw Al Doomis and Shorty being led toward a waiting cruiser.

When Doomis was ten feet from Jack he turned, and their eyes met. For a moment the two young men stood and stared at each other.

"You're pretty quick after all, sport," Doomis said. "You had to be, to outsmart me this bad."

Jack thought that over. "I'm close to one-forty, I imagine."

"I.Q., you mean?"

"Words a minute," Jack said.

NEWTON'S LAW

The old man was popping the last of the breakfast biscuits into his mouth when the door crashed open. Deputy Newton Hobbs burst into the one-room cabin, slammed the door behind him, and leaned back against it, his eyes closed and his chest heaving. "Apaches," he said. "Other side of the river. At least a dozen."

Old Amos Bassett, who had already jumped to his feet, spit out half his biscuit and swallowed the rest whole. The third person in the room, a long-haired man named Jack Fountain, stood also, but a little more slowly: His wrists were handcuffed behind his back.

"Did they see you?" Amos sputtered.

"Don't matter," Hobbs said. "They saw our smoke." He glanced around the interior of the cabin. It was an old line shack, dark and rundown and smelling like years of woodsmoke and unwashed cowboys. His gaze stopped on the rope-handled bucket, still empty, that he held in his right hand.

He stared at it blankly for a second, then flung it into a corner. "Let's get movin'. If we can make it to the woods and double back to the river . . ."

The old man was already gathering his gear. "What about the horses?"

"Leave 'em." Hobbs took out his pistol, spun the cylinder, holstered it again. "We'll have to go out the back window—"

"Give me a gun," Jack Fountain said.

Both the others stared at him. "What?" Hobbs asked.

"You heard me. Take off these cuffs and give me a gun."

Newton Hobbs regarded him a moment. "Let me explain something to you, Fountain. I'm the Law, he's the tracker, you're the prisoner. Prisoners don't get guns."

"Yeah, well, I ain't no regular prisoner, Deputy. For one thing, I ain't really been arrested yet, have I. And if that's Red Shirt's bunch out there"—Fountain nodded his shaggy head toward the closed door—"you'll need all the help you can get."

Before Hobbs could reply, Amos Bassett said, "He's right, Newt. We're just supposed to bring him in for questioning, you said so yourself."

Hobbs turned to the old man. "So what are *you* saying, Amos? Give him a gun so he can kill us like he killed them two women in Hays?"

"I didn't kill *no*body," Fountain snapped.

The old tracker swallowed and lowered his voice. "What if he's tellin' the truth, Newt? One of the Cado boys did say he saw him in Dodge at the time."

All three men fell silent, thinking their own thoughts.

"Come on, Deputy," Fountain said, turning and jingling his handcuff chains. "We're wastin' time."

Still Hobbs hesitated. Finally he muttered, "God help us," and nodded to the old man, who fished a key from his pocket and unlocked the cuffs. When that was done, Hobbs pulled a second pistol from his belt, flipped it over, and handed it to the prisoner. "Head for the window, I'm right behind you," Hobbs said. He turned to grab some jerky and a canteen from the table-top.

When he turned again, stuffing the jerky into his vest pocket, he froze.

Jack Fountain had taken two steps back, and was standing alone in the center of the room. The borrowed pistol was point-ed straight at Newton Hobbs's chest. Amos already had his hands high in the air, and was gawking at the gun as if hypno-tized.

"What's this?" Hobbs said.

Fountain cocked the pistol and studied both of them a moment. His lip had curled into a cold, bitter smile. "Let me explain something to you, Deputy," he said. "You're a dead man, he's a dead man, I'm a free man. As of right now. And free men don't get taken back to hang."

Hobbs nodded. "So you did kill 'em."

"You bet I did. Enjoyed it, too."

Old Amos suddenly spoke up, sounding hurt as well as scared: "But Sam Cado said you was in Dodge that day, with him . . ."

Fountain's gaze flicked to Amos. "I'll give you some advice, old man," he said, still smiling. "Don't believe every-thing you're told."

With that, he raised the revolver, aimed it at Hobbs' head, and pulled the trigger.

The hollow CLICK sounded loud in the confined space of the cabin. For an instant Fountain just stood there, staring in disbelief. Before he could recover, Deputy Hobbs' own gun was drawn and cocked and ready.

"Jack Fountain," Hobbs said, "you are under arrest for the murders of Clara Garvey and Janie Sims. Amos, take his gun and cuff him again."

The old man, who was every bit as stunned as the prisoner, blinked and nodded. While Hobbs held his pistol pointed at Fountain's heart, Amos retrieved the empty revolver and with trembling hands snapped the cuffs into place.

In the silence that followed, Jack Fountain's twisted grin returned. "Pretty cute, Deputy," he admitted. "But you're still dead men. Red Shirt and me go way back, but you and your tracker'll be scalped and roasted by noontime."

Amos Bassett swallowed again, and glanced over Hobbs' shoulder at the closed door. "He's right, Newt—it's too late to run now. What about the Indians?"

Keeping his eyes on Fountain, Hobbs backed up until he was leaning against the doorframe. "Let me put it this way, Amos: So far he's only been right about one thing." Without looking, Hobbs hooked one of his spurs into the crack of the door behind him and kicked sideways; the door swung open again, to reveal a wide deserted clearing, a shallow river, and plains that stretched flat and empty all the way to the distant mountains.

"Don't believe everything you're told," Hobbs said.

BATTLEGROUND

"Do you think he knows?" Jenny asked.

Twenty feet away, Drew Pennebaker stood with his hands in his pockets, staring out over the barren landscape. After a moment he turned, took a Sprite from the cooler they'd brought along, and sat down beside her on a shelf of rock. He rolled the cold can between his palms, his eyes on the eastern sky. Within the last five minutes it had gone from a dull pink to a hard, brilliant orange. The sun was up; it wouldn't be long now.

"No," he said. "I think he suspects something—he's no fool. But I don't think he knows." Drew popped open the can and took a long swallow, then leaned back against the still-cold rock behind them. "If he did, he wouldn't have invited us along."

"I guess you're right," Jenny said. "Maybe it's just my nerves." She sighed and shifted position, her brown eyes studying the surroundings.

What a godforsaken place, she thought. A moonscape of

crags and canyons and scorpions, a vast nothing in the middle of nowhere. Not a tree or a plant or a single speck of green, as far as the eye could see. A hundred yards from the open area where they sat, a deep ravine twisted snakelike through the sand and rubble. A boulder the size of a schoolbus spanned the gap, and offered the only visible access to the jagged line of mountains several miles to the east.

It was there, she remembered, gazing across at the rocky slopes, that Willard was headed. He had told her about it two days ago. *Go with me*, he had said. *It'll do you good to get away from the hotel. I'll ask Drew to come along too.*

As it turned out, Willard had been here once already, years ago, long before he'd taken over the Company. He'd dabbled a bit in archaeology even then, and in the ugly sawtoothed mountains to the east he'd made several finds—nothing significant, but enough to whet his interest. He had described them to her in detail, a faraway look in his eyes. This was at last a chance, he said, to do some further exploring there. All he really wanted to accomplish was to relocate the sites and make some rough sketches for a followup expedition.

Both Jenny and Drew had agreed, and the more she thought about it, the better it sounded. Willard's business meetings would be over soon, and they'd be heading back to the States. This might be her last chance to see more of Africa, and take some good slides for home.

And to be with Drew.

Yesterday afternoon Willard had informed them of the plans. The three of them would drive out in Drew's Jeep—a hardtopped, air-conditioned Wrangler. It was only a few hours' trip across the desert. Jenny and Drew could wait in the hills near the Jeep while Willard did some scouting around, and they'd all get back to civilization before the heat went off the scale. How did that sound?

Both of them had shrugged. Why not? It made no real difference to them. It was only later that night, in the hotel lounge long after Willard was asleep, that the first shadow of an idea entered their heads . . .

***

The sun was well above the horizon now. Jenny shivered despite the rising temperature and tucked her legs underneath her on the rock.

"Where'd Willard go?" she said. "If he's using the john someplace, he's taking a long time of it."

Drew Pennebaker took another swig of his Sprite, then tipped his head to the left, toward the quarter-mile maze of slabs and boulders they had crossed on foot twenty minutes ago. Their Jeep was parked on the other side, out of sight from here. "He went back to the Jeep. Said he'd forgotten his backpack."

"What?" She grabbed his arm, her eyes wide. Part of his drink sloshed out onto the sand. "What if he does know about us, Drew? What if you're wrong? He could take the Jeep right now and leave us here—"

"Calm down. He's not going anywhere." Drew's left hand, which had slipped into his pocket, came out again. The silver keychain glittered in the early rays of the sun.

"Nobody outsmarts me, Jenny—not even Willard. If I'm wrong, as you say, and he is onto us . . ." He shrugged. "Then it's war. Between us and him. And in a battle of wits, my dear"—Drew smiled and jingled the keys—"he's no match for me."

She swallowed and nodded, easing her grip on his arm. Then she stiffened again. "Here he comes," she whispered.

Drew turned to follow her gaze.

At fifty-six, Willard Martin was twenty years older than Jenny and Drew. He was a ruggedly handsome man whose square jaw and close-cut gray hair made him look like a short Lee Marvin. His arms and legs were tanned a deep walnut from the sun, and years of outdoor hobbies had lined and weathered his face like a sailor's. It was an image of which he was oddly proud. Walking toward them now, in a faded cotton shirt and Bermudas, the very last thing he resembled was what he actually was—the chairman and CEO of one of the largest mining conglomerates in the world.

And that was only one of Willard's accomplishments. He was also a gourmet cook, a concert pianist, and the author of three books on amateur archaeology.

In addition to that, he was Drew's boss.

And Jenny's husband.

"Hello, darling," she said, forcing a smile. "I was beginning to worry about you."

Willard stopped several feet away, his chest heaving. "Had to fetch my pack. I'd left it in the back seat." He hitched the old backpack higher on his shoulders, sat down on the cooler, and began to unlace his hiking boots. "How're you two doing so far?"

Jenny shrugged. "Fine. It's really not as warm as I thought it would be."

Willard chuckled. "That's because it's seven in the morning," he said, massaging his toes. "Remember what I told you yesterday? In four hours it'll hit one-twenty. By early afternoon . . ." He shook his head. "But we'll be back at the hotel by that time. Sipping daiquiris by the pool."

"I could use one now," Drew muttered, staring at the sun. His Sprite can sat empty and forgotten on the stone beside him.

Willard grinned. "You'll be okay. Just keep your hats on, both of you, and drink plenty of water. Snap a few pictures if you get bored." He finished relacing his boots and stood up, taking a short pick-axe from its resting place against a boulder.

His own camera lay where he'd left it earlier, in a leather case beside his binoculars on the rock slab next to Jenny's leg. He bent to retrieve them, pulling the camera case strap over his shoulder, and gave his wife a peck on the cheek. She smiled and squeezed his hand.

"Be careful," she said.

He looked about him for a moment, taking stock. "I won't be more than two or three hours." To Drew he said, "Make sure she's comfortable, okay?" Drew nodded, and without further ado Willard turned and strode away from the sandy clearing, his eyes fixed on the ridge that bisected the rugged line of hills to the east.

Silently they watched him go. It was only after he had reached the ravine and crossed its natural bridge that Jenny spoke.

"What do you think?" she asked.

Drew glanced at her, then checked his watch. It was 7:10. "Half an hour. No longer." He raised his head again, resuming his vigil. Willard was already making his way up the slopes.

After a moment, Drew turned once more to face Jenny. She looked at him. He was smiling.

"How about a game of gin?" he said.

***

Halfway up the ridge, Willard Martin lay motionless on a red shelf of rock, watching the two figures in the distance. His binoculars were Bushnell 10 x 50s; he could see every move they made.

They were sitting facing each other, Drew on the bench-like stone where Jenny had been earlier and she on a towel spread out on the sand. Between them was the cooler, and they appeared to be playing cards on its top. As he watched, Willard saw Drew check the time and take a long look in his direction before resuming the game.

Willard pulled himself up onto his elbows and lowered the glasses. Leaning to his left, he unslung the camera case from his right shoulder and set it down on the rock beside him.

The leather case was expensive and well-worn. Besides the camera, it contained a separate compartment for batteries and extra lenses and a pouch for spare film. Willard kept his eyes on the scene below him as he unzipped the pouch, reached inside, and removed a flat black object from below the rolls of film.

It was a tape recorder, a miniature Panasonic he had bought a week ago in Johannesburg. It used a 45-minute micro-cassette; the tape inside was still moving. He switched it off, rewound it to the halfway point, and pressed PLAY.

A snatch of conversation. His wife's voice. That was good: The machine was working.

He hit REWIND again, waited a few seconds, and started it up once more. This time there was only silence. That made sense; when he had first planted the recorder and headed back toward the Jeep, Drew Pennebaker was alone in the clearing, a tattered map of Africa open in his hands. Jenny's gear had been lying on an outcrop of rock nearby, next to Willard's own, so that's where Willard had decided to place the camera case and recorder. The slab of rock actually resembled a bench, and was the natural choice of a place to rest; he had felt sure that when his wife returned from nature's call she would sit there. It was a chance he'd had to take.

Once again Willard raised the binoculars. Nothing had changed. Jenny was dealing another hand. For a full five minutes he lay there in the sun, watching them, listening to the empty hiss of the tape.

He prayed he wouldn't hear what he expected to hear. There was still time to go back.

It was getting hotter. His elbows, propped on the rock,

began to throb. A drop of perspiration ran into his eye; he blinked and wiped his forehead with a shirtsleeve. Ten feet away, a lizard as thick as his forearm scurried underneath a stone.

When the recorder finally spoke, it was so sudden Willard almost dropped the glasses.

"Well," Drew's voice said, "it's almost time." A short pause. Willard spun the volume all the way up. "Any regrets?" Drew asked.

Willard heard his wife's voice next. It was much louder and clearer than Drew's. Evidently she had, as Willard had hoped, sat next to the camera case. "None," she answered. "How about you?"

A long sigh whooshed out of the recorder. "Only one. Only that we didn't do something like this sooner."

There was no sound for several seconds. Then Jenny's voice: "Look at it this way, sweetie. He's worth even more now than he was last month. Or last week."

"Like gold," Drew said.

"That's right." She laughed then, a throaty chuckle that Willard had once loved. For an instant, his composure broke. He squeezed his eyes shut and swallowed, clenching his teeth till they hurt. Then she spoke again, and the moment passed. He opened his eyes and stared at the recorder. "It won't damage your ego, will it," she was saying, "to have a lady support you after we're married?"

"A lady? Who did you have in mind?"

She must have pinched or prodded Drew then, because the recorder issued a sharp male grunt, followed by playful laughter. Willard listened in stony silence.

He wondered what Mrs. Pennebaker, who was also an employee of the Company, would say if she heard this.

Minutes passed. The tape ran quietly on. Below him, the

card game continued. Willard Martin watched and listened.

Soon his hair was soaking wet. He took off his hat with his free hand and fanned himself with it. The binoculars never left his eyes.

He wondered how long they would wait.

"Drew?" the recorder said.

"What."

Willard heard her sigh. "There's no way this can . . . back-fire, is there?"

"Not a chance," Drew said. "All he'll take with him besides maps and sketchpads, he told me, is some digging gear and a few books and magnifying glasses in case he stumbles onto something. And one canteen of water." A short silence, then the clink of aluminum cans, and the ka-choo of one being opened. "Here," he said.

"Thanks."

After a moment Drew's voice continued: "I figure we should stay here for a while after he leaves, give him at least enough time to get over that ridge"—there was a pause here, and Willard could imagine both of them turning to look into the distance—"and then we take off. We walk back to the Jeep and get out of here for good. In this heat he won't last till nightfall."

Jenny must have hesitated, then said, "What about later? When they find . . . the body?"

Drew chuckled. "They won't. That's the beauty of it. Nobody knows exactly where we went—not even his pilot, according to what Willard said to you yesterday. We'll tell the police we all went north, toward the Ngana plateau. You and I got separated from him, searched for him frantically, and final-ly had to go for help. They'll look for him there, not here. And it's roughly the same distance from town, in case anyone decides to check the mileage on the Jeep." He paused. "If the body is found at all, Jen, it'll probably be a hundred years from now—by someone like him, digging for bones."

Willard lowered the glasses. That was it, he said to himself. He'd heard enough. All they'd needed was the opportunity; when it presented itself, they had taken advantage of it.

It was logical. He'd been suspicious of them for months, and ninety percent certain for weeks. Now he knew for sure.

He had had to be sure.

"Drew?"

The tape recorder startled him. Willard had almost forgotten it, for the moment.

Drew Pennebaker's answer was unintelligible. He must have moved away, or had his back to the recorder.

"About us . . ." Jenny said.

After a moment, the reply, barely audible: "What about us?"

"Do you think he knows?" she asked.

Silence.

Once again Willard heard the clinking of cans, the rumble of ice. Then Drew spoke, and his voice this time was clear. He had moved, apparently, to Jenny's side. "No," he said. "I think he suspects something—he's no fool. But I don't think he knows." There was a sharp fizz as another can was opened. "If he did, he wouldn't have invited us along."

"I guess you're right. Maybe it's just my nerves."

Another silence followed, broken only by the whisper of the tape. Below, in the clearing, Jenny Martin was shuffling the cards. Drew looked at his wristwatch. Willard put down the binoculars long enough to do the same. It was 7:36.

The tape played on. Willard heard his wife ask where he was, heard the alarm in her voice after Drew told her Willard had returned to the Jeep for his backpack. Little had she known, Willard said to himself, that he couldn't have done what she feared; not then. He hadn't been certain about them then.

Peering through the glasses, he saw Drew put down his cards and rise to his feet, his eyes on the ridge above Willard's perch. Drew couldn't see much from that angle, Willard knew: The sun was in his eyes. Apparently satisfied, Drew glanced again at his watch. His mouth moved soundlessly as he spoke. Jenny nodded in response and rose from her seat. Together, wasting no time, they began to collect their gear.

Willard continued to watch them, absorbed in their actions, only half listening now to the recorder. Suddenly something Drew had just said caught his attention. Willard rewound the tape for a second or two and played it back again.

"—it's war," Drew was saying. "Between us and him. And in a battle of wits, my dear"—Willard heard the jingle of keys—"he's no match for me."

Willard lowered the binoculars. For the first time that day, the first time during his long, hot vigil, he felt a grim satisfaction.

With half his mind he heard Jenny tell Drew that Willard was approaching, and a moment later his own voice, answering his wife's question. "Had to fetch my pack," he heard himself say. "I'd left it in the back seat—"

Willard switched off the recorder. He rose stiffly to his feet and removed the tape from the machine. He no longer felt any remorse. He stared at the cassette for a long moment, then tossed it away into the rocks. By noon, the heat would melt it to jelly.

He raised the glasses one last time. The man and woman on the other side of the ravine had finished gathering their things. They were walking quickly away toward the west. Toward the Jeep, which was parked and waiting a quarter of a mile away.

Willard was impressed. It had been a well-planned, well-executed operation.

They were leaving him to die.

He put the recorder in his pocket, replaced the binoculars, and swung the camera case over his shoulder. Adjusting his backpack, he turned and continued up the rocky slope.

It was a quarter till eight.

***

The pilot licked the point of the yellow pencil, leaned forward, and printed the six letters C-Y-G-N-E-T. A baby swan. There was only one more to go, down in the bottom corner. Sixty-three across: a four-letter word for "Spanish pot." And wouldn't you know, it was one of those where all the intersecting words were poetic terms or foreign contractions or mythological names.

The pilot struggled with it for five more minutes, then flung the folded newspaper aside. Damn waste of time. For that matter, this whole trip was probably a waste of time.

What a place this was . . .

Chris, the pilot, had been reared on a hundred-acre ranch two hours from Albuquerque, and had always held the opinion that the ugliest scenery on the face of the earth lay within the boundaries of their home county. That opinion was wrong, as it turned out. What was visible now through the tinted glass of the parked helicopter was enough to make the New Mexico badlands look like the Boca Raton Country Club.

And there seemed to be no end to it. It stretched away forever to the right and left, a brownish-yellow sea of stone and sand and emptiness. Behind the chopper, a row of sawtoothed mountains marched like giant camels across the western horizon. Ahead, twenty yards from the windshield, was the landmark—a huge pillar of stone, two hundred feet tall, easy to spot from the air. The chopper had circled it once and landed in its shadow.

The instructions were simple: Remain here alone, beside

the pillar, until twelve sharp. If there was no contact before that time, leave for town, following the same roundabout flight path.

The pilot checked the clock on the instrument panel. 10:55.

The heat, even here in the retreating shade of the pillar, was oppressive. Chris had just remembered the bottle of Jack Daniels, and was rummaging for it under the seat—one little nip wouldn't do any harm—when someone spoke.

"Olla," the voice said.

Chris's head whipped around.

Willard Martin stood framed in the passenger doorway, a weary smile on his face. His cheeks and forehead were grimy, his eyes red, his clothes soaked with sweat. "Sixty-three across," he said, pointing to the puzzle on the seat. "A Spanish pot is an 'olla.' If you're interested."

Chris let out a lungful of air. "You look like you've been in a war."

"Well, a battle, at least," Willard said, a faraway look in his eyes. Then his face cleared, and he climbed inside. "Help me off with this thing, will you?"

Obediently, the pilot took the backpack as Willard shrugged free of the straps. Like its owner, the pack was covered with a film of dirt and sand. The loose buckles were too hot to touch. As Chris upended it to toss it into the storage area behind the seats, two items were visible in the open pouch. One was a clear plastic toolkit, the kind you might carry in your trunk for emergencies.

The other was a little less common.

Chris stared at it a moment, then glanced at Willard, whose attention was elsewhere. He had found the bourbon and was swilling it from the bottle.

Chris hoisted the pack the rest of the way into the storage bin and faced front. Willard was leaning back in his seat now, eyes shut against the glare of the sun. Streaks of perspiration cut vertical scars through the layers of dirt on his face. The bottle, its level sharply altered, lay cradled in the crook of his arm. He looked like a drunk in a Bowery alley.

"Willard?"

Slowly he opened his eyes.

"Is it true?" Chris asked.

An even deeper weariness seemed to tug at Willard's face. "It's true."

Chris pondered that for a moment. "So what happened?"

"What happened," Willard said, "is they think I'm dead."

"And what about them?"

Willard turned to face the pilot. "They're together now."

The statement seemed to echo in the quiet of the cockpit. For a while neither of them said a word.

"Any regrets?" Willard asked, still studying Chris's face.

"Not a one."

Willard nodded, then turned again to stare straight ahead. Moments later, under Chris's steady hand, the chopper rose through a cloud of swirling sand, banked around the stone landmark, dipped its nose, and headed south. After a mile or two Chris glanced again at Willard, who was half asleep already, his head bobbing lazily with the movements of the aircraft.

And as the pilot watched Willard's profile, a shaft of sunlight caught one of the buckles on the backpack behind the passenger seat, turning Chris's thoughts again to the strange object inside it.

Willard was something, all right. He was one of those people who could always find a way to solve a problem, whether it involved ancient history or corporate mergers or crossword puzzles.

And what a solution.

Chris Pennebaker broke out a slow smile.

A distributor cap. Of all things, an electrical distributor cap, with the coil and spark plug wires still attached. In fact, it looked like one Chris had seen several times herself, back home in Johannesburg. Behind her home, actually. In her garage.

Under the hood of her husband's Jeep.

RAINBOW'S END

I met Jenny Bartlett two days ago, standing on my doorstep at six in the morning. She had driven up in a new white Corvette, her hair wild and her eyes red and swollen. I knew who she was; her husband Jake had shown me her picture a dozen times.

"He's dead," she said.

I stood there stunned, holding the door open. "What?"

"It's a long story."

Inside, sitting at the kitchen table with both hands locked around a coffee cup, she told me Jake had been found two hours ago in a Fourth Street alley, with a bullet in his head. The last thing he'd said to her was that he thought he was being watched. Apparently he was right.

"I can't believe it," I murmured. "I saw him last week."

"I saw him last night," she said. She looked ready to start crying again.

I watched her a moment, waiting. "You said it was a long

story . . ."

"It is." She wiped her puffy eyes with the back of her hand. "I need you to help me get the money."

I had been wondering which of us would mention it first. Jake and I had hit two banks in Anchorage last week; the stolen cash had gone into a strongbox in his basement. We had planned to meet in Eagle River tomorrow, to split it up. "Where is it?" I asked.

"Two days ago we took his boat out," she said. "He hid the box on an island in the Sound."

"He what?!"

"I told you, he was jumpy. He said he had to hide it and lay low a while."

"Did he plan on telling me about this?"

"He was coming here today." She took a shaky sip of coffee and looked me in the eye. "Can you drive his boat?"

"You sound desperate."

"I need the money, Charlie. I could use Jake's share."

I studied her a moment. "Why didn't you keep it *all*?"

"What?"

"You could've asked someone else to help you get it. Why me?"

"Because half the money's yours."

"Are we being honorable here?"

"We're being logical," she said. "What's your share? A hundred grand?"

"About that."

"Well, I figured you might be coming to see me about it, eventually."

"A good guess," I agreed. "When do we leave?"

***

Ten minutes later we were heading south along Turnagain Arm. Jenny drove while I studied a nautical map I had found underneath a bottle of liquid soap and an ice scraper in her glove compartment.

We left her car at a tiny depot near Portage, rode the Alaska Railroad through the tunnels to Whittier, gassed up Jake's Bayliner at the harbor there, and headed east. The sky was overcast, the glaciers blue, the water calm. We had only one rough stretch, as we turned south at the end of Passage Canal. I noticed her watching me maneuver.

"You ever driven a boat?" I asked her.

"Not one this big. What's that thing there?"

I showed her the controls and let her steer us through the maze of narrow channels along the way. She seemed to be enjoying herself. Around two o'clock we reached her mark on the map.

It was an ideal spot to hide something. One of a thousand rugged islands dotting the waterways of Prince William Sound, it was uninhabited and probably unexplored. I once heard that some of these places had never felt the tread of human feet. Looking at this one now, with its fog-shrouded peaks and tangled forests, I could believe it.

"Rainbow's End," Jenny murmured.

"What?"

"I just named this island."

I checked the map. "You're right, it's unnamed."

"Not any more."

We stopped in a cove a mile long and half a mile across. After lowering the skiff and going over her directions again, we stood together in the stern awhile, watching the shoreline. A dozen waterfalls roared in the distance. High on one of the slopes, I saw what looked like a furry brown boulder shuffling through the trees.

"Can bears swim?" she asked, following my gaze. We had already decided she would stay with the boat while I fetched the strongbox.

"Jake's rifle's inside," I said, grinning. "If one comes aboard, I'll hear the shots and come save you."

"I don't think you could," she said.

"Save you?"

"Hear the shots."

She was right. Even at this distance, the waterfalls were loud; where I was going, they'd be deafening.

"Then you're on your own till I get back," I said, and stepped down into the skiff. When she handed me the oars she leaned over and gave me a kiss. It surprised me.

"Be careful," she said.

***

The muddy shore was fifty yards away. A light rain was falling when I beached the skiff and trudged inland. I followed a streambed for half a mile, then turned north along the base of a cliff. Twice I saw signs of bear. Finally, near a thundering waterfall, I found what must have been the clearing Jenny had told me about. What I couldn't find was a lone pine she had described, with a hollowed-out trunk.

I looked everywhere; it wasn't there.

The truth hit me like a slap in the face.

I ran all the way back, the rain in my eyes and the roar of the falls in my ears, but when I reached the cove the boat was gone and so was Jenny, and my skiff had four bulletholes in the hull. She'd been a fair shot, at that distance. I found myself wondering what kind of bullet they'd found in Jake's head. If he was really dead at all.

I stood there in the mud awhile, then sighed and sat down on a rock. It was my own fault, really.

Even now, two days later, as I sit here shivering in a cave, eating salmonberries and writing these words on the back of my map, the only two things that really bother me are the Corvette and the bottle of liquid soap. I mean, she tells me she needs money, yet she drives up in a brand-new Corvette? And the soap, I realize now, was to make her eyes red. I should have caught both those things.

But whoever said crooks were smart?